DU

on the

ALTAR

This is a work of fiction. All of the characters, organizations, places, and events portrayed in this novel are either products of the author's imagination or are used fictitiously. Any resemblance to actual persons, living or dead, organizations, events, or locales is entirely coincidental.

Published by Mariposa Bookworks
Glendale, AZ

First edition: October 30, 2020

Cover design by Jake Clark
Developmental edit by Leah Brown
Copy edit by Tammy Salyer
Back cover blurb edit by Jennifer Jarrett
Interior design by Mariposa Bookworks

ISBN 978-1-7349543-3-3 (Paperback)
ISBN 978-1-7349543-1-9 (ebook)
ISBN 978-1-7349543-0-2 (Kindle)

To my mom, for instilling in me a love for books, for teaching me that kindness matters, and for showing me the correct answer to "Have you seen where I put my book?" should often be "Which one?"

To Ralph, for supporting me while I found my way through this journey, for always listening to me, and for only giving me a little crap about disappearing into my writing cave.

To my kids, Josh and Ryan, in the hope that if you never love books as much as I do, you can at least look to this book as a reminder that following your dreams is always worthwhile.

Dust on the Altar

Michelle Winkler

Mariposa Bookworks - Arizona

CHAPTER 1

The last thing Jade expected to do on her lunch break was make news headlines, but apparently all you had to do was help defend one Witch from price gouging and suddenly your loyalty was in question. She hadn't noticed the news drone until it was too late. Only when she turned around to leave did she see its beady little eye staring her down in judgment. Its AI brain quickly decided she was newsworthy, and it beeped twice at her, the red light on its dome signaling that it had transmitted the footage to all the major news outlets. It turned and sped off in search of another news story.

Jade trudged up the wide steps and into her office building's lobby. Its cold glass and marble were a stark contrast to her mood. She always tried to stay out of the spotlight, and getting involved with Witch's rights was not the way to do that. The elevator ride back to her office was torture. The steady *ding* that repeated with each passing floor began to sound like a ticking clock, counting down the seconds until the judgment began. *I really hope April didn't see that.* Maybe she was too busy with the reports she asked her to edit to even take a lunch.

She stepped out of the elevator on the fourteenth floor. The receptionist's desk was barely there, only a single sheet of clear CircuitGlass that curved up from the floor, then bent and traveled horizontally for about a foot. The monitor was a holographic image hovering above the glass at a comfortable viewing angle. The receptionist glanced up and gave Jade a brief smile before returning to her work.

Jade relaxed. *No judgment there. If she didn't see it, maybe April didn't see it either. Or it didn't make the final cut.* Not all videos sent in by the drones made it to broadcast. Most did, though, and were looped several times before something new replaced them.

She turned toward her office. Through the glass doors she could see April standing next to her desk outside of Jade's office. Her blonde hair was pulled back tightly into a bun, emphasizing the scowl on her face. She stood with her arms crossed, tapping her stiletto on the white tiled floor.

"Great," Jade mumbled to herself.

"What was that, Ms. Cerridwen?" The receptionist smiled politely at her.

"Nothing." Jade took a deep breath and headed through the doors.

As Jade walked past her, April asked quietly, "What did you do?"

Jade tried to put off the inevitable argument as she quickly entered her office and went to her desk. "I know, we agreed I'd try to eat healthy this week, but you know how much I hate the cafeteria food. Sammy's has the best burgers in Sun City." Jade sat in her desk chair. The autumn sun's rays streaming through the glass wall warmed her shoulders. She placed the to-go bag on the edge of her desk. Its seamless black glass surface woke, and the greeting *Afternoon, Jade* glowed in the center.

"I couldn't help it. It's just one meal. You'll forgive me." She gave April her best pout, pushing out her lower lip, batting her lashes, and trying to make her green eyes look as sorrowful as possible. "Won't you?"

April stood with her hands on her hips, glaring at Jade. "Not that . . ." She swiped her hand across the desk surface, then tapped an icon among the group that appeared. "That." She pointed at the three headlines that sprang into existence, hovering an inch parallel to the glass: "Local Woman Shows Her True Colors—Witch Black," "Unifiers at Work Again," and "Not Even Sun City Is Safe From the Witch Invasion."

Jade countered, "Those could be about anyone."

April nodded once, then tapped the first headline, causing a holovid to play between her and Jade. The 3D video showed a woman yelling at a cook in a food truck. Though she was impeccably dressed in a dark blue pantsuit, her wavy brown hair was caught by the breeze, making her look a little on the crazy side as she launched her verbal attack.

Jade cringed as she watched herself on the video. In the background a pale woman dressed all in black, with a black *W* on her forehead, looked on. You could clearly hear Jade say, "I know exactly what you did. It may be common practice to charge Witches more, but it's not going to happen here. Whetstone Enterprises is the biggest company in the country, Sammy." She pointed a finger as she finished. "If you don't want to lose our business, then you'd better follow the Accords to the letter. Clear?"

Jade stopped the video on her desk and closed all the headlines. "I couldn't help it. He was charging her twice as much just because she's a Witch. It's barbaric enough that they brand the ones who work here, but there's nothing I can do about that, it's in the Accords."

"They don't brand them," April said, rolling her eyes and plopping down in the chair across from Jade.

"They tattoo them on their foreheads!" Jade countered.

"It's temporary!" April replied. "Once they leave the city limits, it dissolves. It doesn't even hurt them."

Jade looked down at her lunch. She'd had many conversations and arguments with April over the years about how Witches were treated, and it always came down to one important fact: April was a Citizen, born and raised. She would never be able to understand what it was like to be looked at as inferior. Jade had been treated as a Citizen for almost twenty years now, but the truth was still there, hanging over her head every day.

April picked at the hem of her skirt as she said quietly, "I know it's horrible. I get it, Witches deserve our respect." She looked up at Jade. "And hopefully the next election will give us leaders who feel that way. But for now, the laws agreed to in the Accords are clear; we have to have some way to tell them apart from Citizens. It's just the way it is."

Jade sighed. "I know." She appreciated how hard April tried to understand, how she sympathized with her yet didn't let her wallow in the hopelessness of it all. She grabbed her bag and opened the top. Taking a big sniff of the steam rising from within, she reveled in the smell of charbroiled burger. "I get so testy when I'm dieting." She got the smile she wanted from April and proceeded to take her burger out and flatten the bag to use as a plate. "It's all this talk about the Accords being contested. I feel like ever since they became law, there's been unnecessary attention placed on the Witches here. What if"—she lowered her voice—"what if they find out about me?"

April frowned for a moment. "First of all," she whispered, "why are we whispering? It's just me." Jade relaxed at this, and April continued in her normal voice. "Second, if you're worried about attention, the last thing you should have done was get on the news cycle by defending a Witch's rights. Now you're going to be seen as a Unifier."

Jade frowned down at her untouched burger. Of the three political groups, the Unification Party wanted the most changes to their current system. Because of this, their supporters were often thought of as disloyal and were under the most scrutiny. Being associated with them was not something she wanted.

April's blue eyes softened, and she said gently, "Look, that's something we can easily fix. I'm just saying you should have thought of that before you went off the handle at Sammy. As far as them finding out about you, I don't think you have anything to worry about. Your aunt and adopted parents were very careful to make sure the official record shows you being born in Sun City. The only other people who even know are me and Mr. Whetstone." She smiled sympathetically. "I don't think either one of us is going to say anything."

Jade nodded. "You're right. You're right." She took a huge bite of burger and smiled while she chewed, grease dripping down her chin.

April laughed. "You're so gross." Shaking her head, she got

up and left.

As the door closed behind April, Jade called after her with a mouth full of burger, "Yeah, but you're still my friend!"

***

Jade finished eating quickly and once again was grateful her desk was typical of those in her company. Molded from solid black CircuitGlass, it didn't absorb spills or stains, so she only needed to wipe it once and there wasn't a trace of her messy burger on the streak-free surface. She washed up in the half bath attached to her office, then returned to her desk and picked up the proposal April had dropped off for her to sign.

She held the thin sheet of CircuitFilm and paged through the document. When she finished, she laid it on her desk and pressed her index finger to the signature box at the bottom. A perfect replica of her signature appeared on the line next to it.

A gentle chime went off and her desk lit up with *City Solar meeting in ten minutes. Conference Room 4.* She picked up the proposal and grabbed her tablet off the edge of her desk as she walked out of her office.

Stopping by April's desk, she handed her the proposal. "Nice work, April. It reads much better now."

"Thanks, boss," April said, grinning when Jade winced. "You never will get used to that, will you?"

"Nope," Jade replied and walked off to her meeting. "Not if I live for a thousand years."

***

The meeting had gone as most did; they voiced concerns about what a merger would mean for their workers, how their reputation might suffer, and so on. Jade allayed all their worries, using her ability to sense future events to guide her. It wasn't a very strong sense, more like an intuition. It was the one part of Sugar Hill that she couldn't leave behind. She hated it, that last tenuous connection to her past, but no matter how hard she tried, it refused to let her be. So, she used it.

In the end they signed, as she'd known they would. She'd praised their foresight and sent them off more hopeful for their future than when they'd arrived. Everybody won.

Jade stepped out of the private elevator on the top floor and exchanged a brief smile with Mr. Whetstone's secretary as she passed her desk.

As she approached the large ornately carved wooden doors of Mr. Whetstone's office, she heard him speaking with a woman. She didn't recognize her voice and couldn't make out what they were saying, but he didn't sound very happy. She knocked loudly, then slowly opened the door. He was alone. No one sat in the chairs across from his old-fashioned mahogany desk, and his old-fashioned phone rested still in its cradle.

Jade looked around. "Mr. Whetstone? Am I interrupting something?"

Mr. Richard A. Whetstone looked up at her from behind his desk. His frown vanished, replaced by a warm smile that created creases at the corners of his brown eyes. His close-cut salt-and-pepper hair belied an older gentleman, but he rose from his desk with ease. "Jade," he said cheerfully, "not at all." He fastened the single button on his perfectly tailored suit jacket as he walked toward her. "It's always a pleasure to see you. Come in."

The CEO's office was the largest in the building, with his desk at one end and a fireplace at the other. There were a low coffee table and couches in front of the fireplace, creating a cozy living room environment. He often held business meetings with his most important clients in that space. "A comfortable opponent is an unprepared opponent," he often told her.

"How was your weekend?" They hugged briefly, and he motioned to the chair in front of his desk.

With one last glance to make sure they were alone, she replied with the customary, "Fine, Richard. And yours?"

"Oh, it was wonderful." He walked around to his seat on the opposite side. "The weather was perfect for sailing. I really wish you and April had decided to come with us. You both would have loved it. It reminded me of that weekend on the lake after you graduated from Harvard." He smiled fondly at her.

She laughed. "Richard, that was four years ago."

"So? It was a perfect day."

Jade smiled at the memory, just one of many they'd gathered over the years. "Yeah, that was a beautiful day." A sudden chill ran up her spine. Jade looked behind her, half expecting to see someone standing there, but the room was empty.

She turned her attention back to him, smiling weakly. "Um . . . I'm sorry we couldn't make it. We'll go with you next time. I just wanted to decompress after the past week, and April had some political function her parents wanted her to attend." The feeling wasn't going away. She did her best to ignore it.

The frown returned to Mr. Whetstone's face. "Ah yes, the Redeemers Ball. Governor Bishop can't seem to take no for an answer these days. Of course, one doesn't have to say no if one never officially receives the invite." He winked at her, and she caught his meaning.

Mr. Whetstone knew all the players in the city and what moves they would make long before they did. Dodging an invite to an official ball was child's play to him. Jade had known him since the day she arrived in Sun City and found the games he played with his political rivals amusing.

She handed him the City Solar contract. "Mr. Zato signed the contract."

"Of course he did." He took the document and placed it aside in a short stack of other CircuitFilm. "I've learned over the last seven years to never doubt you. I knew from your first year interning that you had a gift."

Something seemed to flash through his mind, a thought or a worry, but it was gone before Jade could understand the expression. His countenance had shifted though. "Now, on to more important matters."

Jade recognized that tone. He was done being friendly with her. He was now in boss mode. As he tapped away on his keyboard—an actual, physical keyboard, unlike the CircuitGlass light show that nearly everyone in Sun City used—Jade tried to sense where the conversation was headed. He frowned at something on his monitor, thin and wireless but still a physical object on his desk.

She realized what it was about: the headlines. Sure enough, when he turned the monitor around to face her, there she was, wagging her finger at a frightened cook while an equally frightened Witch looked on. Jade felt heat rising to her cheeks. She hated disappointing him, but something in her felt the need to stand her ground and defend her position. "The Accords clearly state 'All people within the city walls will be charged the same prices whether Citizen or Witch, with no exceptions.' I was simply upholding the law." Jade straightened her spine and raised her chin, meeting his gaze.

He remained silent, and for a moment it was a battle of wills, neither backing down. Soon the anger in his eyes started to unsettle her. She felt danger, a faint tingling sensation on the back of her neck, like the draft from a cellar doorway was creeping toward her. She suddenly felt like she needed to run and hide. She had seen him threaten others like this, but never her. A wave of dizziness began to creep in. Little pinpricks of light sparkled in the corner of her vision.

"Jade, are you all right?" His eyes were narrowed, and he was leaning back with his fingers steepled in front of his mouth.

Had he been talking? she thought. *He had.* She struggled to remember about what. Jade felt panic start to tighten her throat. "I . . . uh—" She blinked several times and tried again as her vision slowly cleared. "I-I'll be fine. I'm sorry, what were you saying?"

Mr. Whetstone leaned forward and examined her closely. "I was saying you should know better than to draw attention to yourself when it comes to Witch's matters. I was also saying you should tell me right away when there's a problem so that we can get ahead of it." He tilted his head, studying her for a moment. "I expect you to go home early today," he said abruptly as he rose and walked around to her chair.

"What?" she asked, startled.

"Go home and get some rest." He helped her to her feet and as he guided her toward the door, she slowly started to feel better. "Between your outburst this morning and your dazed episode just now, it's clear you need to take better care of yourself." The dizziness was gone by the time he opened the door for her. "I may be the boss, but we both know this company would fall apart without you." He was always telling her that. "Now go home. That's an order."

"I will," she replied as she walked away.

But she didn't go straight home. Instead she kept right on working. She should have left after maybe another hour of cleanup work, but she had far too much to do. Besides, the strange dizziness and weakness had not returned, so she saw no need to leave. The sun was nearly set when Jade finally closed her computer and packed up to head home. She did, however, tell April she needed to skip their usual after-work dinner. She went straight home and fell asleep before her head hit the pillow.

***

She's running as fast as her twelve-year-old legs can carry her through the dark, her feet crunching on the gravel driveway. Her breath comes in short gasps as her lungs struggle to take in air.

She's kneeling in her favorite blue dress and pounding her fists on the burnt floorboards as she sobs giant, silent gasps of despair.

The house is on fire, and she crosses her arms up in front of her face, the heat burning her forearms.

A woman screams.

CHAPTER 2

Jade's eyes flew open, and she bolted upright in bed, the echoes of a scream still fresh in her mind. Breathing heavily, she looked through the wall of glass at the city below. The sun was still below the horizon, and the darkest hour of morning blanketed the city in an eerie stillness. She sat there in the dark for a moment, trapped in the intensity of the dream—the heat of the smoldering house, the bruises to her fists from pounding the burnt floorboards. She rubbed her hands and tried to steady her breath as a bead of sweat dripped down her temple. Jade rarely remembered her dreams, and they were never this vivid.

She was usually an early riser, but the fear of the nightmare still lingered. Instead of rising quickly to start her day, she took a slow deep breath and told herself, *You're safe in your bed. The past is past. It can't hurt you now.*

Across the river only a handful of windows were lit. She stared at those small dots of light, silently willing more of them to shine. The seconds dragged on like hours until finally the sun began to lighten the darkness and the buildings' outlines could be seen against the pale blue morning sky. Jade closed her eyes and waited for her body to relax. The sun's first rays crept into her room, bathing it in their gentle warmth.

Grounded in reality once more, Jade leaped up and said, "Cancel alarm." The many sensors in the room marked her motion. The windows frosted over for privacy, the white marble floor lit up dimly so she could see where she stepped, and the green and blue bedsheets, the only bit of color in the room, were yanked off her bed to be laundered. The bed folded into the wall, replaced by a small gray couch with a large painting of a forest hanging above it. The doors to her walk-in closet opened for her, and she breathed in the cleansing smell of the cedar walls. Stepping onto the plush gray carpet inside, she said, "National news."

The wall of windows in her bedroom became a TV screen. The newscaster was cheerfully reporting, "Today Senator Cane announced a new bill calling for the registration of Witches. Data for the registration would be gathered at checkpoints through scanning, allowing Sun City to gain a more accurate count of Witches within city limits."

Jade passed by her modest selection of casual attire and stepped up to the one black CircuitGlass panel in all the cedar. It sprang to life with options of clothing. She navigated through to business attire and found a sharp-looking blue and gray pinstripe pantsuit. Sliding her finger down to select it and pressing her thumbprint to confirm, she instantly received confirmation her suit would be delivered to her office building within ten minutes.

She passed through the closet and grabbed a pair of gray sweats just before entering the glass and marble area of her bath suite. The TV announcer appeared on the left panel mirror, not having missed a beat in her reporting of reaction to the bill. Normally she wouldn't shower before her run, but her gray silk pajamas clung to her, soaked with sweat from her battle with the nightmare.

As the hot water pummeled her tight shoulders and back, she could just make out the reporter's voice above the noise of the water. "Governor Bishop lauded the bill as 'forward thinking,' but Senator Quinn cautioned that his Statesman Party would undoubtedly see it as a move to give the Redemption Party a stronger foothold."

Jade stuck her head outside the shower door and yelled, "TV off!" then went back to showering. Usually when the news turned to politics, she could turn a deaf ear to it, but not today. When she noticed her arm turning red from scrubbing, she stopped and gave a deep sigh. Finishing up quickly, she threw on her sweats, made up her protein shake, and was out the door in record time.

***

There was a walking trail that ran a loop. April would run to the park benches in front of Jade's penthouse apartment, and Jade would join her for the rest of the run, traveling over the bridge to their office building downtown. During their run, they would talk about anything other than work. It was a Tuesday routine that Jade thoroughly enjoyed, except for the running part.

When April arrived, she was barely breathing hard, as usual. Jade quickly tossed her empty shake cup into the recycle bin next to the bench and started on their route without a word. She was determined not to say anything about the nightmare. She just wanted to forget it. She couldn't stop thinking about it though, and when they stopped at the café in their building's lobby, she hesitated at the door.

April frowned at Jade. "What's the matter? Are you still mad about not being able to go the whole way without stopping? I told you, not everyone can be Olympic material like me." She gave Jade a nudge and a smile but only got a halfhearted grin in return.

"No, it's not that," she replied as April opened the door. "I'll tell you later."

The usual crowd was there, and they all turned to smile at April. The barista had their usual drinks ready when they reached the counter. "Large unsweetened green tea for Miss Jade, and a large caramel-vanilla blended coffee for Miss April." He pushed forward their drinks with a friendly smile.

"Thanks," they said in unison and headed for the door.

There were two women seated there, both impeccably dressed in business attire. Jade recognized them from the copy room. "The Gossipmongers" some people called them.

As Jade held the door open for April, she heard one tell the other, "Didn't you hear? Three, no, four Witches were caught trying to sneak past the city checkpoint . . . with grenades."

Aghast, the other woman replied, "There's no way. Governor Bishop would never allow it."

Jade tried to slam the door shut, but the magnetic bumpers quickly turned it into a gentle closure.

When Jade and April stepped into the elevator, it was empty, a rare sight. April took the opportunity to confront Jade. "Okay, what's up with you? I heard what they said in the coffee shop, but you can't be mad about that. It's obviously a false rumor. You've told me townsfolk aren't violent."

"Usually it doesn't bother me." Jade sighed and crossed her arms, trying to put her frustration into words. "For some reason today, it seems worse. It's just annoying. Never mind, I'll get over it."

The elevator doors opened, and three men from accounting entered, in the midst of conversation. "Not to mention, Cane may have a point." At the others' groans, he added, "No, hear me out. If we knew more about the townsfolk, we could get them the help they need. You know, start a conversation that could lead to some sort of fair agreement, one that's better than the Accords. Maybe even get them to let us send them support. Goodness knows they need it, living out there."

The tall one turned to him in surprise. "Joe, you're starting to sound like," he whispered, "a Unifier."

Joe was quick to argue. "No! No. Look, I'm just saying—" The third one elbowed him and tried to subtly nod in Jade's direction. It wasn't subtle enough. He pulled himself up short. "Oh. Hello, Ms. Cerridwen, April. I, uh, didn't see . . . I mean I was just telling them—"

Jade said, "Don't worry about it. Mr. Whetstone is the one who cares if you talk politics at work, not me. I won't say anything to him, but maybe confine these talks to the break room next time?"

They nodded their agreement as the doors opened, revealing Mr. Whetstone standing next to the receptionist's desk. He looked up as everyone stepped off the elevator and went their own ways. He smiled politely to everyone as they stepped out. "Good morning, Jade, April."

They both replied, "Morning," and continued toward the women's locker room, where Jade's suit was waiting for her in her locker. After they showered and changed, April stopped at her desk, while Jade went into her office and stood staring out the window.

Between all the high-rises, she could just see a sliver of green and blue by the river's edge. *All this talk against the townsfolk, they have no idea what they're talking about. Unifiers, Redeemers, even the Statesmen—they've got it all wrong.*

She heard April's stilettos clicking on the marble floor behind her and turned, forcing a smile. "So"—she attempted to sound cheerful—"what's on the agenda for today?"

April closed the door, then approached Jade with a serious look. "All right, what's wrong?"

"I'm fine."

"Now, look. I know we agreed a long time ago to keep our working relationship and friendship separate, but I can tell something's seriously bugging you."

Jade asked with a smile, "And how do you know that?"

"I knew the minute I saw your face when you came out of your apartment. I let it slide, thinking you'd tell me when you were ready, but you have a really busy day scheduled, and if you don't get whatever it is off your mind, it's gonna affect your work." She sat in the chair in front of Jade's desk. "You said at the coffee shop you'd tell me later. It's later. I'm your friend now." She placed her tablet facedown in her lap. "So spill."

Jade sat in her leather chair. April waited patiently across the desk, sitting ramrod straight.

"I just . . . " Jade hesitated. "There's always been gossip about Witches, but lately it's gotten worse. I don't like how they talk about them. It's not like they're doing anything wrong. They just want to live their lives the way they want. Statesmen are okay with that, why can't everyone else be?"

"Um-hum." April nodded slowly. "And that's what's bugging you today?"

"Well, yeah. Look, if Senator Cane gets his bill passed, paying more for burgers will be the least of their problems. They've already managed to have every Witch in the city marked while they're within the border wall." She raised her hand to stop the counterargument April always threw her way. "I know, I know. They agreed to it, they didn't have to sign the Accords. My point is, every time another restriction is put on the Witches working here, what they're really doing is taking away another basic human right the rest of us get to keep. Do that enough and suddenly they'll be seen not as people but as things. The Redeemers have been trying for years to do just that, and now Cane is paving the way for them." She paused. She hadn't really thought this out until now. "It's like I said yesterday, what if they come after me?"

"No one is going to come after you." April was quiet for a moment. "I admit, there's been some tragic losses on both sides, but that was decades ago. For the most part, the Redeemers are kept in check by the other two parties now. As long as you don't go yelling in the streets about Witch's rights again." April leaned back in her chair. "So, why don't you put all this political talk behind you and tell me what's really got you freaked."

"You know, one of these days I'll be able to keep a secret from you."

April breathed out sharply, crossing her arms in front of her. "I wouldn't bet on that." She winked at Jade. "What's up?"

"I had a nightmare. That's all."

"About what?"

Seconds ticked by and finally Jade stated, "When I was twelve."

April's eyes widened slightly. "Oh. Well, a lot happened when you were twelve." She prompted, "Anything in particular?"

Jade appreciated her vagueness. She always let Jade take the lead in talks about her past. Jade had never even asked her to, she just knew she should. "It was about the night they died. I was there watching my house burn down, and my parents were inside." A lump formed in her throat, and she took a sip of her tea.

"It was just a dream, right? Maybe you're just imagining what the police report described—that they died in a house fire?"

Jade nodded. She wasn't sure though. She hadn't had proper visions since she was a kid. And that had felt a lot like a vision. Still, it was something that had happened in the past. Her distant past, and her visions had always been about the future. "Maybe. It felt real though."

"Dreams can be weird that way. You weren't even there when it happened, right?"

Jade frowned down at her hands. She hoped it was a dream. That would be much easier to deal with than the alternative. She had worked hard to put magic behind her.

"Don't worry about it now, it was just a dream," April said, interrupting Jade's thoughts. "You have a meeting with Starlight holosuites in fifteen minutes, and Mr. Whetstone wants you to send him the Marshfield report."

"Thanks." Jade breathed an inward sigh of relief and opened several screens to start work. She just had to focus on work and ignore the strange feeling she had that something wasn't right.

April walked out of Jade's office and closed the door. Jade had time to open one email and read the first sentence when April opened the door and walked back in. Jade smirked at her as she closed the door behind her. "Forget something?"

April stopped at the corner of her desk, leaning her hand on it, frowning down at the tablet in her other hand.

Jade asked, "Yes?"

"I'm so sorry, you had a voice mail while we were talking." April frowned and glanced back at the tablet. "She says she's your grandmother?"

Jade examined the tea bag tag hanging off her teacup. One green leaf stared back at her. She flipped it over. The other side was blank. "My grandmother? Not my aunt?"

"No, it definitely wasn't Joy. She said she 'must speak with you, immediately.' I think you should return her call."

Jade sighed. "I've told you before, I don't want to speak to anyone from my past." She took a sip of her tea.

April nodded. "I know, and usually I would have just deleted the message, but she said it's regarding . . . a death in the family."

CHAPTER 3

Jade went numb. A death in the family could mean only one thing.

"I'm sorry, Jade, I . . ." April gently took Jade's hand. "Are you okay?" After a moment she said, "She left a number for you to call her back."

Jade replied, "Thank you. I'll use my private line."

"Of course. I'll send you the number now." April made a few taps on the tablet as she walked out of the office, closing the door quietly behind her.

On the right side of the desktop, a phone number began to glow. Jade looked at the pulsing green numbers, then over to her left at the old-fashioned black rotary dial phone. Jade hardly ever used her private line. It was triple encrypted, and not even April or Mr. Whetstone had access to listen in. It was also the only physical thing Jade kept on her desk besides a magnetic sculpture she loved to smash and reshape.

Jade stared at the phone for what seemed like an eternity. She hadn't spoken to Grandma Willow since the months after her parents' deaths. Over the years, Willow had sent her letters and her aunt had tried calling, but Jade had ignored them. She thought she'd left magic behind. Apparently, magic had other plans.

She picked up the receiver like she was picking up the weight of the world. She dialed the number slowly, listening to the click, click, click as each digit rotated back to zero.

After only one ring the line picked up and a voice answered that was so familiar it was as though she had heard it only yesterday. "Well, it's about time."

"Grandma Willow?" she asked tentatively.

"Hello, Jade." Grandma Willow wasn't really related to her. Everyone in the tiny township of Sugar Hill called her Grandma because she acted like everyone was her grandkid.

"You'll forgive me if I skip the pleasantries and get right to the point. There's no easy way to tell you this. Your auntie Joy crossed over yesterday."

The light seemed to dim, almost imperceptibly, like a filter had slid over her eyes. Jade swiveled in her chair to face the city. She stood and walked over to the glass wall, stretching the phone cord to its limit. Looking down, she could see people and cars going about their day, and across the way workers toiled in the nearby offices. They had no idea the world had just ended. Some part of her mind scolded, *You knew. From the moment you woke up today, you knew. Pull yourself together.*

"What happened?" Jade closed her eyes, not really wanting to hear the answer.

"We're not sure yet. It came as a surprise to everyone. None of our healers or psychics had any sense this was coming. Crystal said even the Goddess is silent on the matter. Of course, Sun City sent a Lawkeeper, and they ruled it a heart attack, but I don't believe that. I've sent for our shaman to find out what he can. As soon as I hear anything, I'll let you know. In the meantime, you know what this means. We need you, Jade."

She stumbled backward and sat down hard in her chair, feeling more alone than she ever had. The moment she'd been dreading was here. All these years she'd been waiting for it, knew it was coming. It didn't make her any more ready. "My aunt, my last living relative has just died, and you're already talking about my responsibilities to a town I haven't lived in for two decades?" Her voice broke.

Willow explained softly, "I know this is hard for you, but I too have a responsibility to this town and her people. I would love to have the luxury of focusing on you and your mourning, but we don't have time for that at the moment. Without a High Priestess, we're unprotected, exposed to those who follow the darkness. We're already beginning to see the effects her loss has caused on our magic. It's urgent you come home immediately."

Jade sighed. *Might as well get it over with.* "All right, I understand." She looked at her watch. "It's only a couple of hours there, so I'll leave right after work today. Probably be there around eight?"

Willow sounded relieved. "I'm happy to hear you say that. Her Crossing Over ceremony is tomorrow night, so that should give us just enough time to prepare. Of course, we'll have the Ascension ritual Saturday night, which will give you three days to realign yourself with Cerridwen magic."

"Fine," Jade said shortly.

She could almost hear Willow frowning through the phone. "Listen, child, I know it's short notice, but there really isn't any other way."

"I know, I'm sorry. I mean no disrespect. I'm just tired." She tried to smile, hoping Willow would hear it in her voice and not the sarcasm screaming in her head. "I really am looking forward to seeing you again."

They said their goodbyes and hung up. Jade sat looking out the window. Everything had been so perfect here in her glittering city, where everything was explainable, where she had control, where she felt safe.

They're all gone now. I'm the last of my family. I'm alone.

Willow was right, the township needed her. Its people were her responsibility, but she'd found a way out of that trap before, and she would again. Somehow, she would find a way back to Sun City. This was her home.

She tapped the intercom button. "You can come in now, April."

***

The morning flew by for Jade, a blur of meetings and reports. She walked through it in a daze. As she sat at her desk for lunch, pushing a cherry tomato around her plate, April told her that Mr. Whetstone wanted to speak with her.

Jade made the trip up to his office, growing more distracted and weaker the closer she got. By the time she reached his office door, she needed all her strength to push it open. Mr. Whetstone was standing next to the fireplace on the right side of the room, replacing a large snow globe back on the mantel.

"Ah, Jade, I'm glad you're here." He walked toward her. "Jade?" He crossed the remaining distance quickly, gently grasping her arm, worry etched on his face. "You look horrible. Here, sit." He guided her to one of the large chairs facing the fireplace. She sank gratefully into the soft cushions, certain she would not get back up for at least a week. He poured her a glass of water from the pitcher on the coffee table and knelt next to her. "Drink," he ordered.

"Thank you." She managed a small smile and took a couple of sips, handing him the half-drunk glass. "I feel better," she lied, trying to erase his frown. "What did you want to see me about?"

Mr. Whetstone took the glass from her and refilled it. "You." He handed the glass back to her with a pointed look. "Why did you do it?"

Jade knew that look and tone. *Straight to business now.* "Do what?" she replied innocently and took a sip.

He sat on the edge of the couch next to her and regarded her thoughtfully for a moment. "Jade, you know I take the health and well-being of all my employees very seriously. If they're unhappy or sick, they don't perform at their best and the company suffers right along with them." He waited.

Uh-oh. Jade realized what he was referring to. "Yes, sir?" She took another sip. She had learned a long time ago not to volunteer information when she was in trouble.

"Yesterday I told you to go home and rest, but you refused, working far past business hours. Normally it wouldn't be an issue, but this"—he waved his hand at her—"is not normal."

"I'm fine," she croaked. She cleared her throat and tried again. "Really, I'm okay. I just . . . I'm—"

"You're obviously not okay. When was the last time you got a restful night's sleep?"

She thought of the nightmare. The nightmare that immediately preceded her learning her aunt had died. She stared at him, unable to find the words. Her eyes wanted desperately to close, but she refused to let them. *What is wrong with me?*

Mr. Whetstone took the glass from her slightly trembling hands. "Jade, please. You need to take better care of yourself. I understand you've had a family emergency?"

It always surprised Jade how much he knew about everyone in the company, and how quickly. "Yes. There was a death in the family. I need to attend a funeral."

His face paled slightly. "Is it . . . is your aunt . . . ?"

"I'm sorry. She—" The words wouldn't come. Jade thought back to the day Joy had brought her to Sun City. She had promised her that everything would be okay. *Sweet lies for a little girl.* But even then, she knew things would never be okay again. A few days later when she met Mr. Whetstone, he had introduced himself as a friend of the family. He had seemed so tall and strong, so commanding of the space around him. With him, she felt safe.

Mr. Whetstone's face was at war with itself. Grief, anger, and his responsibility as her self-imposed guardian all fought for control. "I'm so sorry, Jade. She was a good woman." He rested his hand on her shoulder gently. "If there's anything I can do for you."

Jade shook her head. "There's nothing to do. I just have to go back and settle her accounts. It may take a few days." She knew lying to him was a mistake, but she couldn't bring herself to go into the long explanation of why she wasn't coming back right away. She would tell him later.

"Of course, take all the time you need." As she stood unsteadily, he gently guided her toward the door. "In fact, if I see you sooner than two weeks from now, I'll fire you."

CHAPTER 4

The moment Jade finished packing, a chime rang out, a lilting tune Jade recognized as the doorman's page. She closed and latched the suitcase on the foot of her bed and turned to face the wall behind her. "Hello, Jerry."

The CircuitGlass panel lit up with the doorman's face. "Sorry to bother you, ma'am, but April is here to see you."

Jade shook her head. *Uncanny timing, as always.* "Go ahead and let her up, Jerry. And would you please arrange a company limo to pick me up in . . . about ten minutes?"

"Of course, ma'am. What destination should I tell them?"

"Sugar Hill." She watched the doorman closely for a reaction, but he only took a moment's pause before responding, "Right away, ma'am." And the panel returned to gray.

Jade quickly stepped into her closet and opened her jewelry drawer. She picked out her favorite bracelet—a simple band made of tiny seashells— and slipped it on, covering it with her sleeve cuff. It had been a gift from April in exchange for the beaded one she'd made for her freshman year of high school.

She brought her suitcase into the front room then went into the kitchen to brew a thermos of tea for the drive. It was only a couple of hours to her hometown, but after all the news reports lately, she thought the checkpoints could take a while to get through.

While she waited for the water to boil, she took two teacups out of the cabinet, placed a tea bag in each, and looked around her apartment. She was going to miss this place. The open-concept space was minimally decorated. Just the basic furniture, bare cement floors, and high ceilings. The cold, hard living space had been a welcome change when she'd first moved in. An escape from her past. Only last year did she feel the need to decorate it. She had purchased two wall hangings, one of a forest and one of a beach. Her aunt would have approved. She loved nature.

Did love it, she corrected herself. *She's gone now.*

Jade heard April's courtesy knock on the door just as the water started to boil. She called out, "It's open," and filled the cups. She heard a thump and looked over to see two suitcases and a handbag dumped on her floor.

"I got your text." April stood there, arms crossed, tapping her foot. "I can't believe you were going to leave without me."

Jade was not in the mood for a fight, but she could see it coming like an unstoppable train. Just the thought of leaving April mad at her caused her to lash out. She let the cupboard door slam shut. "I don't have to do everything with you, April. It's not like we're married."

April's jaw hit the floor. "No, we're not married, we're just best friends—lifelong friends. And no, you don't have to do everything with me, but this isn't just anything, is it?" She walked over to her and yanked her into a tight hug. "Jade, sweetie. You're going to your hometown for a funeral." She held her at arm's length. "That's not something anyone should have to do alone."

Jade turned away quickly, grabbed the honey jar, and plopped it down next to April's teacup. "It's more than just a funeral." She filled April's cup from the teapot.

"What do you mean?" April asked as she spooned honey into her cup.

Jade filled the thermos and her own small teacup. She knew she should tell April she wasn't coming back anytime soon, but she didn't know how. *How am I supposed to say I could be stuck there for the rest of my life? Trapped in a magical township, protecting a magical coven, dealing with their magical problems, when all I want is to stay here!*

She dropped the teacup into the sink, and it shattered. "Damn it!" She grabbed a towel and started wiping up the countertop and front of the cabinet.

April gingerly picked the shards of ceramic out of the sink and put them in the recycle bin under the nearby counter. Once everything was cleaned up, April said, "I'm sorry. I'm not trying to make things more difficult for you."

"I'm sorry too." The lump in her throat made it hard to speak.

April took Jade's hands. "Jade. Talk to me."

Jade looked up into her eyes. She owed April the truth. "It's just . . ." *How do I do this? How do I say goodbye?* Tears threatened to fall. "It's been so long since I've been there, all my memories of it are painful, and it's a township, it's so different from Sun City . . . I don't want to scare you."

"Scare me?"

"They practice magic, April. Real magic."

"And that's scary?"

"Well . . . isn't it?"

April thought a minute. "No. Not really. I mean you've always told me what rumors were true and which weren't. It doesn't sound all that bad."

Jade smirked. "You say that now, but just wait until you see something floating past you."

"What, like we do with antigravity packs?" April's eyes got big.

Jade realized their technology reproduceed the same effects as a levitation spell. April rented airtime every weekend and was always trying to get Jade to go with her. Jade wanted nothing to do with flying, but she usually went to watch her friend back flip and spin, navigating the course like a pro. "Well, what about when something appears right in front of you? Out of thin air?"

"Like in the holosuites." April was looking doubtful now.

"Um . . . yeah, I guess." She was right. In holosuites you could make items appear or disappear. Although they weren't physical items, it looked real enough. And supposedly the government's transportation division was getting close to being able to teleport objects. It wouldn't be long before they could do the same thing as a magic portal.

April scoffed, "Yeah, sounds real scary." After a moment she nodded. "That's settled, then. We'll go together and I'll be there to support you, for as long as you need me. Besides"—she gently took Jade's hand in both of hers and gave a squeeze—"I have a feeling it's for your own good." She smiled knowingly at her.

Jade couldn't help but smile at her best friend's attempt at levity. Maybe she was right. She decided to put her troubles on hold and exclaimed in mock horror, "Oh, no! Not something that's good for me!"

"Yes!" April responded. "Now deal with it, or else!" Her mock sternness, comical in its exaggeration, wasn't lost on Jade.

"Well, since you put it that way . . ." They brought up curved pinkies in practiced synchronicity. "I promise to try to make the best of this." With their pinkies hooked together, like lifelines for each other, they "shook hands" once before letting go.

April said, "Seriously though, maybe it will be good to finally deal with it. You know, find some closure."

"Yeah right. I don't need closure, it's already closed. I moved on and I love my life now. I don't need to connect to my roots or any other tree appendage."

The doorman announced that Jade's limo was ready. Jade quickly washed their cups then grabbed her thermos and walked toward the front door where her bags were waiting. She picked them up and held the door open for April.

Suddenly it all felt real. They were going to Jade's hometown. April was going to walk down the same magical streets she'd grown up on. "You have to promise me you won't laugh at anything you see or hear."

"Laugh?"

"You may see some weird things going on. More than can be explained by technology comparisons. Just promise me?"

"I promise," April replied.

"And you can't tell anyone here—about what you see or hear there." Jade didn't believe she would, but it would ease her mind if she just promised now.

"Of course," April said with a mock-serious face.

"And—"

"Oh, for pity's sake, Jade. I promise to be blind and deaf the whole time. Can we just go?"

"Why are you so excited? We're going to a funeral, you know."

April's grin faded. "I know, but I'll finally get to see where you're from." She leaned into Jade's side and whispered while looking around, "And maybe I'll finally get to meet the mysterious Charlie."

Jade missed the elevator call button and had to try again. "Charlie?"

"Yeah. Remember? A couple years ago he kept trying to call you and you kept being 'not available.' All you ever told me was 'He's an old friend.' He's the only old friend I've ever heard of, so I want to meet him. See what kind of embarrassing stories he can tell about you." She winked at Jade.

"Yeah. Great." The idea of April meeting her childhood best friend made her nervous. "You know, magic wasn't really his thing when we were kids. He's probably not even in town anymore. I bet he relocated." While most cities prohibited any Witches living within their boundaries, a few of the more "progressive" cities allowed them to be residents, provided they didn't practice magic.

They entered the elevator and April said, "Well, either way, it'll be nice to see where you're from."

When they got outside, the driver opened the door for them, and the doorman loaded their bags while they got in the limo. During the short drive to the city limits, April was busy on her tablet, giving Jade time to think.

They stopped at a red light, and the crosswalk barrier was raised, protecting pedestrians from any errant vehicles. Hardly anyone drove anymore, of course. People entering or leaving the city limits needed a human driver since the road sensors stopped at the border, and there were a handful of the richest class, like Mr. Whetstone, who preferred human drivers. All the other vehicles were driven by AI and didn't even have driver's seats.

But crosswalk barriers were still there protecting Sun City's people, a fail-safe for the automated vehicles, automated lights, and tracking that everyone wore on their wrists. A whole system designed with backup after backup, just to keep people safe while crossing the street. Shouldn't a coven have at least one backup plan in case something happened to their coven leader? After all, two High Priestess had died suddenly in one generation. Jade couldn't be the only hope for them.

Why can't someone else take over for me? What about the High Priest? The coven must surely be able to function with one leader. Or maybe there's a ritual we can do to break the bloodline ties. It's worth a try at least.

***

Jade's childhood memories of entering the city were fuzzy, and over the years she had thought the stories of what checkpoints were like must have been exaggerated. Approaching the checkpoint, she was shocked by what she saw. The road in front of them had several barriers that forced the driver to slow down in order to weave between them, and at the end was a large sign that read *Stop Here. Await Orders.* Beyond that, Jade could see several armed guards in military gear standing next to a shack in the center of the road. Surrounding the whole thing and funneling all traffic through the barriers were shock-fences, their edges glowing with the electricity flowing through them. It all gave the impression of a prison or war zone.

Witches and Citizens had reached several agreements over the past few decades that should have made this kind of armament unnecessary. While Jade hated the idea of the Witch's mark, she'd hoped it would finally help mitigate the Citizens' suspicion and fear that one of them could be hiding in their midst. She'd assumed it would be a simple matter for them to exit or enter the city, like entering a nightclub: show your ID, receive your stamp, move along.

They waited at the last barrier to be waved forward for inspection. On the other side of the guardhouse, Witches were being searched, their cars torn apart and bags ripped open. Others were turned away before even reaching the guardhouse.

Even the outgoing traffic was a target. A guard was marching over to the driver's side window of the car ahead of them. He held something up to the window, then opened the driver's door and stepped back, holding his gun at the ready. The driver stepped out with his hands up and was handcuffed by a second guard and dragged away forcefully. The first guard placed a disk on the roof of the car. A flying drone came zooming out of the guard shack and straight into the driver's window. After a moment the car started up and pulled out of the traffic line.

Jade lowered the partition and asked their driver, "Do you know what that's all about?"

The driver said, "The scanner must have registered the driver as being a Witch. Any Witch attempting to leave without their mark showing is breaking the Accords and is arrested."

"They can tell if you're a Witch by scanning you with a device?" Jade felt a lump in her throat growing, but kept her voice as casual as possible.

"Yes, ma'am, didn't you hear? Last week they issued scanners to all the checkpoints, and today they started using them. Supposedly they found out that Witches give off a specific energy signature. Has something to do with all that magic they claim to do." They were being waved forward, and as the driver started up the car, he shrugged. "I don't understand how it all works, I'm just glad it does."

Jade raised the window back up and sat back in her seat. She whispered to April, "If they scan me . . ." Jade was worried what they'd do to her, but even more so for Mr. Whetstone. He had pulled strings to falsify her birth certificate. If she was found to be a Witch now, he would not only lose credibility but could face jail time as well. He could lose everything.

April took her hand gently. "Just stay calm. Remember, you've done nothing wrong." She raised her chin slightly, and Jade copied her posture, although the knot in her stomach didn't buy her act.

They were told to stop right next to the guardhouse, and a large angry-looking guard stepped up to the driver's window. He only glanced at the driver's ID before stepping back to the window on April's side. She rolled it down. His smile didn't reach his eyes as he looked Jade and April over. "Identification?"

Jade took off the thin black wristband all Citizens wore. It served many purposes: watch, bank access, and in this case, identification. She handed hers to April, who had taken hers off as well, and April handed them both to the guard. He scrutinized them for several moments, using a miniature tablet.

"Hmm . . ." He looked back at them and said, "We've had several Witches come through today who haven't been wearing their mark properly." He put their wristbands in his shirt pocket and took out his scanner. "I'm going to have to scan you." He paused, his smile growing bigger. "You understand."

As he raised it toward April's eyes, a second guard came up and tapped him on the shoulder. "Wait!"

The first guard's smile disappeared, and he snapped, "What is it?"

"They've been cleared. Give them back their IDs and let them through."

"But I haven't scanned them yet." He sounded disappointed, like a child who'd been told to come inside for the day.

The guard stepped around him and placed his hand on the scanner, forcing him to lower it. "You want to tell Governor Bishop himself why you're holding them up, go ahead."

After considering a moment, he pulled their wristbands out and gave them to April as he said through gritted teeth, "Our apologies, ma'am." To the driver he yelled, "Move along!"

They slowly rolled away from the checkpoint, and Jade sank back into the seat. "That was close. Why would the governor concern himself with us?"

April said, "I've no idea." She thought for a moment. "Maybe Mr. Whetstone had something to do with it. Didn't you say Governor Bishop was trying to recruit him to their party?"

"And this was what, payment for his joining them?"

April looked out the window behind them. "Probably not. Well, when we get back we'll ask him."

Jade mumbled an agreement and turned back to the window. Beyond the wall the high-rises and office buildings were gone. Now the only thing out her window were forest and fields. She let her eyes lose focus, causing the passing scenery to blur, reducing it to an artistic blending of green, brown, and white streaks. She brought into focus the raindrops on the glass. A few gathered together, merging into larger drops, until they were heavy enough to be moved by gravity and pushed by the wind. As a drop ran sideways along the invisible barrier, she sympathized with it. Completely out of control, at the mercy of the elements around it.

The memories from when she'd lived in Sugar Hill were hazy and dark. In the months after her parents' deaths, Lawkeepers from Sun City had come to try to investigate. Joy and the other town elders had made it crystal clear that they would do their own investigation. One of the clearest memories Jade had from that time was watching the Lawkeepers drive away. Joy had placed a hand on her shoulder and said simply, "We take care of our own, Jade. Remember that."

Jade had been relieved the questions would stop and she could move on, but she couldn't. Everywhere she went she saw her parents. Every store she entered, the bittersweet smile of the townsfolk greeted her, reminding her. Even Aunt Joy wasn't a help. All she'd wanted was to step up Jade's training, in complete opposition to Jade's wishes. She was done with magic. When she'd moved, she had put a solid wall between herself and her past. Now that wall was about to be shattered, and she was helpless to stop it. All she could do was hang on and hope she would survive.

CHAPTER 5

Calling Sugar Hill a small town was an understatement. The shopping mall was Katie's Emporium on Main Street, five hundred square feet of shopping heaven. The movie theater was the wall of the firehouse on Saturday night, and you had to bring your own chair or sit on the ground. The museum was old man Flannerly's house. He could tell you anything you wanted to know about the town's history, or the country's for that matter. He also had several old barns on his property that were completely stuffed to the brim with more memorabilia and trinkets than you could see in a day. The planetarium was Madame Belle's backyard. She knew the name of every star in the sky. Between her telescope and magical talent, she could show you anything in the heavens as if it were sitting in your hand.

The sun had just set by the time Jade and April arrived in town, and as the streetlights flickered on one by one, Jade thought Main Street looked darker than she remembered.

The street also seemed shorter, and in a matter of minutes they were turning right onto the road that led to Joy's house.

Jade looked out the window into the thick woods. She re4membered how the fireflies would dance through the branches, lighting them with a soft glow. But now, all she saw was darkness. Even the last light from the sky seemed banned by the overhead branches she imagined were twisted and tangled. The back of her neck tingled in warning.

"You all right?" April asked.

"Fine. Just a lot of memories."

"Ew, gross," April joked.

Jade smirked and grabbed her hand in thanks. She looked outward again as they pulled into a wide driveway before a towering gate. Memories came flooding back of childhood games she'd played with Charlie in the front yard and huge neighborhood parties she'd attended in the back. It used to be a place of magic and fantasy. Now it was just a dark gray property.

A giant marble lion stood guard on either side of the entrance. Jade looked closer at the one on her side of the car. He was magnificent. Life-sized and lifelike, he stared fiercely through the pouring rain. Rivulets ran through the creases in his mane and over his nose. His form was perfect except for the tip of his left ear, which was broken off. As a child, Jade had always thought of them as being magically alive, able to move or freeze at will. The gate opened slowly, and as the car began moving through it, Jade swore she saw his eyes move slightly toward her. She looked again but he was still. *Must have been a trick of the light,* she thought as the car continued on. She looked out the back window as the lions and gate disappeared into the growing darkness.

The driver parked on the curved driveway in front of the house. Jade looked up at the imposing façade. The house was several stories tall, with a widow's walk, spires on the two corners facing the drive, and small stone gargoyles perched along the roof. What made it even stranger looking were the randomly placed windows. There was nearly every size and shape: big bay, little stained glass, round, square, and octagonal. It made it impossible to tell precisely how many floors were inside, never mind how many rooms.

The dark gray paint was peeling and worn on the main building, but the rest was a multitude of what seemed to be freshly painted colors. The shutters were reds and golds, the trim was shades of blue, and the wraparound porch's posts and railings were various dark purples and maroons. A kaleidoscope of color, offset by the drab backdrop.

The driver unloaded their bags while Jade and April took shelter on the front porch. Hanging from the porch's roofline were several flowerpots. They always contained white carnations, her aunt's favorite flower. Even now in late fall they were blooming. The rain began to lessen, and by the time the driver was done bringing everything to the porch, it was just a misty drizzle. April politely dismissed the driver, and she and Jade picked up their bags. Jade heard the screen door squeak open and turned to see who it was.

The Main Street lights, the darkened woods, and Joy's property all looked so different than Jade remembered. They were faded or muted, somehow lost to time. Willow looked exactly the same. She stood there wiping her hands on the same denim-blue apron, her posture tall and regal, matching the crown of snow-white dreadlocks piled high on her head. Her smile, nearly as white as her hair, contrasted her dark brown skin beautifully. She was still a queen to Jade.

"Jade, I'm so glad you're finally here."

Jade placed her bags back down and said, "Happy to see you too, Grandma Willow."

Willow gave her a sideways glance and said, "Um-hmm." She opened her arms wide, and Jade stepped into a huge hug. She breathed in hazelnut and coffee and comforting warmth that chased away the night's chill.

Willow said, "You aren't really. Not yet, but that will pass." She released her and said, "You'll have a good rest tonight, then tomorrow you can lend me a practiced hand to help with the million things we need to get done before tomorrow night's Farewell Feast."

Jade didn't see how she could be considered "practiced" since she hadn't made much more than tea and toast since moving away twenty years ago. Her adoptive parents had raised her with a full-time cook, and eating out was a regular event. She put off the correction and focused on introductions. "Grandma Willow, this is my friend April. April, this is Grandma Willow."

April held out her hand and said, "It's a pleasure to meet you, ma'am."

Willow looked at her hand with a raised eyebrow and then at Jade. "You didn't warn the poor child about us?" It took a moment for Jade to realize what she was referring to, but by then it was too late. She had grabbed April's hand and pulled her into a hug as big and welcoming as the one Jade had received. "We're wary of strangers in this town, but you're with Jade, so that makes you family."

Willow held her shoulders at arm's length. "And as family I expect you to call me Grandma Willow. It is a pleasure to meet you as well. I just know we'll have loads to talk about." She winked at her, then picked up April's bags and shooed her through the front door with them. "Now let's get inside where it's warm."

As the two entered the house in conversation, Jade took a moment on the porch to look out at the trees. Their vivid fall colors were muted by the dreary twilight. She was far from the sterile comfort of her gleaming city. In this small magical town, nestled in the wild countryside, lived the memories she had tried to forget. She'd spent the months after her parents' deaths trying so hard to return to her normal magical life, but each holiday ritual she'd attended had seemed duller than the last. The magic had slowly left her, leaking out of her life through the hole in her heart.

She shivered as the cool dampness in the air pressed against her thin blouse, and she pulled her light jacket closed. The rain had completely stopped, but the thick clouds remained, covering everything in a cold, wet gray blanket. It was as if the world was holding its breath, watching her and waiting for her to do something. Jade turned and followed April and Willow into the house.

April was following Willow up the long staircase to the second floor. "It really is a beautiful home."

Willow answered with a smile, "Thank you. Jade's auntie Joy was always proud of her things. She was very different from her sister in that. Two sides of the same coin, as they say."

There were sconces every few feet along the wall, and as Grandma Willow approached each one, it lit up and remained lit until all three of them had passed.

Jade took hold of the hand-carved wooden banister and followed them up. Along the wall between the sconces, portraits of her maternal family line stared back at her, their eyes seeming to follow her as she passed.

At the top of the steps Willow stopped at the first set of doors and said, "Kitchen broom fell this morning, so I made up the guest bedroom for company." She opened the bedroom door on the left side of the hall and placed the suitcases gently inside. The lights within turned on. "April, make yourself at home. The bathroom is next door, and there's fresh towels on your dresser." She motioned to a door halfway down the hall on the opposite side and said, "Jade, your old room is just as you left it, except for fresh sheets of course. First on the agenda tomorrow is brunch at the Keepsakes'. Ten minutes with them and you'll be caught up on all the town gossip for the entire year."

Perfect, Jade thought and rolled her eyes.

Willow admonished her, "Don't you dare roll your eyes at me, child. Have you completely forgotten your manners? Mrs. Keepsake is a longtime friend of your family and cared for your aunt very much. She is also mourning her loss, and you will show her respect."

Jade stood up straight, heat flushing her cheeks. "Yes, ma'am," she replied. She smiled slightly though, amused that even after all this time Willow could put her in her place that easily.

"Now, if either of you needs anything during your stay, I'll be in the room at the end of the hall. Since my little home is so far from town, I've been staying here to make arranging everything easier on me. I hope you don't mind, Jade."

"Of course not, Grandma Willow. Why would I mind?"

"Well I didn't think you would, but it's only polite for me to ask the lady of the house." Jade stared blankly at her. "This is your home now, Jade, or will be once the paperwork is settled." She pulled a small silver pocket watch out of the front of her apron and glanced at it. "My, it's getting late. I have one thing to finish up downstairs before I turn in, so I'll say good night and sleep well. I expect you both to be up early, and if you would come downstairs to give me a hand, that would be lovely." She said it as if they had offered to help and she was happily accepting. She squeezed Jade's shoulder briefly and seemed to float down the stairs.

As soon as she was out of sight, April whispered to Jade, "I like her. And they're not as primitive as everyone thinks." She pointed to a sconce. "Look, they even have motion sensor lighting."

Jade raised an eyebrow at her. "Look closer."

April did so. After a moment of frowning, she stood back, surprised. "What? It's not a bulb or a flame—" She squinted again at the small ball of light, hovering within the glass dome. "It's—the light's not connected to anything?"

Jade nodded, amused at her reaction. "I told you, you'd see some weird things. Just like there's technology everywhere in Sun City, there's magic everywhere here."

"Yeah, but knowing you'll see magic and actually seeing it are kinda different." She took a step toward her room, then paused. Turning back to Jade, she asked, "What was that about her broom falling?"

"It's a superstition. A broom falling means company's coming. Just one of the many things they believe here."

"Well, in this case it was true. I think this trip is going to be very interesting." She stepped into her room, looking around in wonder as if in a museum.

Jade grabbed her bags and walked toward her old room. *Lady of the house. My house.* As a kid she had always felt her aunt's house was a second home, but it was still her aunt's house.

She stared at the door with trepidation. Her memories of the time after her parents' deaths were fuzzy at best, and she was fine with that. It had been a terribly depressing time in her life she didn't want to remember. She felt opening that door would be opening her mind to those memories.

Oh, stop being a baby, Jade, she scolded herself and quickly opened the door, stepping inside.

CHAPTER 6

Entering her old room was like stepping back in time for Jade; everything was just as she remembered it. On the opposite wall was a huge pentagon-shaped stained-glass window. Each corner was connected by the leadwork, forming a star. The panels were each a different color and texture of glass. One of the panels was nearly clear and smooth, allowing one to peek down into the driveway.

It was covered by lacy white curtains. When Jade had moved in after her parents' deaths, she'd wanted thick black ones, but her aunt had insisted on something brighter. They compromised by adding a second curtain rod to accommodate a heavy set of forest-green curtains, which blocked out most of the light. Every time Jade would enter the room, she'd close them, and every time her aunt Joy would come in, she'd open them.

She placed her bag on the hope chest at the foot of the bed and turned to look at the right side of the room. While the rest of the room had been cleaned and cared for, this wall was untouched. On the right were several bookshelves, full to the brim with books of every color and size imaginable. She stepped up to the intricate cabinet on the left edge of the wall. Her altar was untraditional, like much of her magical practices had been. The top had curved sides that allowed the lid to slide over it, keeping the working surface out of sight. The bottom was reflective of the house it was in. Shelves and drawers were randomly placed along the front of the cabinet. There were no rows, and each compartment was its own unique size. Her aunt always nagged her about keeping it there. She said room corners were areas that collected all kinds of negative energy. Jade had thought that was all the more reason to have an altar there. Turn the negative energy into positive and use it.

Jade looked over each item on the open top of the altar fondly, seeing past the years of dust that covered them, remembering the way they'd looked when she'd used them regularly. The two white candles looked like the tops had been painted black from so much dust. It clung to the wax rivulets that hung on the sides, emphasizing their shape, making them appear almost alive. The small silver bell and knife were more like iron in appearance from the years of neglect and tarnish.

The tiny black cauldron in the center was the only thing that looked the same, though perhaps a bit duller. She had never cleaned it, at least not with water. After every spell was done, she would dump any ashes into the nearby river, then set it on the open windowsill to bathe in the moonlight and breeze overnight.

Jade focused on the cabinet's surface. The color of the wood was wrong somehow. It was grayish brown, dull and tired looking. She reached out her hand but stopped just short of touching it. Frowning sadly at the one forgotten item in the room, she turned her back on it and went to unpack her things.

***

"Good morning, sleepy head."

Willow's voice woke Jade, dragging her up from the depths. She stretched luxuriously, like a cat after a long nap. She cracked her eyes open to peek at the first beam of sunlight sneaking through the space between the heavy curtains.

Willow asked from the doorway, "How did you sleep?"

"Good." Jade was surprised. She sat up and stretched again. "Really good. What time is it?" Jade squinted at the invasive sunbeam that seemed to follow her every move.

"Early," Willow replied, walking toward the window. "Today is going to be busy. Lots of people want to see you." She threw open the heavy curtains, the sun filtering through the sheer ones, bathing the room in a soft golden light.

Oh goodie, Jade thought to herself. *Lots of people.*

Grandma Willow was tucking the curtains behind black iron hooks on either side of the window. "First thing's first, though. I appreciate you and April helping with some of the food prep for tonight." She walked out the door and tossed a cheerful thank-you over her shoulder as she left.

Jade took much longer than she usually would getting ready. Every few moments she found herself lost in a memory. They were good memories, for the most part. She remembered having a tea party with Aunt Joy one afternoon. They'd sat cross-legged on her bedroom floor, Joy twirling her pendant between her fingers, catching the sun's rays and reflecting them into Jade's eyes. She remembered running into Joy's bedroom one thunder-filled night and being lulled to sleep with Joy's voice as she told her stories of the gods of lightning and thunder. Jade had always felt safe here.

When she was finally ready, she peeked into April's room, but she wasn't there. She went downstairs and found her and Willow laughing together in the kitchen. April was standing at one end of the white marble island, cutting carrots, and Willow stood at the other, kneading dough. The bay windows over the double-basin farmhouse sink were partly shaded by light curtains with a white and yellow flower pattern. The morning sun shone through, casting yellow sunbeams streaming into the kitchen like rays from heaven. Jade took a moment to enjoy the scene. It was like something out of a Rockwell painting, a small-town home setting that worked on your soul like comfort food, warming you from the inside out. For a moment, she forgot why she was there.

Willow asked, "You all right, dear?"

"Yes, I'm fine. I was just trying to figure out what that delicious smell was."

"Oh, you should recognize that, Jade." She turned to April. "She would come running in the back door every Saturday morning, just as I took a fresh batch of stuffed apples out of the oven." She winked at Jade as she put on her oven mitts. When she opened the oven door, the scent of cinnamon and apples filled the kitchen, bringing smiles to both girls.

Willow placed the large pan of apples on the stovetop. "Now, while these cool, you can make yourself useful and get started on peeling those potatoes there, thank you." Willow motioned to the huge tub heaped with freshly washed potatoes next to the sink.

Jade walked over to the sink and began peeling the spuds one by one and placing them in the pot on the other side of the sink. Soon she was lost in a daydream of her past.

***

Eight-year-old Jade ran through the back door of her aunt's kitchen, the worn screen door slamming shut behind her. Joy looked up from her pot of potatoes at the kitchen sink. "Jade dear, you're just in time."

Jade smiled proudly as she trotted over to her aunt. She froze in place, and the smile vanished as she rounded the kitchen island. Charlie was standing next to the compost bin, peeling carrots. "Charlie Jordan, you cheat!"

Charlie gave his most innocent face. "What'd I do?"

"You know darn well." Jade was stalking toward him with her hands on her hips. "There's no way you could have made it here before me without cheating."

Joy stepped in before Jade could reach Charlie and stood as referee between them. "Now how do you know that, Jade? Maybe he's just faster than you."

Jade backed down just enough to show respect for her aunt and tried to calmly explain her side of the story. "Mom said we could come here for lunch. I told Charlie I could beat him here, and he said okay. So, we went on the back porch and I said 'one, two, three, go!' and started running. When I got to the other side of the field, I looked back and he was way behind me. Like, not even at the road yet. So, there's no way he could have got here first if I was that far ahead to start." She crossed her arms and smiled triumphantly at Charlie, certain that she had won again.

"Did you specify he had to run?" Joy stood up straight and played with the pendant around her neck, smiling down at her niece.

"Well no . . . but—"

The road that passed by the field led around a lake to her aunt's house. The path Jade had taken, while straighter, cut through a dense forest with fallen trees and boulders, not to mention the stream that fed the lake. Jade had been forced to slow down as soon as she'd hit the tree line. Charlie would have made it to her aunt's house in plenty of time if he'd gotten a ride right away.

"Fine," Jade said, completely miserable she had overlooked that possibility. "You win this time, but next time, I'm gonna make rules."

Joy smiled and placed a hand gently on Jade's shoulder. "Now you know to be careful how you word what you want to happen. It's like they used to say. 'The devil is in the details.'"

Charlie looked at her, puzzled. "But Miss Joy, you don't believe in the devil, do you?"

"No, dear, but those who did had a valid point; the details are what will usually mess you up if you don't pay close attention to them. Now, why don't you take over spud duty for me, Jade?"

Jade jumped up on the stepstool her aunt placed in front of the sink for her and finished peeling the potato her aunt had left. She looked back to see Charlie peeling his carrots, orange shreds flying everywhere, and her aunt kneading away at a huge mound of dough.

She didn't really mind losing to Charlie and smiled as she concentrated on carefully peeling the potato in her hand. I'll get him next time, *she thought.*

***

Jade snapped back to the present. She knew what that little girl didn't—nothing lasts and people die. She dragged the peeler blindly across the potato and winced when it sliced into her finger. "Ow!" She dropped the peeler and potato into the sink.

"Are you okay?" Willow asked as she came over to her.

Jade looked from Willow to her finger. "Yeah. Um, just distracted I guess." She gave Willow a weak smile.

"Here." Willow pulled the potted comfrey plant off the windowsill and, after bowing her head for a moment, plucked off a small leaf. She put the leaf in her mouth and chewed while she grabbed a small piece of cloth out of a nearby drawer. She gently took Jade's hand, placed the chewed-up leaf over the cut, and tied it on with the cloth. "Now just give that a minute or two to work."

Jade smiled slightly at the familiar old procedure. "You still refuse to use store-bought medicine, I see."

Willow smiled fondly back. "I always will." She gave Jade's hand a gentle pat and returned to her work of kneading the dough on the island.

Jade turned to see April giving her a quizzical look. "Is this one of those things we talked about?"

Jade replied, "Sort of." She went back to peeling her potatoes, at a much slower pace. "Comfrey is used for cuts because it has antibacterial properties and chemicals that help cells grow faster, is all."

Willow put her mound of dough in a bowl and covered it with a kitchen towel. She pushed the bowl of dough aside to rise, then took a large slab of beef out of the fridge.

April asked, "So, is all this food for the wake? Or do you not have wakes?"

Willow told her, "We have something similar called the Farewell Feast." Jade gave Willow a look, hoping she would not jump in with details of communing with the dead. Willow continued with, "It's basically a potluck dinner where everyone shares things they remember most about whoever has passed. I'm making the apples as my own contribution. Being the family's immediate relative, Jade is responsible for the main dish and traditional bread. I've decided stew will be easiest for the three of us to make. We're making enough for all thirteen council members and any guests they bring."

"Well, I've just cut enough carrots to feed the whole town, probably." She giggled. "What's next?"

Willow directed them in gathering and measuring the ingredients into a giant crock pot. After setting it for eight hours, she said, "April, would you please get Jade's coat for her, and grab one for yourself? We need to head out to the Keepsakes', and I believe it's still a bit cold outside."

April nodded and left without arguing.

Jade asked Willow, "What's that about?"

Willow said, "You wanted to talk, so talk." She sat down on a stool opposite Jade at the kitchen island.

"What makes you think I want to talk?"

Willow tilted her head at Jade. "You really have been away for a long time. Have you forgotten I can sense intention more clearly than even your mother could? Every time April asks a question, or I go to speak, you want to stop me from speaking. It's so strong I would probably have a sore throat if you were still connected to your magic."

"A sore throat?" Jade asked.

"Yes. I doubt you could truly silence me. You are decades younger than me, after all. So, what is it you don't want me to say?"

Jade wanted to be tactful, but Willow appreciated blunt honesty as well as manners. "April doesn't know I'm here to become High Priestess. In fact, she doesn't know my parents were coven leaders." Jade held her breath while Willow seemed to consider what she'd said.

"I see. And precisely when, may I ask, were you planning on telling her?" Her disapproving stare cut to Jade's heart.

"I'm sorry. I'm going to tell her, it's just . . . it's hard."

Willow waved a hand dismissively. "There are times to keep secrets, child, but this isn't one of them. The longer you wait to tell her, the more it will hurt her and"—she raised a finger—"the harder it will be to say."

"Grandma Willow—"

"Don't worry, I don't tell other people's lies for them. Just be sure you don't wait too long. You have a lot to go through these coming days, and you'll need her support and friendship to help you. Secrets damage relationships. Don't damage yours unnecessarily."

Jade knew she was right; she didn't like it though.

Willow placed a hand on her shoulder gently. "Trust me, April is more understanding than you give her credit for." She gave Jade a proud smile, then focused behind her. "Perfect timing, April." She grabbed her lace-trimmed white gloves off the chair next to her and pulled them on. "Let's get going, shall we?" Picking up her purse from the table she walked out.

CHAPTER 7

April handed Jade her coat. After putting it on, April linked arms with her, and they followed Willow out. As they reached the front door, Jade felt April pull back on her arm, slowing her down. Once Willow was several paces ahead, she whispered, "She seems pretty happy for someone who supposedly lost her best friend. She told me your aunt and she used to hang out a lot, especially after your parents . . ."

Jade finished for her, "You can say it, April. They died."

"See, that's what I don't get. She's been nothing but friendly and upbeat this whole time, like we're just here on holiday or something. What's her deal? Is it another one of those weird things you said I'd see?"

Jade replied, "That's just how they are. They see death differently than we do because they don't believe it's an ending." She reluctantly continued, "They believe the spirit first moves through a veil, where it's greeted by loved ones who have passed on before."

April nodded. "That's not too weird so far. Citizens used to believe something similar, generations ago."

Jade continued, "Then it gets weird."

They'd reached the car, and although Willow was already in the driver's seat, she asked through the open window, "What's weird?"

April replied, "Jade was just explaining the way you see death differently from us in the city." She hopped in the back seat and closed the door, while Jade walked around to get in the front passenger seat.

The old gas engine roared to life, and Willow slowly steered the big blue boat of a car down the drive as she said, "I'm surprised at you for calling it weird, Jade, since it's what you were first taught. But I suppose after you've lived for years in the city, it would seem a bit unusual. You see, we believe our spirits never die. When your body is no longer able to support it, your spirit passes through the veil between worlds into the Summerland. It's a wonderful place, April. Much like the heaven Citizens used to believe in. You get to see your loved ones again, you don't feel pain or stress. All your worries melt away." She smiled for a moment.

April remarked, "You almost talk as if you've been there."

Oh boy, Jade thought. *Here it comes.*

"Actually, April, I have. Many times. We all have. It's very rare that a new spirit is born. Most people decide to be reborn after they die, so almost all the current population has been to the Summerland before. They just don't remember."

April thought a moment before asking, "You said 'most people.' Can people decide not to be reborn?"

Willow replied, "They have several options. They could become guardians, spirits who guide and support those who are alive. They could remain in the veil or Summerland to help others across. They could even leave Earth altogether and travel the universe."

Jade frowned at the rosy picture Willow was painting. "Or they could become trapped in the veil or on Earth, condemned to live for eternity as a ghost, growing angrier and more vengeful as time goes on."

Willow gave her an admonishing look. "Child, you know that's a very rare occurrence and not nearly as frightening as you're trying to make it sound." She glanced at April in the rearview mirror. "There are times this happens, but it's rare. It's simply because the spirit refuses to move on. They continue hanging on to their former lives and cannot pass through the veil. That's why there are people who help spirits cross."

April said, "Well, that all sounds very . . . reasonable. It would be nice to believe something like that were real. I mean, not that it's not real, necessarily. I don't mean to offend."

"Don't trouble yourself. I know you mean well. It's difficult to see another's viewpoint when you've no experience with it yourself. You'll learn in time." Jade was about to ask what she meant by that when Willow said, "Ah, here we are."

They pulled into the Keepsakes' driveway and April exclaimed, "Whoa! And I thought your aunt's house was big." She turned to gape out the window.

Jade smiled at her reaction. She'd forgotten how huge the house could seem the first time you saw it. Her aunt's house was like a haunted mansion, large and forbidding with the promise of secret passages. The Keepsakes' was like a castle. Made of stone and marble, it promised elaborate galas and the spoils of wealth.

They walked up the front steps and stopped on the landing. After a moment Willow turned to them and said, "That's strange. She always opens the door when we approach." She knocked several times on the door, but no one answered. "Let's go around back."

Jade and April followed Willow around the right side of the house to the backyard. The path they followed was the most perfectly manicured Jade had ever seen. It was a stark contrast to the mostly wild and slightly overgrown winding paths of Joy's property. This footpath of square flagstone was ruler straight. Not a single blade of grass dared break the lines of blue-gray stone. The backyard was a rolling field of green dotted by statues and topiary. The marble patio had a round iron table and chairs set for five, with delicate flowered china.

As they passed the bay windows looking out from the kitchen, a high-pitched scream came from the house. Jade turned toward the window and could barely make out someone waving furiously inside through the reflection on the glass.

A moment later, a bustling bundle of energy exploded out the French doors, all waving arms and high-pitched squeals of joy. Mrs. Keepsake trotted over to Jade and enveloped her in a smothering embrace. "Aaah! Y'all made it! I'm so happy to see you, darlin'!"

"I'm happy to see you too," Jade replied, then mouthed to April, *Sorry*. She had wanted to warn her that Grandma Willow's greetings were nothing compared to Mrs. Keepsake's, but their talk about death had pushed it from her mind, and now it was too late.

Mrs. Keepsake released her hold on Jade, her silver shoulder-length curls leaving the scent of cinnamon in their wake. "Of course, I do wish it were better circumstances, but you're here now. Oh!" She practically bounced on her toes. "We have so much to catch up on, I almost don't know where to start."

Willow said, "I apologize for just walking into your yard, but you didn't answer our knock. Is everything all right?"

"Yes, that is strange, isn't it?" Mrs. Keepsake said. "Well, we've all been having issues with our spells lately, haven't we? I'll just have a look at it later." She turned toward April. "Now, who have we here?"

Willow said, "May I introduce Jade's friend April, from Sun City."

As Mrs. Keepsake turned toward April, Jade was surprised to see her stand straight and hold out her hand formerly to her. As April shook it, she said, "Welcome to Sugar Hill, dear."

"Thank you. It's a pleasure to meet you," April replied.

Mrs. Keepsake said, "Likewise. It's such a lovely morning, I thought we'd take our brunch on the back patio." She waved toward the iron table. "If y'all have a seat, I'll be right back with the first course." As they sat, she trotted into the kitchen and returned with a tray of muffins and a flowered teapot that matched the teacups and pattern on her dress exactly. Mrs. Keepsake sat the tray in front of her seat, then leaned toward April, offering her the plate of muffins. "I am expecting one more guest, but I don't think they'll mind if we start without them." She glanced at Willow.

Jade saw the look and became instantly nervous. "What's that look for?" she asked warningly.

"Look? What look?" Mrs. Keepsake replied innocently, then winked at April.

"*That* look. You look mischievous, and when you look mischievous . . . well, it's not good."

Mrs. Keepsake looked past her for a moment, then laughed and said quietly to Jade, "Jade dear, it's not about being good, it's about doing what is for your own good." She rose and said in her most cheerful voice, "There you are! We were starting to think you'd gotten lost."

A deep male voice chuckled behind her. "Of course not, Mrs. K. I could find your lovely home blindfolded."

There's something familiar about that laugh, Jade thought as she rose with Willow and April. As Mrs. Keepsake walked with him back toward the table, Jade looked him over. He was only a couple of inches taller than her, and muscled but not overly so. He wore a black leather jacket and blue jeans, with a dark bloodred crew-neck shirt. As he turned to the side to greet April, Jade noticed a small copper earing in his right ear and an iron band on his right index finger.

When he turned to greet Jade, her heart nearly stopped. His chiseled features and dark curly hair contrasted starkly with his pale blue eyes. As she looked into them for the first time in years she was mesmerized. *Charlie?*

The last time she had seen him, he was running after her car, tears streaming down his face as she was driven out of town and headed for Sun City. How had that young boy managed to become the current handsome man she saw now?

She felt the heat rising in her cheeks as she managed to croak out, "Hello." *What is wrong with me?* So, he was good looking. She'd met men hotter and certainly more powerful than him and hadn't been fazed. Here was her old friend, her companion and sometimes punching bag, and suddenly she was a mess.

After a moment she cleared her throat and tried again. "Good to see you, Charlie. It's been a long time."

Something in his eyes sparked. "Yes, it has." He took her hand gently but firmly, and Jade relaxed into its warmth. He was so familiar and yet so foreign to her. And she couldn't stop staring at his eyes. They had always been blue, but she hadn't remembered them being so stunning.

After another heartbeat, he released her hand with a smile and looked at Willow as he stepped back toward the empty seat. "Grandma Willow, it's so good to see you again."

They all sat down at the table, and tea and muffins were passed around. Mrs. Keepsake was the first to speak. "It's a shame we have to meet under such circumstances, April. I do hope you are able to enjoy your time here. Just let me know if there's anything you need. Since you won't be able to accompany Jade to the Crossing Over ceremony—"

"Funeral," Jade mentioned to April.

"Uh . . . yes, funeral, tonight. Maybe this evening I can show you round town and you can catch me up on how our Jade's been doing all these years. It's almost a shame really. Charlie does the most beautiful ceremonies and rituals. But we must stick to tradition, and only family is allowed." She brightened. "Maybe you'll get to see him at work during the Ascension ritual Saturday. Usually the whole town attends those, so I'm sure you'll be able to go."

April asked, "What's an Ascension ritual?"

Willow explained, "The Ascension is what designates a High Priestess and High Priest to lead the coven and binds their magical energy to it. It's the most important ritual a coven can perform since it serves so many functions, including protecting the coven."

Jade's brain finally caught up to the shocking part of what Mrs. Keepsake had said. "Wait, Charlie's rituals?" Charlie had never shown any magical abilities, and she never would have imagined him leading a ritual. She asked Willow, "He's leading rituals now?"

"Yes, he is," Charlie replied. "A lot has changed since we were kids. Including my becoming High Priest."

Jade was dumbstruck. *There's no way!*

Charlie smiled at her expression, but it didn't reach his eyes. "I've been studying. Had to since you left."

"I don't understand," April said.

Willow explained, "Every coven must have a High Priestess and High Priest to lead them. Without leadership it soon falls apart and disbands. When our last High Priest died, that role needed to be filled."

"And the most qualified person for the job was Charlie?" Jade asked. "He was ten years old!"

"Eleven," Charlie corrected. "And so what? There have been High Priests younger than that before. That's why we have an entire coven of elders. They make the hard decisions and train the High Priestess or Priest until they're ready to lead."

"True, but potentials usually begin training from the time they can talk. And aren't you an Esolate, anyway?"

"Esolate?" April whispered to Mrs. Keepsake.

"Opposite of a Natural, who's someone who barely needs training, like Jade. An Esolate is basically someone without apparent magical skills. They have to train hard to become adept at magic."

Jade turned back to Charlie. "Look, it doesn't really matter. I was just surprised that someone who never did a single spell when we were kids would be capable of becoming High Priest."

"Well, I am. Joy sacrificed everything to make sure I would be more than capable."

"Sacrificed? In what way?" Jade suddenly had a weird feeling of being watched pricking at the back of her neck. She glanced at Willow and could tell she was sensing something too.

Charlie glared at April before giving Jade a pointed look. "It's complicated. We'll talk about it another time. After all, we're here to prepare for Joy's farewell." He turned to ask Mrs. Keepsake something, completely dismissing Jade.

As the heat rose in her cheeks, Jade crossed her arms and sat back in her chair. "No, Charlie. We have time." She lowered her voice slightly. "Explain it."

Nervous looks of varying intensity flew around the table. Willow rested her hand on Jade's shoulder. "Jade, perhaps Charlie is right." She glanced at April. "We have a guest."

Jade was not calmed. If anything, she was angrier. She felt she was being treated like a kid and her friend was the enemy. "April is your guest, but she is my best friend. Anything you can say to me, you can say in front of her."

Charlie glared at her. "No. As High Priest it's my duty to protect this coven. She's heard enough. All you need to know right now is that we had no choice. You were gone."

This was the moment she dreaded, explaining her leaving to Charlie. "I had no choice either."

"You had a choice. You just didn't want to choose the hard route."

"You think what I did was easy? I left the only home I ever knew, moved to a city where I knew nobody, and left behind my best friend."

"You see, that's just it. Best friends don't leave each other without saying goodbye. And no, I don't think it was easy, but I do think it was easier than staying."

"I wanted to! I tried to! That day, I made them wait for you to come home. I told them I wasn't going anywhere until we said goodbye. When you finally got there, you walked right past me. You looked past me, like I wasn't even there!" She struggled against the tears that she felt welling up inside her heart. "You just went right in the house." She swallowed hard and turned the sadness inside into anger and aimed it at him. "You didn't even care I was leaving."

"Why should I have?" Charlie frowned at his teacup. "I could see it in your face, your mind was made up and there was nothing I could have said to change it." He looked up, glaring straight into her eyes. "You never did listen to me."

Jade couldn't believe he was acting like this. Her voice was low and dangerous. "You don't know anything."

She stood and addressed the rest of the table as if Charlie had never been there. "Thank you, Mrs. Keepsake, for having us over, but I'm afraid I've lost my appetite. Grandma Willow, we're going to wait in the car. If you'll excuse us." She gave April a pointed look and turned to walk away, imagining everyone at the table staring after her.

She heard April push her chair back, and as her footsteps caught up, she faintly heard Mrs. Keepsake say, "Well, that could have gone better."

CHAPTER 8

Jade sat fuming in Willow's car, replaying the fight in her head. Charlie was High Priest. Charlie. That was surprising, shocking even, but it wasn't what upset her. *"You never did listen to me"? How could he say that? How could he think it?* Jade always listened to Charlie. Sure, she may not have done what he wanted most of the time, but she always listened. It was definitely not the reunion she had envisioned. More than that, they had treated April like an outsider. Of course, she was, but April had always been there for her. It didn't matter if she was from the city, Jade expected them to treat her with respect.

"So, that's the mysterious Charlie." April wiggled her eyebrows at Jade.

Jade smirked at her. "Don't do that. Eyebrows should never be allowed to move like that."

"Well, tell me about him."

"What's to tell? We used to be friends, now we're not."

As Willow got into the car, Jade began to speak but was shushed. *Grandma Willow actually shushed me?*

"April, I'm sorry you had to witness that. Jade and Charlie should have dealt with whatever issues they had privately. We are not in the habit of being so open with outsiders. We are happy to answer any questions you have, but I hope you will understand that some of the inner workings of our coven must remain private."

April replied, "Of course. I didn't mean to pry. I was just trying to understand what I could."

Willow smiled at her and turned to Jade. "And you, Missy. You may be an adult, but I am still your elder in both age and council status, at least for now. You will show me the respect I have earned."

"I apologize."

Willow straightened. "We'll say no more on the subject."

The whole ride home Jade felt like they were all frozen inside that car, waiting to be freed. As soon as the car stopped, Jade got out and managed to refrain from slamming the door. "I think I'd like some time alone. If that's all right."

"That's fine. Remember the feast is in a couple hours, so don't go far."

"I won't," she replied and headed up the steps to her room.

She threw herself across the bed and lay there for what seemed like forever. The tears she felt welling up inside just wouldn't come. She rolled over and stared up at the ceiling. Before her parents had died, Aunt Joy had set this room up for her so that she could come visit any time she wanted. She would spend hours here, completely cut off from the world, yet a part of it all at the same time.

She looked over at her dusty altar in the corner of the room, then got up and walked over to it. The roll top was open and the items laid out for a cleansing spell. The day she left she had cast one to release herself from the pain of her past and start her life anew. Turning away from the altar, she pressed her back against the wall between it and her bookcase, willing herself to disappear, to go back in time, anything to stop the pain.

She felt a draft on her left arm and had a vague memory of there being a door here. *No, not a door exactly, but there was another room . . . wasn't there?* She reached her hand behind the bookcase and pushed, wriggling her arm after it and soon her head. Her whole body slipped through, and she emerged on the other side of the wall. *My secret room!* The memories came flooding back as she struggled to see in the darkness.

Jade had spent so much time there as a kid that she knew its dimensions by heart. It was only four feet wide but as long as her bedroom was, and the ceiling was far out of reach. The room was completely empty, with nothing on the walls and no outlets or light switches.

She had always felt safe there, even in the days after her parents' deaths. It was the one place she could count on to make her feel everything would be all right. The problem was when she left, whatever had been bothering her was still out there, waiting for her. She leaned her head back against the wall and closed her eyes. *Just for a minute,* she promised herself, sliding down to the floor.

She let her mind drift, not pushing it any one direction, not really thinking of any one thing. She entered a trance state, neither awake nor asleep. As she sat there, she soon realized she was unable to move. Then the sensations came.

The footfall of someone running on gravel.

The salty taste of tears.

The silky texture of burnt wood.

The acrid smell of smoke.

Danger. Pain. Struggle. Sacrifice. Power so overwhelming she began to shake.

A woman screamed.

Jade's eyes flew open and she stared blindly into the dark. She waited, breathing heavily, wiping the sweat from her face. A blanket of calm descended on her. She took two deep breaths, smelling the cool dusty air around her. She hadn't had a vision like that since she was little. Back then they happened regularly, though usually not as frightening.

She stood and began to feel her way along the wall for the opening to get out. She passed her hands back and forth, feeling only the smooth texture of the wall. After several moments her fingers felt a draft. She quickly pushed toward it and tumbled into her bedroom.

She picked herself up just as April appeared in the doorway. "I'm sorry I can't go with you to the funeral . . . I mean Crossing Over ceremony, but I get it. Even though I don't really understand your traditions, I do respect them." She gave a small smile. "Oh, and Grandma Willow wanted me to let you know 'Guests will be arriving soon, and if you don't get down here and lend a hand setting up, I'm gonna tan your backside, grown-up or no.'" She gave Jade an embarrassed smile. "Her words, not mine."

"I know. She was always threatening that when I was little. I never gave her the opportunity to follow through though."

"Sounds like you were a bit of a troublemaker." April smirked. "What happened to you?"

"Life," Jade replied, and they headed downstairs.

***

As Jade and April entered the living room, Willow and Charlie were talking in hushed tones.

Willow said, "April. Just the person I wanted to see." She walked right past Jade with only a brief smile to acknowledge her presence. "You're so kind to help me with something in the kitchen, thank you." She took her arm, and they disappeared through the kitchen door. Jade was left standing with Charlie.

As she took a step toward the kitchen, Charlie spoke, a little too loudly. "I don't think I've said yet—" They made eye contact, and he froze in midsentence. He swallowed hard, then continued in a softer tone, "I'm sorry." He took a step toward her, but she backed up. He nodded and stepped back. "About your aunt, I mean. She was a good woman. Strong, kind. She didn't deserve—"

"Thank you," Jade said shortly. She didn't want to talk about her aunt. She just wanted this day to be over, and it was a long way from being that. She took another step toward the kitchen door.

"Jade." Charlie stopped her with a gesture. "Willow told me not to say anything to April about your role in the coven. While I will honor that request, there's something we need to discuss." He lowered his voice, turning away from the kitchen door slightly. It brought his face only inches from hers, and she felt the tension rise in her back. "You have a choice to make, and there's really no time to hesitate."

"What choice?" She had an idea what he was referring to.

"The Ascension."

Yup, that's the one. "No," Jade answered sharply, trying to keep her voice down. "I don't have a choice. I've been forced into accepting responsibility for a coven I haven't been a part of in years. But since I'm the last of my bloodline, I have to. I hate it, but there's nothing I can do. So, I'm here. I'll do the Ascension, I'll lead the coven, you win, okay?" She started toward the door again, and Charlie blocked her path. She crossed her arms and glared at him. "What?"

He sighed. "You know how important it is for us to replace Joy with a proper High Priestess as soon as possible. Every day we wait leaves our coven in danger."

"Danger? What do you mean? Is there something going on I don't know about?"

"There's a lot you don't know about. What you should know now is that without a High Priestess we're not at full strength. We need you, Jade. Your coven needs you. We've been struggling since you left. Losing both leaders at once is a devastating blow to a coven's Essence."

"Essence?" She hadn't heard the term used in relation to a coven before.

"Yes." He gave her a quizzical look for a moment. "You were so powerful before. I keep forgetting you didn't finish your training. Magic isn't really inanimate. It's connected to the living spirit of every Witch who uses it. In a coven that connection is amplified and consolidated. It becomes a living thing of its own. We call it Essence. When a coven is healthy and strong, so is its Essence. Spellwork comes easily and the coven members are happy and powerful. When a coven is wounded, its Essence suffers." Charlie paused, and a pained look washed over his face.

"And losing a High Priestess wounds a coven?"

He nodded. "Or a High Priest. Usually the transfer from one coven leader to another is prepared for and done while they're still alive." He looked away from her, seeming to become lost in his own thoughts. "Losing Joy came at the worst possible time." He frowned at her for a moment before softly asking, "Do you remember what happened just after we lost your parents? How everyone seemed affected by it and even Grandma Willow was struggling to cast spells?"

She gave Charlie a warning glare. "Of course, I remember. Everyone in town loved them." She looked down at the dining room table, its surface pitted and scarred from generations of use.

"That's true, but it was more than that. When we lost your parents, it hurt our coven's Essence almost to the point of collapse. With both our leaders gone at once, we were holding on by a thread. We only survived because Joy stepped in. I don't know how much you remember of what training you had, but not just any Witch can lead a coven. At least not without consequences. Many factors contribute to a Witch's compatibility, but bloodline is most important. As Rose's sister, Joy was part of the Cerridwen High Priestess bloodline, but she hadn't been trained for it like your mother had, or you had started to be."

Jade could see where this was headed. She placed her hands on her hips. "Enough with the history lesson, Charlie. Just tell me what you want from me."

"I want you to make the choice to commit to being High Priestess. I want you to commit to leading this coven."

"I said I would." She took a step toward the door, and Charlie blocked her yet again. She tilted her head at him, her voice low and threatening. "You know, you really should stop doing that."

"I will, when we're done talking." She took a step back and crossed her arms again, so he continued, "Saying you'll do something and committing to it are not the same. I think you're planning on going through the motions, doing the Ascension ritual and getting the coven back on its feet, then going back to the city and being an absentee leader. The problem is coven magic doesn't work like that. You have to not only be here, but be—"

"Committed. I heard you."

"I hope so." The fierceness in his eyes was replaced by sorrow. "Because if you don't, you're not the only one who will suffer."

Before Jade could reply, April entered. "Willow said she can use some help in the backyard."

Charlie held Jade's gaze for a moment more, then passed by April into the kitchen.

April watched him go, then gave Jade a concerned look. "Hey, you all right?"

"Not really, but what can I do?" She gave her a weak smile and looped her arm in April's. Squeezing it close to her, she leaned her head on April's shoulder for a moment and said, "I'm just grateful you're here."

April squeezed back, and as they walked out the door, she replied, "Always."

CHAPTER 9

As they entered the kitchen, Jade was overwhelmed. White carnations were everywhere. There were five oversized bouquets, as well as an individual flower for each place setting. She looked over at Willow, who stood at the end of the kitchen island directing the last flower into a vase without touching it. April had been looking across the room and hadn't seemed to notice. "April and I are here to help."

Willow said cheerfully, "Good, you can go out back and help Charlie set up the tent, tables, and chairs. Soon as April and I finish these place settings, we'll be out."

"I'm sure Charlie can handle that himself. Why don't we both help you?"

Willow stopped and stared Jade down. "Go outside, now." She then smiled at April and said, "April, I appreciate you handing me that ribbon next to you, thank you."

"Don't worry, I'll be fine." April picked up the green-and-white-striped ribbon off the counter and brought it to Willow.

Jade opened the back door as Willow asked April, "How are you at tying fancy bows?"

Jade walked out onto the porch. The view was dominated by a huge pentagon-shaped tent set up in the yard. The cream-colored canvas of the roofline glowed orange in spots, as if a light string were underneath. Jade knew she wouldn't find any wires, like the sconces in the stairway. Several of the glowing dots flickered, as if struggling to stay lit. Charlie was tying back a flap on the tent door, while five round tables marched in an orderly line into the tent.

Jade blinked several times at the scene in front of her, then glanced behind her. April was still engrossed in tying bows to all the vases. She'd been okay with the mysteriously lit sconces, but Jade worried seeing walking furniture might be a bit much. She wanted to ease her into magic, not smack her in the face with it.

She ran down the steps and confronted Charlie in a low voice, "What the hell are you doing?"

He raised an eyebrow at her. "Tying back the doorway so we can actually enter the tent? What's your damage now?"

Jade rolled her eyes and pointed forcefully to the last table marching past them. "Tables don't walk! At least not where we're from. You can't let her see this."

Charlie had finished tying the flap out of the way. "First of all, you are from here. Second, April won't see anything she's not ready to see."

"What does that mean?" She looked at the back door of the house again.

"It means Willow spelled her."

Jade turned slowly toward Charlie. "What?" Her face flushed hot and there was a tingling in her extremities.

"Willow put a spell on April to keep her from seeing any magic she wasn't prepared to deal with."

The tingling in her hands turned to warmth, and she clenched her fists tightly, resisting the urge to wrap them around his throat. "She put a spell . . . on my best friend . . . without her permission?"

Charlie looked down and his eyes grew wide. "Looks like you're starting to connect to your power."

Jade looked down. Tiny blue sparks were dancing across her knuckles, like static electricity gone wild. The moment she realized what she was seeing, they began to fade. She stretched her fingers out, looking her hands over front and back. Her hands had grown warm, but she hadn't felt the sparks. She wasn't surprised she was raising power, just that she wasn't consciously controlling it. Magic without control could be deadly.

She wrung her hands and flung them downward, releasing the last traces of energy. "I'm not connecting to any power," she lied. "That was . . . it was a mistake. It won't happen again."

Charlie tilted his head and said softly, "Don't worry about April. It's a mild spell, easily broken by willpower. Willow was only trying to take one worry off your mind. She would never put her in danger."

Jade gave him a sideways glare. "Of course not. That's not the point."

"What's not the point?" April asked from the porch. She was carrying a large vase in each arm as she walked carefully down the porch steps toward them.

Jade breathed a sigh of relief that the tables had already settled into their positions inside the tent. "Oh, nothing. Coven business." She waved a dismissive hand in Charlie's direction, then quickly approached April. "Here, let me help with those." She took one of the vases and followed her into the tent. They each placed one in the center of a table, and Willow brought out two more.

"April, it's so kind of you to grab the last vase out of the kitchen, thank you."

April nodded and hurried out of the tent. Jade put on her best fake smile and said to Willow, "I hear you spelled April?"

Willow raised an eyebrow at her and said in a voice far too cheerful, "Why yes, child, I did. And I'll spell you too if need be. Now, I suggest you climb down off that high horse you rode into town on and stow your pride in a box. You knew what you were getting into when you came back, and I'm guessing if you really care about April as you claim, you prepared her as well. We have bigger issues to deal with than me putting a mild glamour on your friend."

She flicked her wrist toward the tables. A breeze blew through the tent, chasing sparkling lights, which swirled over each table like glitter on the wind. As the sparkles passed, full place settings appeared in their wake.

The last table was set and the glittering light show swooped out the door just as April entered with the last bouquet. "I think I hear a car—what?" She looked around at the tables. "You guys are fast." She smiled at Jade as she placed the bouquet on the last table.

Willow said, "I'll go greet our guests. Charlie, you know where the serving dishes are. It's so nice of you three to plate our part of the meal, thank you." She waltzed quickly out of the tent and up the porch steps.

***

For the next half hour Jade had no time to be worried or angry. The guests seemed to arrive all at once, each family bringing their own addition to the meal. By the time all the serving plates were filled and everyone started to take their seats, Jade had forgotten about April being spelled.

The five tables in the tent formed a circle. All thirteen of the coven members had come, as well as a few important guests. The head table was at the back of the tent. It was oval, and Jade, April, Charlie, and Willow all sat on one side, facing everyone else. April was going to be seated at one of the other tables, but Jade had insisted that as her guest she wanted April next to her. Willow and Charlie had agreed without complaint.

As Willow was sitting down at the other end of the table, a young woman dressed all in blue came up to her and said, "Ms. Scrivener asked me to tell you she's running a bit late and we should start without her."

"Thank you, Crystal," Willow replied. The woman left to take her seat.

April leaned over and asked Jade, "Are we missing someone?" She nodded toward the empty chair on Jade's left, between her and Charlie.

"A place setting is left open for the guest of honor, in this case for Joy." Jade refused to look at the chair.

Charlie stood and gently tapped the side of his glass, the sound much louder than expected. When everyone was nearly quiet, he said, "Coven members and friends. Welcome to Joy's Farewell Feast. Tonight, we celebrate her life and contributions to our community, and say farewell as she prepares to cross through the veil."

Everyone spoke as one: "Merry meet, merry part, and merry meet again."

Out of the corner of her eye, Jade could see him turn toward her. She knew what was expected but she couldn't move. She just stared at her plate. Empty.

After a moment he turned back and continued, "I'm sure I speak for Jade when I say, we will miss Joy very much. She was a mentor to both of us. In coven traditions, magical practices, and life lessons. When I was called to take up the mantle of High Priest, Joy was right there with me. She took on High Priestess with such poise and strength and led me through those early years." He bowed his head for a moment, "I would have been lost without her. Thank you, Joy, for your guidance." He raised his glass toward the empty chair.

Just then a tall thin woman in a prim pinstripe gray suit entered the tent hurriedly. Ducking her head, she half whispered, "My apologies." Hugging her thick briefcase to her like a shield, she shuffled past the empty seat next to Mrs. Keepsake and straight to Willow's side.

Jade struggled to hear what they were saying. The woman whispered something about, "We have a problem . . ." Willow tilted her head, and after several words were exchanged, Jade heard the woman say, "No, I looked there too." Willow pressed her hands downward in a kind of *calm down* gesture and turned toward the crowd.

"It seems something has come up, and we're going to have to move things along. Please forgive the disruption. Enjoy your dinner while we adjourn for the reading of the will." She motioned to Charlie and Jade to rise and follow her.

Jade grabbed April's hand and whispered, "I'll be back in a little bit. You'll be okay here?"

"Of course," she smiled.

Jade rose and followed Willow and the woman in gray out of the back door of the tent, a door Jade could swear hadn't been there moments before.

The door led to another room, like a smaller version of the main tent. There was only one table in the center of the room, but the same lights followed the roof's perimeter as in the large tent. Several of them started flickering. As the tent door closed, the lights slowly faded out, and the thick canvas of the tent blocked most of the daylight.

"Not to worry," the woman said as a light flared up in front of her. "I come prepared." A flame hovered just above her palm. She pulled a white pillar candle from her purse and dipped it into the flame, which left her palm and stayed with the wick as she turned it back upright. She whispered, "Lux." *Light*.

The flame duplicated itself; each new flame shot out toward one of the four iron candelabras standing in each corner. Soon the tent was once again enveloped in the soft candlelight. She placed the pillar candle in the center of the table. Charlie and Jade each took a seat, while Willow and the woman in gray spoke quietly off to one side.

When Jade's parents had died, she'd been too distraught to attend their will reading. The thought of hearing her mother's voice channeled through someone else was too much to deal with. Instead, she'd refused to go and had stayed the evening in her aunt's house, watched over by Mrs. Keepsake. After it was over, Joy came back and insisted she go to the Crossing Over ceremony. "You'll regret it if you don't go," she'd said.

Charlie broke through her thoughts. "What do you think she left you in the will?"

"Other than the house? No idea." Jade's family wasn't one to place a lot of value on material possessions. Even Joy, who was always building one collection or another, placed little financial value on them. Joy might have left her some magical tools, but considering how long she'd been away, she thought that doubtful.

The two women stopped talking, and as they took their seats, Willow introduced them. "Jade, this is Ms. Scrivener. She is decidedly the only lawyer your aunt trusted and therefore the executor of the estate. She'll be the conduit for Joy today. Of course, you know Charlie."

Ms. Scrivener nodded at Charlie, then addressed Jade. "Pleased to meet you, Jade, although I do wish the circumstances were better." With a warm smile she reached across the table to take Jade's hand in a gentle but firm embrace. "Your aunt spoke so highly of you. She loved you very much."

"Thank you, ma'am," Jade replied. Her throat tightened as she realized soon she would be talking to her aunt again. Would she scold her for leaving after her parents had died? Would she be disappointed in her for not keeping in touch all these years?

Ms. Scrivener said, "As you may know, your aunt wasn't very fond of the city's legal system. In our tradition written wills are not often used. The only reason she made one was to protect her land and certain valuables from the possibility of being seized by the city. She's said her goodbyes to everyone else. You and Charlie are special to her, and being the next coven leaders, what she left for you was too important to be done unofficially."

She laid her briefcase on the table in front of her and started to unhook the clasp, then stopped and looked over her right shoulder. After nodding once, she said, "Well, apparently she is anxious for you to hear what she has to say." She closed the clasp and pushed the briefcase aside. "Let's get started, shall we?"

She placed her hands flat on the table and closed her eyes, tipping her head back slightly. Her lips were moving, mumbling something Jade couldn't quite make out. The string of lights in the tent flickered dimly and the candles brightened. A whistling could be heard, like a strong wind had picked up outside, but the tent wasn't moving. Jade noticed Charlie staring at the center of the table. He was frozen still as a statue, his eyes wide.

"What's wrong?" she asked him.

"I don't know, but something's not right."

Jade followed his gaze to the candles. At first, she didn't see anything wrong, but then she realized the flames were moving too slow, like seaweed underwater. The realization sent a body-shaking shiver up her spine.

Charlie was facing Ms. Scrivener now, rocking back and forth slowly with his eyes closed. Jade put her hand on his arm gently, but he didn't respond, just kept mumbling under his breath.

Jade looked at Ms. Scrivener. She had her head down now, arms straight and fingers gripping the table so hard her knuckles were white. She was rocking in time with Charlie and moaning quietly. Willow had stood and was walking around them all in a circle as large as the space would allow. She had a crystal ball in one hand, made of amethyst, and in the other she held an athame, a small knife. Jade vaguely felt the energy in her wake, like the warmth from a distant fire.

Sacred circles were often raised for ceremonies as a way to protect against harmful spirits or energies. Jade wondered why they hadn't raised it before they started. She felt it then—a different energy, cold and dank, coming from Ms. Scrivener. It felt unwanted, dark; it put Jade's nerves on edge.

Grandma Willow was about three-quarters of the way around. The closer she got to completing the circle, the wilder Ms. Scrivener's movements and vocalizations became. She began slapping her hand on the table repeatedly and mumbling, "No no no no, you can't. It's mine. Me! Why? Ha ha ha!"

She suddenly opened her eyes and stared viciously at Jade. "YOU! Little lamb."

CHAPTER 10

Ms. Scrivener sneered at Jade across the table. "Think you're so special. Think you can—"

Willow took the final step, closing the circle, and turned toward Ms. Scrivener. Standing behind her with her arms raised, looking up, she murmured something.

Ms. Scrivener said, "No! No no no no no no." She shook her head violently, her once perfect hair now flailing around her.

"Repellere!" *Repel!* Willow said forcefully.

Ms. Scrivener went quiet and dropped her head to her chest. She sat there, breathing heavily at first, then slowly her breath normalized. Willow collapsed into her seat. Charlie stopped rocking and sat back with a sigh.

Ms. Scrivener opened her eyes and returned her head upright. She looked around the table, playing with her necklace. Her eyes settled on Willow, and she said in a soft voice, "Well, that was not what I expected."

Willow nodded. "You should probably hurry. You may not have as much time as we thought."

Ms. Scrivener squinted around the table, and when her eyes found Jade, she let go of her necklace and beamed. "My dear girl." Her voice was still her own, but she sat up straighter, and her eyes beamed a little more when she smiled. Ms. Scrivener was channeling the spirit of her aunt.

"It's so hard to know where to begin. There's so much you don't know about your family, about yourself even. After your parents died, I spent countless hours consulting with the Goddess, trying to decide what I should tell you and when. Then suddenly you were all grown up and living a different life, so far from our magic. I thought you were safe. I thought we both were. Unfortunately, things happened that I didn't foresee. The point is, now we have an opportunity to put things right.

"Before you were born, there was a girl named Abigail who was being trained to become coven leader. She didn't have quite as much power as you, but she did show promise, and she was part of the same bloodline." Ms. Scrivener paused as if the memory was real to her and causing her pain. "Abigail was my daughter."

"What? I have a cousin?" Jade wasn't sure if she was more surprised at the revelation or the fact that she hadn't seen it coming. Her intuition should have at least given her a hint that something would surprise her. Regardless, she now had a chance. Since her cousin was also in line to become coven leader, then that was her chance. All she had to do was talk her into taking over for her. She looked at Charlie. "Did you know about this?"

Charlie shook his head. "I'm as stunned as you are."

Ms. Scrivener played with her necklace as she explained, "A few years before you were born, when the Accords were first signed into law, a delegation from Sun City came to explain the new rules to us and have us sign our township's agreement to abide by them. One of the young Citizens in the group was named Andrew. He was so different from the stories I'd heard about Citizens. He listened to us, was polite, respectful. We fell in love.

"Unfortunately, your grandparents were too set in their ways. They couldn't accept I had fallen in love with someone who not only didn't have the natural talent for magic but also was from the city. We were young, though, and decided to elope. I left town with him, and shortly afterward we had Abigail. A few years later your grandparents passed over, and your mom reached out to me to return home. We did, and your mom helped us settle in.

"You were born a year later. Abigail loved to help Joy take care of you, even called you sister. The next year . . . Abigail . . . died in a car accident." She paused, a frown crossing her face. "She was seven." Her voice broke and she took a moment to compose herself.

Jade felt for her aunt, but she couldn't help feeling sorry for herself too. It meant she was right back where she'd started, the only one who could become High Priestess.

Ms. Scrivener continued, "While it was heartbreaking to lose her so young, because of my faith I was able to come to terms and move on. Unfortunately, Andrew was devastated. He had heard about resurrection spells and was convinced that was the answer."

Jade nearly gasped. Her whole life she'd been taught that death was a natural part of life. Bringing someone back from the dead was the worst thing a Witch could do. Even worse than killing. It was the darkest magic, and no one in the coven was allowed to perform it. At least not since her grandparents' time.

Ms. Scrivener paused, looking distant. "I tried to explain how wrong that kind of magic was, but he wouldn't listen. He began taking daily trips to the city to consult with some of his peers who had begun theorizing magic was an undiscovered form of energy. When his science failed him, he began researching all kinds of dark, twisted spells, trying to find the one that would bring her back. When he exhausted our library of magical spells, he started asking everyone in town. Of course, no one would help him. Not only was what he was trying to do wrong, but without the proper Witch's training, spells that strong can easily backfire.

"Eventually, he went to your parents for help. I suppose he thought as coven leaders they would know how to bring her back, and he could use my being family to persuade them to do so. They refused, of course, and he attacked them. Even though he was not raised as a Witch, he had some powerful spells at his disposal, and I suppose through watching me he'd picked up enough to use them. Although, I always wondered how he had learned battle magic spells." She looked directly at Jade. "Your parents fought as hard as they could, but they were overpowered."

Jade clenched her fists under the table, wishing she had April's hand to hold. She was always able to calm her down, and right now she needed calming. After all this time she finally knew: her parents had been murdered, and by someone in the family, by a long-lost uncle she hadn't even known about until now. No one had ever mentioned him to her, not even in passing.

After a moment Ms. Scrivener continued. "When I heard what Andrew had done, I searched for him to bring him to coven justice, but he was nowhere to be found. I never heard from him again. In the days before my death, I'd sensed that someone was watching me. I had a premonition that I wouldn't see another full moon. It appears I was right."

Jade had never realized her aunt had premonitions too. She had so many questions. Were her premonitions painful, like they sometimes were for Jade? Did they always come true? How old was she when they first started? Instead she asked, "Do you know how you died?"

Ms. Scrivener shook her head. "No. I mean . . . I'm not sure. I was out in the garden when I felt a presence behind me. It felt familiar, but before I could turn it was over." She gripped the table, closed her eyes, and shook her head slowly. She opened her eyes, but they were completely white. Through gritted teeth, she said, "No . . . Willow?"

Willow jumped out of her seat. "Charlie. It's back." She moved to stand on Ms. Scrivener's right, and Charlie went quickly to her left. They both placed their hands on her shoulders and back, bowed their heads, and began chanting "dimitte" *dismiss*.

After a moment Ms. Scrivener began to shake, just slightly at first, then harder and harder. Soon she was shaking so hard she was falling out of the chair.

Willow took a step back and lifted both hands to the ceiling. Looking up, she cried in a low voice, "Enough!" and slammed both fists down to the ground. The whole floor shook. The Sacred Circle Willow had cast around them flashed visible for a moment, like a dome of lightning, brighter at the floor, fading but still visible at the top. Willow,

Charlie, and Ms. Scrivener, who had fallen to the floor by now, were all panting heavily.

Ms. Scrivener pulled herself back up to her chair. "Goodness. That wasn't fun at all."

"Was that what I think it was?" Charlie asked.

"Another spirit? Yes, a powerful one. It seemed they tried to come back just then, but the connection broke."

Jade said, "I thought mediums were protected while channeling."

"We are. Not only does the Sacred Circle protect against malevolent energies entering our space, but I have my own personal defensive spellwork in place." Most spirits are respectful of such measures and stay away. However, if a spirit's strong enough, they can find a way to break through." She looked at Willow. "She was stronger than any spirit I've encountered."

"She who?" Willow asked.

"I don't know. I've never communicated with them before." Glancing at Charlie, she warned, "But you have a more serious problem to deal with. The Keys are gone."

CHAPTER 11

Charlie asked Ms. Scrivener, "Gone? What do you mean, exactly?"

"I went to the coven altar, but they weren't there." Ms. Scrivener shook her head. "With the coven's power waning, perhaps the protection spells on them were failing." She looked pointedly at Jade. "That can definitely happen when it's without a High Priestess long enough. Between that and the dark spirit that just tried to break through, I'd say your coven is under attack. Or is about to be."

The four Keys of the Ascension were holy relics, items used in ritual to channel power. They weren't just used for Ascension rituals; they were a vital part of any coven rite. Their being missing was a serious problem, not just for the Ascension, but for everyday coven life.

Jade turned on Charlie. "How could you have lost the Keys? You're supposed to be the High Priest and all, aren't you responsible for them?"

Charlie frowned at her. "I didn't lose them. Joy felt like she was being watched and suggested we keep them at the altar, and I agreed."

"Why there?"

"Because the coven altar is the safest place in town."

Jade crossed her arms. "Well, that theory's just been blown out of the water."

Charlie rolled his eyes. "It *is* the safest place. Trust me."

"That's it? 'Trust you'? That's all you have to say?"

Charlie straightened in his chair. "Yes, trust me. I'm the High Priest of this coven!"

Willow raised both her hands. "Children, enough. Charlie is right. The Keys should have been safe there. It seems not having Joy's successor take over immediately is affecting our magic faster than I thought it would."

Jade crossed her arms. "Is that why the spirit was able to interrupt the séance and why you had to go all warrior and purge the circle?" Jade hadn't seen battle magic since leaving Sugar Hill, but there was a particular charge to the air that she still recognized.

Willow straightened her posture and spoke in a measured tone. "Let me assure you, child, you have never seen me 'go all warrior.'" She smiled sweetly. "If the need for that ever arose, there would be cause for concern indeed."

Ms. Scrivener said, "In any case, she's gone now. Our more immediate problem is finding the Keys. Luckily, they have been with this coven for centuries, meaning their magic is tied firmly to this coven and this town. Whoever took them won't get far. The magic within them will see to that. You should finish putting Joy to rest. Once that's done you can go after the Keys and whoever took them." She took two items from her briefcase and placed them gently on the table. One was a small black velvet box about the size that would hold a necklace, and the other, something about a foot long wrapped in dark brown leather.

"Whoever has them must have used some powerful magic to retrieve them from the chapel's safeguards. Charlie, you and Jade should work together to find them. If you had both gone through all the proper training, it would be a simple task to share energies. Since this isn't the case, I think you should keep these on you." She picked up the black box and handed it to Charlie. "They have been used by our coven's leaders since the beginning as a way to connect and bond. Keep them safe."

Charlie took the box but didn't open it. He slipped it into his inner coat pocket. Jade glared at him, but he just smiled. It was going to drive her crazy not knowing what was in the box.

Ms. Scrivener looked to Jade. "What Joy left for you was originally your mother's." She reached down to her side and lifted a bundle of thick red fabric onto the table. In the center, a circular silver clasp was pinned to the fabric. She gently passed the bundle to Jade, who took it reverently and placed it in her lap.

She ran her hand over the material. It was soft and thick, dark red like blood. Realizing what it was, she lifted the bundle and buried her face in it. The smell of lavender and vanilla brought back memories of her mom performing ceremonies dressed in the Witch's cloak. *April would have loved her,* she thought, smiling against the fabric. The thought they'd never meet caused a twinge in her heart.

As Jade lowered the cloth back into her lap, she looked down at the silver pin. It was a penannular brooch, three wires twisted around themselves in the shape of a ring, one end of a straight pin looped around them so that it could slide freely. A gap in the ring was punctuated on either side by two triple spirals that kept the straight pin from sliding off.

Ms. Scrivener gently opened the leather package, laying it out flat on the table. It was a rolled parchment. The edges were rolled around wooden stakes with hand-carved ends. They were simple in design but high quality. She reached into her briefcase and pulled out a small stack of papers, laying them next to the parchment. She sat there with her hands on both items for a moment.

She looked at Jade and seemed to decide something. "There's a bit more information I think you should have. Joy didn't specifically mention this, but I doubt she'd mind me telling you. I'm not sure if you reached this part of your training, but you should know that becoming High Priestess gives you access to not only the entire coven's power but divine power as well. There are safeguards of course, and for most things the High Priestess can use her own power and magic or work together with the High Priest. In some rare instances, however, the higher level of divine magic is needed."

Jade couldn't imagine what would need that much power. Or how it would be controlled. She knew most of the coven members were very old, and Witches grew in power as they aged, regardless of how frail their bodies might get. "Why would you need that much power?"

"There are a few reasons, but the most important one is in the protection of the coven." Ms. Scrivener sat back. "I did research on your coven before taking this position. Your grandparents, and the generations before, followed the old ways of secrecy, keeping the coven's power secret and a low profile in general. That meant those who seek to steal power didn't take much notice of your coven. When your parents became coven leaders, they changed that. They began holding public rituals for the High Holy days and trading with neighboring covens. It brought the attention of some pretty dark forces. They saw your coven, and your family, as a target."

Jade's blood went cold. "I thought you . . . Joy said my parents died because Andrew killed them. Now you're saying they died because someone was attacking the coven?"

"Your parents *were* killed when Andrew attacked them. However, I believe Joy's death may have been the result of dark magic. That suggests another coven's attack.

"When Joy died, Sun City sent a coroner to examine the body. He couldn't find any cause of death, so he just ruled it a heart attack. I got word back from our shaman just before I came here. He said that when he examined her, she was covered in dark magic residue."

Jade asked, "You're talking about magical energy signatures?" One of the first things Jade had figured out about magic was that it left a residue or afterimage on whatever it touched. She had explored this and eventually learned to detect it. Later in her training she'd been told it was called a "signature." It was very faint and faded over time, but each type of magic had a different one: battle magic, healing magic, dark magic, you could learn to tell them all apart.

Ms. Scrivener nodded. "Joy's body showed no trace of her defensive battle magic. Usually Witches die from old age, illness, or accident, but murder is almost unheard of."

Suddenly the briefcase fell over and crashed down to the floor. Everyone jumped noticeably. Ms. Scrivener picked it up, and everyone looked around nervously. Jade's whole body shivered. She had that same creepy feeling of a cellar door being open and the draft creeping up her legs as she had in Mr. Whetstone's office.

"Is it possible that spirit came back?" She rubbed her thighs, trying to massage the goosebumps away.

Willow had taken a round stone out of her pocket and was looking through the hole in the center. She scanned the room, and when she reached the space between Jade and Charlie, she stopped. "No." She lowered it and nodded to Ms. Scrivener. "But we have a different kind of unwanted visitor."

Ms. Scrivener reached into her briefcase and tossed a handful of dust at the candles in front of her. After a brief flash, all the lights went out momentarily.

When they relit, the room seemed slightly darker but nothing else seemed different. Then she noticed a shimmer pass over Charlie's face. The cold cellar-like draft wafted up her back and over her left shoulder. It pressed through her shirt and into her skin.

Jade said, "That's not a spirit, is it?"

Charlie placed his warm hand gently on her left arm. "Don't worry, it can't hurt you."

"No, but if it doesn't back off soon, I may suffer frostbite," she said through gritted teeth.

The cold presence withdrew, then she saw it, a dark shadowy figure walking around the table.

It stopped next to Ms. Scrivener. She squinted at the shimmer a moment. "If by spirit you mean a dead person, then no. This Witch is very much alive."

A Witch could project their spirit out of their body, sometimes to great distances. When young Jade had learned this, she'd been excited to try, but found she could only hold it for a few seconds.

Ms. Scrivener said, "Yeah, that's not gonna work, my friend. I only allow the dead to speak through me. Whatever you want to say, you're gonna have to put forth the effort to do it yourself."

The figure moved back around the table toward Jade, her stomach turning as she watched it approach. Projection or not, the dark presence was not welcome. She reminded herself that Willow was here. Charlie nodded to her, and she found herself taking comfort in his presence as well. Straightening her spine, she glared at it defiantly.

It was definitely humanoid, but there were no facial features, as if a hood was pulled forward and the shadow hid what lay beneath. Then it whispered. "Jade, how you have grown." The whisper was definitely male, though she didn't recognize it.

In a firm voice she asked, "How do you know me?"

"All in good time." He began to fade slightly, like smoke dissipating in a breeze. He solidified again and whispered, "What is important now is that you find the Keys I took. You'll need to connect to your magic and that of the elements to find them. Then you may become High Priestess and gain all the power that comes with it."

Willow asked, "So she can help you bring Abigail back, Andrew?"

Andrew's form darkened, becoming nearly solid looking, and turned toward her. "You do not get to speak her name!" Andrew's voice was gruff, as if he had lost it and it was just starting to return. The candles flickered, then regained their strength, though the room remained dim. His form faded again until it was barely there.

He whispered, "I didn't mean to kill your parents, but they left me no choice. They refused to help me." Part of his shadow-form reached up toward her cheek, like he was reaching out his hand. "But you will not refuse me, will you?"

Jade backed up slightly, and he lowered his ghostly arm. "You killed my parents? What makes you think I would ever help you?"

He stayed motionless, and for a moment Jade had the distinct impression he was glaring at her. "Because, you have no choice. Your coven depends on it. The longer you're without both coven leaders, the weaker your coven will become." He began to fade away. "Remember the Witch's Pyramid," he said before disappearing completely.

Charlie asked Jade, "Are you all right?"

"Relatively speaking. Just . . . trying to wrap my head around what just happened." She'd always wondered how her parents had died, but to know that a relative, someone trusted, had betrayed them—it made the situation all the more tragic. *Then, to top it off, he has the balls to show up asking for my help?*

"There's no way in hell I'm helping him."

Willow said, "Of course you're not. We'll deal with Andrew later. There are things that must be attended to first." Jade stared blankly at her. "Your aunt's Crossing Over?" she prompted.

Jade deflated. She felt the need to do something now, and the Crossing Over ceremony would require quiet contemplation. She sighed and resigned herself to putting her revenge on hold. "Fine. What's first?"

Ms. Scrivener pushed the rolled parchment and stack of papers toward her. "I need you to sign these."

Jade took the parchment and carefully unrolled it partway. It felt warm and seemed to hum beneath her fingers. The yellowed material was thicker than paper, almost like linen. At the top, in big bold calligraphy letters, it said "Deed of Trust." At the bottom was a signature line, and below that several columns of names, each in different handwriting.

Ms. Scrivener said, "Your aunt didn't have any other children, and her marriage to Andrew was made void a year after he disappeared. She left all her material possessions to you, including the house and property. The scroll is for the house and property, the other papers are for the items inside the house, just to be thorough. Just sign and it all belongs to you."

Jade took the pen she offered and signed her name. Almost the instant she finished, her signature seemed to glow. The ink started to drip, pouring downward. It flowed to the top of the block of signatures below. As it moved, all the signatures shifted to make room so that her signature became the first on the list.

Ms. Scrivener said, "Your family has owned the property since the town was founded. Your ancestors formed a bond with the land that can never be broken, so each owner remains a part of its history."

Jade looked down at the list of names and saw Joy's and her parents' signatures below hers. She knew she should have been comforted by this, but she only saw it as another reminder of how alone she was. A long line of powerful Witches that ended with her.

She handed the scroll back to Ms. Scrivener and quickly signed the stack of papers she handed her. Those signatures stayed fixed. She handed back the pen and stood. "Is that all?"

"That's it. I'll put these in the house safe."

Willow stood at the edge of the circle, pointed at the ground, then drew a line with her finger in the air, up over her head, over a couple of feet, then back down again, cutting a doorway.

Jade asked Willow, "Why don't you just disburse the circle?"

"Ms. Scrivener and I need to discuss some things in private. I appreciate you two going back to the dinner to wait for us. We'll join you shortly."

Charlie held the tent flap back as Jade passed through into the main tent. As soon as she stepped over the threshold, she realized they had been in near silence. Suddenly the sounds of a party assaulted her ears. Lively music, laughter, and glasses clinking. She was supposed to be remembering the good times with Joy, appreciating how she'd affected her life, and saying goodbye so that she could cross into the Summerlands. Instead she was filled with dread. She wanted Joy to hold her close and tell her everything would be fine.

Jade sat down in her seat and grabbed April's hand.

April frowned at her. "You okay?"

Jade looked out over the merry group. Over and over people took turns toasting to Joy, listing the qualities they loved most about her. Her kindness, her intelligence. Someone yelled, "Her Joy!" and everyone laughed.

She was joyful though, Jade thought. Not in an "always has to smile" kind of way, but in a "deep down in her bones so that she practically glows" kind of way. They were all speaking of her in the present tense, holding their glasses up to the main table as they toasted, as if she were actually seated there, right next to Jade. But she wasn't, at least Jade couldn't see her, or sense her. She stared at Joy's empty chair, plate piled high with untouched food, and the glass full of wine she would never taste again.

Death is just one part of the cycle, she reminded herself. *What's more important is April. She deserves the truth.* She was hoping she would have more time to find a way out, but April was looking at her expectantly, and she knew her friend wouldn't let it go. She told her about Andrew, his relationship to her and his ultimatum: find the Keys and become High Priestess to help him. April listened quietly, glancing at Charlie a couple of times.

When Jade was done, April pulled her hand away and nodded. "I see."

"April, I'm so sorry."

"Sorry I found out," she countered.

"No. Well, not really. I was going to tell you, I just wanted to find a way out of it before I did. I will find a way." April wasn't even looking at her, pushing her food around her plate. "April, say something."

"What is there to say? Your mom was High Priestess and you were supposed to take over for her, but you decided to hide that along with all the other parts of your past you didn't want to share with me."

"It's not that simple."

"I'm not trying to make things harder on you. You have a lot to deal with right now. It just doesn't sound like a temporary situation to me, and you should have told me."

"I know. And it's usually not, but this is different. I promise I'll find a way out of it. This is not permanent."

April smirked and narrowed her eyes. "Right. To be continued, I guess." She turned to her plate and picked at her food.

The food smelled delicious, but Jade couldn't bring herself to have any of it. She just sat there looking at her empty plate. *Empty.* She felt that way inside too, like her heart had gone numb to its own heartbeat. She felt like she should be crying, should be sobbing hysterically, wailing even. But there were no tears. Nothing but the emptiness.

She thought over all that had happened since arriving here. She'd been so hopeful she would find a way out of the Ascension ritual. That she would attend her aunt's Crossing Over ceremony, cry, maybe get some antique silver at the will reading, cry some more, and head home. But April had found out about her family's position and her eventual role in the coven at the worst possible time. Not to mention she'd learned she had an uncle and cousin she never knew about, that some dark spirit who was powerful enough to breach a Sacred Circle was lurking around, and the very Keys needed to perform the Ascension ritual had been taken. Her coven needed more than just one Esolate Witch and whoever they found to replace Joy; her coven needed a bloodline High Priestess. They needed her.

And what about the box Charlie had received? Why hadn't he opened it? She didn't mind working with him but, *Connect and bond? What was that about?*

When Willow and Ms. Scrivener entered the tent, it felt like both an instant and an eternity had passed. Jade had no concept of time now; she only knew she was being told it was time for the Crossing Over. It was time to say goodbye to Joy.

CHAPTER 12

The Crossing Over ceremony was held at the old cemetery near the center of town, and by the time Jade and Willow arrived, the sun was nearly touching the horizon. Jade used to love this place when she was little. The property was bordered by a knee-high stacked-stone wall covered in moss and lichen. The main entrance had a rusted gate that was barely hanging on its hinges and remained open all the time. Most of the tombstones were ancient, overgrown, and decrepit. Some had fallen over, and many were nearly unreadable from centuries in the elements. She had always been able to feel the power of those buried here though. As a child the presence had made her feel she was surrounded by life and loved ones.

As Jade stood looking at the gate, she felt nothing. No presence. No life. Just a dark plot of land covered with tombstones. Jade and Willow walked in the entrance to gather with the other coven members. After a couple of minutes, they formed a line and began walking down the wooded footpath.

The cemetery was laid out in a circle within the square outer border wall, the corners being left to grow wild. The outer rings of the circle had graves of average townsfolk, and the most influential, powerful families were buried in the inner rings.

In the very center was an almost perfectly circular mossy clearing, bordered by another three-foot-high stone wall and topped with a wrought-iron fence. There was a gap in the stone wall on each of the cardinal compass points. Charlie stood at the southern entrance, greeting the coven members as they entered and took their places in a circle around Joy's casket. Faint music could be heard coming from all around them, and the solemn beating of the drums kept time with their footsteps.

As they approached, Jade was determined to keep her composure. She hadn't cried at the Farewell Feast. She hadn't cried when she went into the house to change into the ceremonial robes Willow had laid out for her. She hadn't cried when she said goodbye to April on the front doorstep, assuring her they would talk everything through when she got back. She hadn't cried when she entered the cemetery and saw her family name, Cerridwen, listed on the gate with the other founding families.

Only when Willow stepped aside and Jade was faced with Charlie's somber expression did the tears finally come flooding out. She fell forward and Charlie caught her, holding her steady as she cried into his shoulder. His arms wrapped around her, pulling her close. She felt grounded and her tears slowed.

He gently murmured the customary greeting, "Merry meet."

His voice was warm and comforting, but she couldn't gather the strength to reply. She clung tighter to him, her spirit starving for his calm strength.

He spoke her part for her. "Merry part." After a pause he gently grasped her shoulders and pushed her away to look into her eyes. "Merry meet again."

It was a greeting that was used for every occasion but was most meaningful at a Crossing Over. Jade followed Willow around the clearing to her place in the circle.

It was tradition to use this area for certain types of gatherings. The crypts of the five founding families were built at even intervals along the clearing's edge. If you drew a line from crypt to crypt, it would form a pentagram with Jade's family crypt on the northern point, where her aunt Joy would be laid to rest with Jade's parents. The building was almost as old as the cemetery itself. Vines grew up the stone walls, and the windows were intricately hand-formed stained glass, their colors muted by the dirt of time. A large wrought-iron gate secured the inner carved wooden door. It was truly a beautiful building.

Joy's casket was in the center of the clearing with the head facing the northern crypt. It was lifted waist high by thick tree roots, which twisted out from the ground and wrapped around like fingers of some giant hand. The lid of the casket was resting on its side on the ground next to it, leaning against the roots.

As Jade took her place next to Willow, she couldn't look at her aunt's casket. Instead she stared at the ground.

Charlie finished closing the Sacred Circle's doorway and positioned himself at the head of the casket. He raised his hands and the drumming stopped. She could still feel it, though, in the background, like a heartbeat.

Four coven members stepped out of their spots and walked around the perimeter, Willow among them. They each took up positions at a different compass point, facing inward.

Willow stood behind Charlie in the north. She turned to face outward and tilted her head back, holding a white pillar candle in front of her. "Guardian of the north, element of Earth, I call on you to guard this space and bear witness to our rite. Bless us with your strength." The candle in her hand lit by itself.

A slim lady Jade vaguely recognized stood in the east. Baby's breath flowers were tucked into a messy wreath of gray braids circling her head. She turned outward and tilted her head back, speaking in a singsong voice, her French accent thick, "Guardian of the east, element of Air, I call on you to guard this space and bear witness to our rite. Bless us with your wisdom." Her candle lit.

In the south stood an old man with scraggly long gray hair and an equally scraggly gray beard. His voice was gruff as he said, "Guardian of the south, element of Fire, I call on you to guard this space and bear witness to our rite. Bless us with your power to change." His candle lit.

Mrs. Keepsake stood in the west. "Guardian of the west, element of Water, I call on you to guard this space and bear witness to our rite. Bless us and purify us." Her candle lit.

Charlie said, "The gates are sealed, the circle raised, let only love enter here."

"So mote it be," everyone said in unison. As the coven members let go of their candles, they remained in the air, hovering. The members returned to their places in the circle.

"My fellow coven members, the time has come. Please step forth to say your final goodbyes and cut any personal ties with Joy, so that she may cross the veil in perfect love and perfect trust."

One by one, each of the thirteen coven Witches walked up to the coffin and spoke quietly to Joy. Some placed things in the coffin with her. When Willow returned to her place in line, they all looked at Jade. She stared at the coffin.

Willow leaned over and whispered to her, "Jade, you must."

She had only been to one other Crossing Over ceremony—her parents'. At that one she had felt their presence. All other magical energy had eluded her after their deaths, but on that day, she could feel them as if they were standing next to her. It had been comforting to her. She had talked to them throughout the ceremony, and when the final prayer ended, she felt them go.

Jade took the few steps until she was looking right at Joy's face. Only it wasn't Joy. She felt nothing. No presence. It was just a body. A shell. Empty.

A sudden fear came over her. Something inside her screamed to run, to get away from this thing in front of her. She turned and took a step toward the clearing entrance.

The instant her eyes left Joy's body, the horrible feeling retreated. She could still feel it haunting the edges of her consciousness, a knowledge of emptiness, but she wasn't afraid anymore. She turned and walked sadly to her place in the circle. She looked once more at the dimly lit coffin and Joy, who wasn't Joy. "I'm sorry," she whispered, uncertain who she was speaking to. Tears fell from her eyes and she closed them, willing the tears to stop.

When Jade opened her eyes, she saw Charlie bent forward, both hands gripping the end of the coffin, his forehead resting on the rim. He was mumbling something, talking to Joy. For a moment Jade could imagine that Joy was just asleep, and Charlie was telling her goodnight. Their profiles were the reverse mirror image of each other. He lifted his head and looked at Joy. "Thank you. Rest well."

He took a step back and, after a moment, raised his hands skyward. His voice wavered at first, becoming stronger as he spoke. "Oh, Great Spirit! We come before you, having said our goodbyes to Joy, to thank you for our time with her. We ask that you take her spirit safely across the veil to dwell with you in the Summerland."

"Goddess, hear our prayer," the coven members said in unison. They all joined hands, and as Willow took hers, Jade felt a spark like static pass between them.

Charlie continued, "We thank you for her untiring support and ask that you bless her and give her rest."

"Goddess hear our prayer."

"We thank you for her devotion to family and friends alike and ask that you comfort her, so that she may let go of her past and those she's leaving behind."

"Goddess hear our prayer."

"We thank you for her sound advice and ask that you grant her wisdom and guide her in choosing the path her spirit will now take."

"Goddess hear our prayer."

"We thank you for letting us know her and gratefully give her back to you."

"So mote it be. So mote it be. So mote it be."

Jade waited for something to happen. Anything. After a few moments of deafening silence, Charlie lowered his head. "Merry meet . . . "

Everyone around the circle followed suit, and Jade repeated with them, "Merry part, and merry meet again."

The instant the closing words were finished, Jade quickly rose and headed straight for the southern entrance. She had to get out of there. Her aunt wasn't here, so how could she say goodbye? It was all a waste of time.

Grandmother Willow called out to her just as she reached the invisible circle's parameter. "Jade, no!"

Jade stopped immediately. She had been so intent on leaving she had forgotten about cutting a doorway. When she was young the sacred circle was as solid as brick. Right now, she felt the only thing stopping her was respect for Grandma Willow and the other coven members.

She turned to glare at Charlie. She wasn't really angry at him; he was just the easier target. Charlie nodded to Willow. She walked over to Jade and drew a doorway in the air with her finger in front of where Jade had stopped. She motioned her through, and Jade ran away.

CHAPTER 13

Jade didn't stop until she came to the small lake behind her aunt's house. She ran down the long dock and plopped down at the end, dangling her feet over the side. As she sat facing out toward the water, the moon was just above the horizon, and a cool breeze caressed her face and dried the few tears that had managed to escape as she ran.

She looked out over the peaceful scene, but she didn't feel peaceful inside. Not only was her heart racing from the run, but it was breaking as well. She wanted to keep running all the way back to Sun City, back to a time before any of this had happened. But she couldn't, she was trapped. Trapped in a town she no longer felt was home. Her parents were gone and now her aunt was too. She was alone.

Footsteps sounded on the dock behind her, and she turned to see April walking slowly toward her. When she reached the end of the dock, she said, "I saw you from the kitchen window. Do you feel like company?"

Jade nodded once and looked back out to the lake while April sat next to her. They remained that way for a while, and Jade relished her silent company. With April in her life, she never felt lonely. She could almost pretend they weren't fighting.

Jade closed her eyes for a moment and slowly leaned her head against April's shoulder. She had half expected her to pull away, but apparently April was just as happy to pretend things were normal for the moment. Jade relaxed into the strength she felt emanating from her friend. As she felt April lean her head against the top of hers, she thought more tears would come, but they seemed to have dried up. She never really cried while living in Sun City, at least not with anyone else present.

Jade watched the stripe of moonlight reflected on the lake surface shimmer and dance as the gentle breeze formed small ripples. "Dragonfly Lake," she said quietly.

Without moving, April asked, "What?"

"That's what I used to call it." She sat up straight and raised her chin toward the water. "Each summer when I was little, I saw fairies riding the backs of dragonflies, dueling each other like knights at a jousting match. They would chase each other around, like some kind of complicated dance, trailing fairy dust behind them that glittered in the sunlight." She smirked at the bittersweet memory and looked around the lake. Even this late in the year, there should have been a few out. They loved the full moon, and tonight it shone brightly, even with the scattered clouds. She couldn't tell if they were missing because they were gone, or if she just couldn't see them anymore.

"I saw magic everywhere back then. Most kids can, even Citizens. The games they play, make believe, and imaginary friends, it's all them seeing the real magic that's around us every day." April looked at her as she continued, "But when a Citizen grows up, the ability to sense magic fades. It's just part of becoming an adult. Sometimes they can still feel it, like when you know someone's about to call and they do. Moms often sense it when they know their kids are hurt miles away from them." She paused, and April nodded solemnly.

"I know you don't believe in the power of magic. But I did. I grew up not only believing but practicing it every day. When I moved to Sun City, I tried to stop believing. I gave up practicing, stopped following the holy days. I made a conscious decision to turn my back on magic and everything I had been taught. And it worked. I've been able to put everything behind me and start new.

"But then my aunt died, and I had to come back to this . . . place. It feels different here. I feel different. The house, the séance, it all feels—"

"Magical?" April smirked at her.

"Yeah. But that's the danger. It's all 'ooh, look at that light.' And 'ooh, a real séance.' Next thing you know you're standing in the middle of a cemetery, talking to a corpse, and watching people wave their hands in the air for no reason."

"It wasn't for no reason," April said gently. "Traditions are important, whether you believe the reasons behind them or not."

"That's not the point." Jade hung her head and closed her eyes.

"Then what is?"

"Before we left, I told you I had a nightmare about the night my parents died. It wasn't a nightmare. Not exactly. It was a vision. Or part of one. I used to get them all the time when I was little, and they always came true. But ever since that night, I've been having visions of the past. Like a memory, but stronger, more real."

"Nightmares can feel very real."

"No, it wasn't a nightmare." She felt she had to make April understand. *If I can just make her understand what I'm going through, she'll see that I don't want to stay. That I want to leave but can't. Then maybe she can forgive me.* "The night my parents died . . . I was the one who found them, their bodies I mean. It was the last night I ever tried to cast a spell. I tried to bring them back." April was staring at her with wide eyes. "You've got to understand, I was just a child, but I was powerful. I didn't care that bringing someone back was forbidden. I just wanted my parents to live." Her voice wavered and April took her hand.

She looked down at their entwined fingers. April was always there for her, not matter what. She continued, "It didn't work though, of course. My parents had always told me I could do anything, and with magic all things were possible. I realized that night they'd lied to me. All the power I had didn't mean anything if it didn't work when I needed it most."

"I'm so sorry Jade. I . . . I had no idea you were the one who found them. That must have been . . ." She shook her head. "I can't imagine."

"You're still not getting it. People die, and yeah it sucks I found them like that, but death is a part of life. The problem is that when I needed magic it failed me. It would have been wrong to bring them back, but what hurt more is that it didn't work at all. Trying to bring them back was an impulse act of a child, but what I learned from it was that everything I've ever believed about magic was a lie.

"When Witches grow up, they don't lose their ability to sense magic like Citizens do, it gets stronger. Today, I should have been able to feel it. I should have sensed my aunt's presence, so I could say goodbye, but I felt nothing. I thought that's what I wanted. Today I had to say goodbye to my aunt, and she wasn't even there."

"I'm not sure what to say."

"You think I'm crazy."

April pursed her lips. "I don't think you're crazy. I believe you believe in magic. But I'm a Citizen, Jade. My parents raised me to believe that only science can give us the answers we need, only science can truly create the miracles we seek. I'm sorry you couldn't feel her presence like you thought you would, but that's what every one of us goes through when we lose someone we love."

She draped her arm across Jade's shoulder and pulled her close. "It's cold, and harsh, and it hurts like hell, but you will get through it. Just like everyone does. You're not alone, Jade. It may feel like it now, but you're not."

You're a better friend than I deserve, Jade thought. She sat up straight. "I have to tell you something. You're not going to want to hear it, but you deserve the truth."

"You're not going back to Sun City." Her dark expression revealed the pain she kept out of her voice.

"April, I'm so sorry. I thought I could get out of it."

"Of course you did." Her smile didn't reach her eyes.

"What?"

April stood. "Why don't we go inside?"

Jade rose and said, "Just tell me what's wrong."

"You're not going to like it."

Jade tilted her head.

April sighed. "Fine. Since you brought it up, I knew you weren't going back. I figured it out a while ago. What's wrong though is . . . you say you thought you could get out of it. Really? You thought? Or were you just telling me that to put off having to confront me?"

"What?" Jade blinked at her.

"Well, you're pretty much an expert at running away from things."

Jade's cheeks burned. *Why is she being so mean?* "That's not fair."

"Isn't it? You ran from your hometown because your parents died, you ran from school when they teased you, you've run from every good man or woman that ever wanted to date you."

Jade turned and began walking down the dock.

"Prove my point, run away!"

Jade froze in her tracks and faced April. "What do you want from me?"

"What do I want?" Tears welled up in her eyes, but her expression was one of anger. "I don't want anything from you. I don't care where you live or what you do, I don't even care that you're the High Holy Priestess or whatever. That's not why I'm mad." She pinned Jade with her eyes. "I'm mad at you because you lied to me, you kept secrets from me, you basically ran from me. You always run from your problems, but you promised you'd never run from me. Not from me!" Her voice broke.

"April, I'm not running from you!" She slammed her hands on the railing, gripped it tightly, and let out a frustrated growl. She was angry at her aunt for leaving her in this situation. Unfortunately, her aunt wasn't there to yell at. April was. "I'm sorry I lied to you. We agreed when we met that my past would stay past, and I'd only tell you things when I was ready. But my parents being coven leaders is not something you ever needed to know."

"Need to know? I'm not a spy for the government, Jade, I'm your best friend. Any time in the past twenty years you don't think you could have said, 'Oh, hey, April. You should probably know my parents used to run an entire coven, and oh yeah, I'm expected to go back home and take their place someday.' That would have been nice to prepare myself for."

"I'm sorry, okay! What do you want me to say? I love my life in Sun City, and I love you. You're more than my best friend, you're like my sister. If I could leave right now and go back to the way things were, I would, but I can't."

"Why not? You find a way to avoid hardship, confrontation, anything that's out of your comfort zone. Why is this any different? What would happen if you went back, if you didn't take on this responsibility? I mean, bloodlines must die out sometimes. Don't they have a contingency plan for that?"

"The coven doesn't just deal with managing the town, they're kind of . . . they have a symbiotic relationship with its magic, and it all ties into the bloodline, my bloodline." She sighed. "It's complicated."

April replied, "Family usually is."

Jade heard footsteps coming down the dock and turned to see Charlie, still in his white ritual robes, walking slowly toward them.

Jade rolled her eyes and said, "Great. Just what I need." At April's raised eyebrow she explained, "I kind of left the ceremony abruptly. He probably wants to yell at me more than you do right now."

April looked at Charlie, then back to Jade. "Do you want me to stay?"

Jade shook her head. "No, I can handle him. We'll talk later?"

April nodded but stood still until Charlie reached them. She said, "I'll be just inside if you need anything," then glared pointedly at Charlie before pushing past him and striding down the dock.

Charlie pointed after her with his thumb as he asked, "What's with her?"

"She's a little protective of me sometimes." She walked back to the end of the dock and sat down, staring at the ripples in the water below her feet, their edges silver from the moonlight. She studied them carefully, watching each wave pass under her toward the shore. "I'm sorry I left so quickly. Have you come to beat me up too?"

Charlie sat next to her and copied her pose. "Um . . . no. Everyone deals with loss in their own way. While it would have been nice of you to stick around, you didn't do anything wrong." He glanced behind them. "I wanted to apologize for my part in our argument at brunch this morning, and at the will reading. I've been dealing with some personal issues lately, which have me on edge. When I start sensing a dark presence right about the time a stranger starts asking questions about our coven, it only makes things worse." He paused, looking down at the water for a moment. "What I'm trying to say is, I know this is hard for you, and I didn't make it any easier. I promise I'll try to be more supportive, and I hope you can try to see things from my perspective."

She nodded. He had a point, but she didn't understand why he had been so rude toward April. "What part of your perspective made you glare at April like that? She was only asking what anyone who grew up in the city would."

"I know, and I realized that after the fact," he explained calmly. "Like I said, I felt a dark presence. When I looked at her, I thought I felt a wall go up, but after talking with Willow, we realized it wasn't from April specifically."

Jade scoffed at his explanation. "Maybe she did put a wall up because she thinks you're all nuts for practicing magic but is too polite to say so."

He visibly relaxed and chuckled. "Maybe, but I meant what I said about protecting the coven. She may be your friend, but—"

"Don't worry. I got the point. The super-secret ancient mumbo jumbo is safe from nonmagical hands."

"Oh good. And the magic wand and decoder ring are still in the magic box? Don't forget, Falcor needs to be home before dark or he'll turn into stone."

"Okay, smart ass. I get your point."

Charlie sat still for a few moments, obviously lost in thought. He turned toward her with a serious look on his face. "Jade, you are the most powerful person I've ever met, bar none." Jade began to say something, but he stopped her with one finger in the air between them. "You know I'm right, whether you admit it or not. I may not be a Natural like you, but I have been trained in the arts long enough to be able to sense power. Trust me, you have it."

"Maybe I used to," she mumbled to herself.

"No, you still do. It's locked away inside you. Deep in the part of you that hides your childhood, but it's there."

Jade was taken aback by how sincere and understanding he sounded. She had thought he hated her, but now she wasn't sure. She turned away and stared into the darkness. A few clouds had developed, and the moon was partly hidden. A silence fell between them, wavering between comfortable and uncomfortable. "I'm sorry I left you. I didn't want to hurt you, I wasn't even thinking of you. I was just in so much pain myself, I felt I had to leave."

Charlie clenched his jaw and frowned at the water. He closed his eyes and sighed. "I know. You were young and didn't know how to cope. But things are different now. Now that you're back we can find the Keys, become High Priestess and Priest, and together we'll protect our coven from whatever comes our way."

"Even though that's exactly what Andrew wants?"

"Are you having second thoughts? I thought you agreed to become High Priestess."

"I did, but what if I can't connect to my magic anymore, or if once I do, I can't control it? What if we can't even find the Keys?" She was reminded again of how she felt at the Crossing Over ceremony. Not a spark, not a shimmer, nothing to show there was magic anywhere around. Sure, she'd generated static in the feast tent, but she hadn't meant to then. When she needed to feel her aunt's presence, it had abandoned her, again. She jumped up and started walking down the dock, stopping after only a few steps. She turned to face him. He had stood as well but hadn't moved and was just calmly watching her. He seemed so contained, while she felt her insides churning. It infuriated her.

"What happens if I don't become High Priestess?"

The question seemed to surprise him, but after a moment he answered quietly, "Then the coven will die."

"Die? You mean everyone in it?"

Charlie shook his head quickly. "No, no. Sorry. What I mean is the magic of the coven will return to the Earth. People can still practice personal magic, but we won't be able to perform any of the rituals and spells a coven should; we will basically disband. There will no longer be a Sugar Hill coven."

Jade couldn't picture it. In Sun City she never thought about magic. It wasn't a part of her life there. But in the back of her mind, Sugar Hill was the place where magic lived, and the coven was its home. She couldn't imagine the town without it. It was just wrong. "But there must have been a time when the High Priestess didn't have a child, or they died. There has to be some way to continue if the bloodline is broken."

"If it's broken, yes. But it's not broken, you're alive. If you were to die . . . technically the coven could choose anyone, but that's not really an option, is it?"

Great. Time for last resorts. "If the coven disbands, what will happen to the town?"

"I don't know, but it's possible Sun City will incorporate it into their city limits."

"Can they do that? I mean, I've never heard anyone mention anything like that."

"That's because the Accords have protected us. Part of the Accords states that no city may incorporate any township's land without approval of its coven. Without a coven, we have no way of stopping them. And they would definitely want our land. We have some of the richest soil in the region. They would quickly turn most of it into massive farmland to feed the city's population, or dig it up to take our natural resources like oil."

Jade imagined the pristine countryside being plowed over and dug up for the city's benefit, the trees clear-cut for their wood. She loved her glittering city, but there was something peaceful and sacred about the wilds of Sugar Hill. Imagining a world where places like that didn't exist hurt her heart.

She stared down at the water. It was shallow enough at this end of the dock to see the bottom during the day, but now the water looked black. *Clear as mud,* she thought. Jade turned to see Charlie staring across the lake. He looked so peaceful with the moonlight bathing his face in its cool silvery glow. She looked out at the lake with him, trying to feel the peacefulness she used to share with him as kids.

After a few moments he said, "It's getting late, we should head in."

They slowly walked down the dock and along the path back to Aunt Joy's house. *My house. That's going to take some getting used to.*

Jade was in no hurry. The cool night air was mild enough to be comfortable. Their footsteps settled into a rhythm, the silence surrounding them like a buffer, keeping the world and all their problems at bay.

When they reached the back-porch steps, Charlie stopped her. "I want you to know something. No matter what happens, I will always be your friend. I know you've lost so much but I wanted you to know you will never lose me."

"You can't promise that. What you can promise is that you'll protect April."

"Willow already spelled her from not seeing magic until she's ready."

"No. I'm talking about Andrew. When he appeared at the will reading, I got the distinct impression that no one is safe around him. If anything happened to April—" Her throat closed around the words she didn't want to say.

"Hey." He took her hands and stepped close, looking intently in her eyes. "Nothing's going to happen to her. I promise I will protect her. Besides, anyone stupid enough to mess with a friend of yours is the one who really needs protection."

Jade smirked. "Yeah, right. I haven't done magic in years. I'm no threat to anyone."

"You may not believe in your power, but I do. More than that, I have faith in you."

Jade stared back into his eyes, a comforting calm washing over her.

April's voice from the doorway startled them both. "We were starting to worry about you guys." Jade stepped back from Charlie, and he quickly let go of her hands.

Charlie replied with a brilliant smile, "No worries, April. I was just making sure she got home safely."

"Grandma Willow wanted me to tell you she thinks Charlie should stay here tonight. She said that way we can get an early start looking for the Keys in the morning, without waiting for him to drive all the way from across town."

Jade frowned at Charlie. "Don't you still live at your parents' old place?" It was just across the river, an easy walk.

"No," Charlie replied. "It's a long story. Let's just say I moved."

Jade shrugged and passed April on the porch. She walked into the house, stopping momentarily in the kitchen. She was about to say something to April when she realized she wasn't behind her. She turned to look through the open doorway. Charlie was towering over April, and she was staring back at him unfazed. Jade couldn't make out what they were saying and slowly stepped closer to the door, careful not to let them see her.

". . . none of your business," April said. Jade watched as she tried to sidestep Charlie, but he blocked her path.

He said something she couldn't make out. April raised one eyebrow and tilted her head, placing her hands on her hips as a smile crept over her face. "I'm only going to say this one time: do not hurt her." She waited a moment and then walked straight toward the steps, making him move out of her way.

Jade quickly backed away and flew down the hall and up the stairs to her room. She ducked inside and shut her door. It had been one hell of a long day, and she guessed tomorrow wouldn't be much easier.

CHAPTER 14

Hooded figures in the dark.

Whispers of promises kept, and vows broken.

Laughter becoming cries.

A woman screams.

When Jade's alarm went off at seven o'clock, she groaned and hit the snooze button a little too hard. The dream seemed distant already, its details fading into an overall feeling of dread.

She looked up at the curtains and the faint reddish light sneaking from behind them, making them appear to glow. She rose slowly in the dimly lit room and threw open the heavy curtains. Blinded by the light, she shaded her eyes with her hand. Slowly things came into focus, and she was shocked at what she saw.

The east side of the property held a small apple orchard. Beyond that, thick forest went for miles. The sky seemed made of blood and fire as the angry sun rose from its bed of red and orange flames on the eastern horizon. It cast an eerie rust-colored haze over the trees, as if the Earth herself had been betrayed and was hell bent on revenge.

Jade stared at the frightening sunrise from her bedroom window. In Sugar Hill the old sayings weren't just quaint wives' tales but life lessons and rules to live by. The one that came to mind in this case was "Red sky at night; sailor's delight. Red sky in the morning; sailors take warning." There was a storm coming. Jade just wasn't sure what kind.

There was a gentle knock on the door and April asked, "Jade? Can I come in?"

She called out, "Door's open."

April opened the door in her typical morning jogging suit of skin-tight pink Lycra tank top and black boy shorts. "Morning. I was thinking maybe we could go for a run. You know, like we do back home? Clear our heads a bit before we have to face the day."

"Yeah," Jade replied. "I guess. Give me a minute to change." While April waited on the bed, Jade stepped into the bathroom to change into her modest baggy blue sweatshirt and sweatpants.

The winding country roads were a nice change from the boring grid of city streets they usually traveled. Sun City had parks of course, but they didn't come close to the serenity of unmanaged nature. The only thing that threatened to ruin it was the ominous red sky. It was lighter now but still tinted everything a bit orange, as if it had bled down and tainted the world.

As their run took them through town, they still hadn't talked about Jade staying in Sugar Hill. Jade was starting to wonder if April had just given up when she slowed to a brisk walk.

"All right, Jade. Spill. How is it you haven't asked for a break yet? You're usually panting louder than a steam engine by now." She walked with her hands on her hips, not exactly out of breath.

Jade realized she was right. She was breathing heavily but not nearly as bad as normal. "I don't know. I'm just not that tired. Maybe we should talk now?"

"Start with how your visit with Charlie went last night. You were looking pretty deep into each other's eyes when I stepped onto the porch."

Jade ignored the barb and filled her in on the bad news about becoming High Priestess.

April's face darkened again, and she spoke in a near whisper, "Is it always this dead on a weekday?"

It wasn't the reaction Jade had expected. She became aware of a chill in the air that had nothing to do with temperature, and glanced around nervously, trying to find the source of her unrest. The handful of storefronts hardly counted as a town, but it was enough for the people living nearby. The cobblestone street was barely wide enough for two cars to pass.

While there was never a crush of people on the streets, you could always count on Katie's Emporium to be lit up and the faint sound of music leaking onto the street. They were right in front of it and only silence greeted them.

"No. We'd better head back."

When they finally crossed the boundary of her aunt's property, the dread fell away as if banished from going any further.

"Grandma Willow?" Jade called as they entered the house. They found her in the kitchen, standing at the back door and looking out. "Grandma Willow?" Jade asked hesitantly. She took a couple of steps closer and realized Willow was mumbling something, her hands slowly lowering in front of her. With a final motion upward, she turned and smiled broadly.

"Hello, Jade, April. Did you enjoy your run?"

"It was lovely," April replied. "The woodlands around here are beautiful, and the main street is so quaint." She frowned, looking out through the doorway behind Willow. "That sunrise is a bit creepy though."

"A storm is coming," Willow said with a slightly ominous tone. After a moment she smiled warmly. "Don't trouble yourself, now." She put her arm around April and pulled her close. "You're safe with us."

Charlie walked in and asked, "Anyone else feel that?"

"Feel what?" April asked.

"Darkness."

Looking pointedly at Charlie, Willow said, "Don't frighten the girl." She gave April's shoulders a squeeze. "Once we've completed the ritual, I'm sure everything will be fine. It's probably just because we haven't had a permanent High Priestess for so long. Nature doesn't abide imbalance."

Jade sensed Willow wasn't telling her everything and pushed, determined not to let it go. "What aren't you saying?"

Willow took a deep breath. "Today's sunrise is not the only sign we've had lately. The last few months we've received message after message, and they all say basically the same thing: prepare."

April said, "Now look who's scaring the girl."

Willow smiled, then closed the door and turned to face Jade. She put her hands on her shoulders and looked into her eyes. "I have faith that you, even with all your self-doubt, are the most powerful Witch I know." She winked at April. "Next to me, of course. And whatever comes our way, we can handle it. Now, you have a long day ahead of you. Go change and I'll get breakfast ready."

Jade and April raced up the stairs and parted ways to shower and change. While the hot water flowed over Jade's sore muscles, she thought about what life would be like without April. While she combed through her damp hair, she remembered how lost she'd felt at the séance without her hand to hold. By the time she opened the door to her room, she'd made her decision; if she was going to become High Priestess and leave Sun City forever, she would spend every moment she could with April until then.

After the breakfast dishes had been cleared, Grandma Willow asked April and Jade to sit with her and Charlie.

They took their places around the dining room table. As Willow opened her mouth, Jade jumped up. "I have something to say." All eyes were on her now, and she felt her nerves withering away. For a moment she doubted she was doing the right thing. She looked down into April's blue eyes, reminding herself why.

"I've been thinking, about Andrew, and the Ascension, and the coven . . . and I've come to a decision." She looked at April one more time. Things were about to get difficult between them and she wanted to remember how she looked now, before she felt betrayed. "I will become High Priestess and stay in Sugar Hill to protect the coven, with one condition . . . April goes where I go. She hears what I hear. No leaving her out, no keeping secrets. You want me to be coven leader, consider April a coven member."

"No way," Charlie said. "No offense, April, but she's a Citizen, an outsider. You can't possibly think it's right for her to know things even township Witches don't."

Grandma Willow asked, "Am I right in surmising you will not back down from this position?"

Jade cleared her suddenly tight throat, "Yes."

"Hmm." Willow looked April over and then back up at Jade, gently tapping a finger on the table. "We accept your condition." She kept Jade's gaze but said with a smile, "Close your mouth, Charlie. It doesn't become you."

He did as he was told but crossed his arms, clearly unhappy with the situation.

"Thank you." Jade sat down with relief. That had gone much easier than she'd thought it would.

Willow said, "April."

"Yes, ma'am?"

"For generations, almost no one from the cities was told anything about our covens. Our way of life was kept secret in order to protect us from those who wanted to persecute us for our beliefs. Occasionally, in rare instances, an outsider would be brought into the fold if they were vouched for by one of our own. It seems Jade has just done this for you."

April nodded solemnly. "I promise to keep anything I learn in the strictest confidence."

Willow smiled. "I know you will." She turned to Jade. "You know that becoming High Priestess is not a simple task, but you have never been told the process that directly precedes it. Traditionally when Witches ascend, they've had years of practice and preparation. They're handed the Keys and allowed three days of quiet contemplation and meditation. During this time, they connect to the Keys and bond to their energies. Andrew has taken that away from you. In having you search them out, it seems he's returned to the old ways when Witches were sent on quests to prove themselves worthy. One for each Key, each one a test of leadership qualities."

Charlie asked, "Can't we just do a locator spell to find the Keys?"

"After the Crossing Over last night, I performed several locator spells for the Keys. Each time I felt I was getting close, I was repelled. There are different ways to sense magical energy. For me it's a flavor. Your mother's magic tasted like white chocolate, your aunt's like apples. When I was close to finding the Keys, I tasted pure sugar. When Andrew stole the Keys, he must have spelled them with your family's magic."

Jade said, "But how is that possible? Andrew wasn't blood related; he was only married to my aunt."

Charlie said, "There are five levels of magic: self, family, elemental, coven, and divine. The personal level—that of the self—is the easiest, and the one all Witches use. Then comes the more powerful, and more difficult, family level. This is done by tapping into the essence of all the family members' magic. Of course, they would have to be in the family to do this, but part of the marriage ritual includes a bonding of magical essence."

Willow said, "Exactly. As far as magical energy is concerned, Andrew is family."

April raised a hand. "There's one thing I don't understand."

"Only one?" Charlie asked.

April made a face at him and continued, "Yes, smart ass, only one. I understand the Keys are needed for the Ascension ritual, and that's the only way Jade can become High Priestess and have access to the coven's power. I also get that by hiding the Keys Andrew's forcing Jade to tap into her power quicker than if they were handed to her. The one thing I don't understand is why doesn't Andrew just use the Keys to tap into coven power himself? Then he doesn't need Jade to do it."

Charlie said, "No, it doesn't work like that. Only a High Priestess or Priest can access coven-level magic. While he could use the Keys to tap into elemental magic, which is more powerful than both self and family, it's not enough power for a resurrection spell. There's also the fact that it's a dark magic spell."

"And that needs more power than elemental?" April asked.

"Sort of. Look, I don't think we have time for this. April, I'm sorry, I'm not trying to be a jerk, but it really is complicated. I'll be happy to explain every detail after we get the Keys back."

Willow gave him a warning look. "Charlie, let's remember our manners, thank you." She looked to April and said, "Each Key is an item that represents a corresponding element. The

Air Key is an athame. The Fire Key, a wand. Water's is a chalice, and Earth's is a disk. Both dark and light magic can be used at any level, but they don't mix well. Trying to use a Key that has been imbued with light magic for dark intentions damages it. It's not that dark magic is more or less powerful than light, it just requires different energy. For now, let's just say the longer the Keys are in Andrew's possession, the more of his dark magic they're exposed to. Which is why we need to get the Keys out of his possession as soon as possible. Jade will need your and Charlie's support to do this."

April replied, "Of course."

Willow rose and walked over to the fireplace. "I think you should start with the Earth Key." She opened a small box on the mantle and took something out of it. Returning to the table, she said, "Because it's more firmly connected to the physical plane than the others, it's the easiest to work with. Charlie, take them to the chapel. Since the Keys were used most often there and that was the last place we knew where they were, you should have the best luck picking up their trail from there."

Jade asked, "Aren't you coming with us?"

"No. I think it's best if you find your way through this without my direct help. Andrew is in the wrong, but he has one thing right; searching out the Keys without our help will force your connection to magic to be stronger quicker. And right now, that's exactly what we need. April, you must listen to Charlie and Jade. Do everything they tell you."

"I'll be happy to help any way I can."

Willow nodded and reached out, taking Jade's hand in both of hers. "I have a gift for you." Jade could feel something metal placed into her hand. "You may find a use for it later."

When Willow pulled her hands away, Jade looked over what she'd given her. It was a pendulum, cone shaped, about one inch long, attached to a silver chain at the large edge that ran about six inches to a small ornate silver ball. The pendant was made of two stones fused together, with their meeting point running the length, one side a pale blue aquamarine stone, and the other a vibrant blue lapis lazuli stone. It was a divination tool used for everything from answering simple yes or no questions to casting location spells. She placed it in her cloak pocket, feeling armed and ready.

And so it begins.

CHAPTER 15

As Charlie's black muscle car rumbled through town, Jade and April stared out the windows at the townsfolk and small shops. Jade was happy to see people actually out and about now. Not as many as usual but at least it no longer looked like a ghost town, more like a nearly dead town. They turned off Main Street and soon were bumping slowly along an unmarked dirt road.

Charlie pulled over at a huge tree that blocked the road. "We walk from here."

He led them down a side path and through the woods. Jade had dim memories of walking this way with her parents, but she couldn't quite place it and was starting to wonder if it had been a dream. The woods slowly became thicker as they went, the canopy overhead blocking more and more light. "I remember this . . . but . . ." She looked behind them at a large oak tree with bark that looked amazingly like a face, then forward to where Charlie was holding back some branches. "Isn't there a footbridge?"

"It's farther up," he said as she took the branches from him. "We're almost there."

As they continued on, April asked Jade, "You've been here before?"

"Once, when I was very little, I think. I remember that strange tree back there, and . . . oh, here it is." They crossed a small stone footbridge over a stream. "Yeah, and there's the hill."

Charlie had reached what looked like a steep bank, about eight feet tall, covered in moss and tree roots. The undergrowth was so thick you couldn't see beyond it. Charlie was leaning against an intricately carved wooden door set into the hillside. He spoke in hushed tones with his head close like he was telling it a secret.

Jade said, "It's called the chapel. We use it for certain special ceremonies. My mom and dad took me here for my Dedication ritual, when I started training to become High Priestess. You're going to love this. It's so pretty inside."

Charlie finished whispering and took a step back. The door opened inward about an inch and stopped. "Well, that's not good."

"What?" Jade asked.

"It should have opened all the way for us." He spoke the words again, but this time nothing happened. He braced his shoulder against the door and shoved hard, the wood slowly swinging inward under his strain. He motioned to Jade and April and stepped through.

Once they were through the doorway, the space opened up. What looked like a dirt mound on the outside was just closely bound roots and tree trunks. Two rows of trees formed a hallway of sorts, like columns in a cathedral. Their branches spread overhead to form a roof and hung down outside the trunks like walls. Colorful glass trinkets and baubles hung everywhere, catching what light filtered through between the leaves, sending rainbows flying. The ground had patches of different-colored moss and lichen, with dainty flowers scattered here and there. It was like walking through the center of a kaleidoscope.

At the end of the passage stood a tall wide-trunked tree. Its roots were mostly above ground and twisted, forming a shallow pool at the base, with stairs leading up on either side to a raised platform above the pool. Water gently poured into the pool from under the roots, appearing to come from the tree itself. A large, circular, dark green stone plaque hung on the trunk.

Charlie was halfway down the natural corridor, but April stood just inside the door, eyes wide, turning in a circle.

Jade grinned at her. "I told you it was pretty."

"Pretty? No, it's beautiful." She continued looking around. "Amazing . . . wondrous. I can't even see outside but there's light everywhere. Calling it a chapel is an understatement. It's more like one of the old cathedrals I've seen in history books."

Jade walked down to where Charlie was kneeling at the fountain. He stood and turned as she approached, holding a large box with its lid open. "This is where the Keys were kept." He held it out to her. "Can you feel their energy?"

"No," she said, staring at the box.

"You didn't even try."

"I haven't cast a spell in years. I'm sure there's got to be more to reconnecting than just trying."

He studied her for a moment, then motioned to the stairway that led to the tree trunk. "Follow me."

She followed him up to the platform. He put the box down on the podium of tree roots that looked out over the hall. April stayed out in the hall, looking over every inch.

Charlie said, "I understand this is difficult for you, but it's not going to be as hard as you think if you only try." When Jade didn't reply he continued, "See this plaque?"

The three-foot round plaque hung from the tree on the other side of the platform. It was carved to resemble a tree of life. Branches and leaves spread out, filling the top third. Within the leaves were birds and flying insects. Under the leaves on the right side of the trunk were several different animals walking along the dividing line that represented the Earth's surface. On the left side, the land dipped down and fish were carved into the space. On the lower half, roots twisted their way through the earth, stretching out toward the edges, making a mirror image of the top half. Here things like worms and bugs had their place.

Charlie said, "This is a tree of life. It shows all nature, all life, being part of the same whole. It's all connected, Jade. And you are a part of that connection."

She sighed. "I remember my teachings; you don't have to quote them at me. I just can't feel what they tell me I should."

He took her hands. "Remember when you first saw the feast tent?" He held her hands up between them. "You generated electricity because you were so upset. That's not simple magic. It requires you to make fire and water—two opposing elements—work in harmony. You weren't even focused on trying to do that. I think you're still connected to magic; you just have to let yourself feel it. You just"—he turned her to face the podium where the box rested and placed her hands gently on the edge of the empty box—"have to try." He took a step back.

Jade took a deep breath, then released it and closed her eyes. When she was little, she never had to try to feel energies. It was something she had always been able to do, even before she had started training to become High Priestess. She knew he was right, she only needed to try and she would connect to the energies. That wasn't the problem. The problem was, she didn't want to.

She let go of the box in frustration. "Can't you do it? I know I need to eventually, but can't you just get us started? Find the first Key, and I'll connect to it once we have it with us."

Charlie didn't reply. He just stood there staring at her.

As the seconds ticked by, Jade became more and more annoyed. Finally, she couldn't take it anymore. "Fine!" She grabbed the box edge and focused on earth, the hard, stable surface they walked on every day, the way it smelled after a rainstorm, its dark rich color.

She had a vision then, a real one, like she used to. The collection of sensations assaulted her. They were real and visceral, and she was helpless while they imparted their message.

Cold hard earth under her feet, sending a chill up her spine.

She coughed, choking as water filled her lungs.

Her skin flushed hot as if burned by a flame.

A stinging wind pushed against her.

As quickly as it came, it all disappeared, leaving a void of sensation and intense loneliness. She let go of the box and opened her eyes, falling back a couple of steps as she reoriented herself.

April had come up to the platform and stood next to Charlie. They waited patiently while she took a moment to catch her breath. Slowly, the knowing came to her. It was by far the most enjoyable part of her visions, mainly because she that meant it was over. "The Keys were taken and separated. They're not being used, they're . . . dormant? No, waiting. The first is . . ." She looked around the structure. The opening to the path she needed to take was like a hole in a tree. She looked down the steps and saw it. To the right side of the stairs was a dark area, like an unlit alcove. "There." She walked down to stand before it, and Charlie and April followed.

There was cool dank air emanating from the space, like the entrance to a cave, only she couldn't see even an inch past the entrance. It was like nothing existed beyond.

Charlie said, "I don't remember seeing this before."

April said, "No. I looked all over this place waiting for you two, and it was definitely not here. There were just tree trunks, like the rest of the walls."

Jade replied, "It doesn't matter. This is where my vision's leading me, so this is where we go." She stepped forward into the darkness.

CHAPTER 16

There was no sound, no light—nothing. "Hello?" Jade whispered tentatively. She blinked in the darkness. At least she thought she was blinking; she was telling her eyelids to blink, but it made no difference in what she saw. She reached out slowly in front of her but found only empty space.

She quickly pulled her hand back. "Wait, guys, we need a light." She reached behind her, and her hand bumped into a dirt wall. She turned and felt around, her fingers crawling along the rough surface. Just above her head was a dirt ceiling. *Was there a cave in?*

"April!" she shouted. She pushed against the wall from where she'd come, sank her fingers deep into it, began digging, pulling the dirt down around her as her breathing began to quicken. *They were just here.* "April! Charlie!" she called. There was no reply, and seemingly no end to the dirt.

She turned around and leaned her back against the wall she'd come through. She felt around blindly: wall on her left, wall on her right, space in front. She whispered to the darkness, "April? Charlie? Where are you?" She listened intently, but the silence pounded against her ears.

She reached as far forward as she could. Nothing but cool damp air brushed her fingertips. Shuffling her foot forward, she leaned farther still. Nothing. She fell back to the wall, her breath racing, the cool damp air pressing against her. The smell of earth filling her nostrils was suffocating. "I've got to get out of here."

She slid one foot forward, then the other, one hand on the cold dirt wall beside her, one hand scanning frantically in front of her and to her side. *There has to be a way out.*

The floor seemed level and as smooth as dirt could be, same with the walls. Her shoes made a scuffing sound as she shuffled along. It was the only sound she could hear besides her breathing.

Her fingers crept along the wall, leading the way into the void. As her hand slipped forward, finding only thin air, she jerked it back, grabbing the edge she had found. Her heart in her throat, she clung to the corner as she tried to slow her breathing.

When she found her courage again, she reached out to the other side of the tunnel and felt along that wall, but it turned sharply left. She gathered her courage and stepped as straight forward as she could and found a third wall crossing her path.

Great. Left or right? She turned her head toward the right tunnel and swore she could just make out the walls. *Oh good.* Moving along quickly now, she was thankful this trial had been so short. Then she ran straight into a wall. Dead end.

What? She held up her hands in front of her but was unable to see them. Desperate to escape, she had been deceived by her eyes making her think she could see.

No, no, no. She turned and went back the way she came, passing the first tunnel at the junction. She passed turns and multiple junctions, stumbling several times. Soon she was completely disoriented.

She grabbed her arms and leaned her back against the wall, focusing on her breathing. *Slow down, you ninny,* she told herself. *Hyperventilating and passing out will do you no good.*

She took several slow, shaky deep breaths. When she felt more stable, she placed her hands on the wall again and tried to remember the turns she had taken to get there, but there were just too many. She stood still, trying to listen, but the silence was deafening.

She chose a direction and started walking slowly, feeling her way. She had no idea where she was headed, but anything was better than standing still. "Charlie!" she called out frantically. She tripped on something and fell to her knees for what seemed like the hundredth time.

Crawling forward several feet, she found herself at another dead end. Reaching out to the left and right, she felt dirt all around her. Sitting on the floor, panic rose within her. Her throat tightened, her hands shook. *They're never going to find me. I'm going to die here, trapped in this underground hell while I suffocate.*

She pulled her knees up tight, squeezing them to her chest and resting her forehead on them as her tears fell. She couldn't do it. It was all too much. "April," she squeaked through her closing throat. "I'm sorry."

After a moment, a sudden calm washed over her. It was as if someone had gently placed a hand on her shoulder and filled her with courage. *No,* she thought. She said it aloud for good measure. "No, I'm not going to die here."

Standing shakily, she faced back the way she'd come. "You have to keep going," she told herself, "there's no other choice."

As she took a step, she realized, *But there is a choice, magic.*

"No," she told the darkness.

But it's why you're here, it replied. *To reconnect to the magic. To find the Keys.*

"I haven't done it in so long, what if it doesn't work?"

There was silence in her mind for a moment. *You just . . . have to try.* Charlie's gentle plea echoed in her mind. Whatever part of her mind she was arguing with, she knew it was right. Charlie was right.

Jade sighed. "Fine. Magic time it is." The lighthearted comment didn't help the lump in her throat. She stood in the dark, hands outstretched, while she searched her memory for a helpful spell. She hated doing this. She hated having to even think about magic.

She wiped the tears from her face and realized she wasn't crying because she was trapped in the dark; she was crying because she was being forced to do something she didn't want to. She was crying like a little girl who was told to eat her vegetables. That made her angry.

She was mad at Willow for making her face her responsibilities. She was mad at Charlie for treating her like she was just another coven member, and most of all, she was mad at her aunt for dying and leaving her alone.

As she knelt with her hands on the ground, she stretched out with her mind, seeking the energy of earth. After a moment she felt it. A cool, stable force at the edge of her senses.

Magic had been so simple when she was young. While most witches memorized rhymes and words of power, she usually just said what she wanted to happen, and the power did her will. But she had been connected to it then and had used it every single day. She could only hope that the same process of spellcasting would work for her now.

She began speaking, quietly at first, her voice rising in volume and strength as she went. "I am Jade Cerridwen, daughter of Rose Cerridwen, last of my bloodline, descended from an ancient line of powerful Witches." She felt the power growing as she spoke, rising up through the ground, through her hands and arms, filling her with confidence and calm, pushing back against the anger raging within her. "I am a woman who was raised in the ancient teachings of the High Priestesses and Witches before me."

The energy of the earth entwined with her own, pulsing throughout her whole body. She felt heavy but not weighed down. "Element of Earth, steadfast and persistent, I call and command you, show me the way out."

She felt the energy pulse down her arms and out under her hands. She stayed there, hands on the ground, as the moments ticked by. Focused on the energy rhythmically pulsing below her, picturing it in her mind as a soft white glow under her palms, she asked quietly, "Please, show me the way out?"

At the same time, she thought she heard something. Since her eyes were no use, she closed them. After a moment she heard it again. Though she couldn't pinpoint its source, it definitely sounded like a drip. The sound changed from a dripping to a trickling, like a spring flowing downhill. The idea the tunnel may start flooding caused her to open her eyes in a hopeless attempt to see where the water was coming from. She stared at one of the many roots lining the dirt floor.

As the sound of water stopped, it dawned on her that she could see. For real this time. Barely. She looked around at the faint spots of pale blue light everywhere. Mushrooms the size of peas were scattered all over, and they were glowing. She chuckled at the absurdity of it.

They were concentrated around her hands on the floor and radiated outward, like sunbeams, mostly in one direction. Back the way she'd come, then down the tunnel to her right. She tried to stand, but her knees gave way and she fell. Her whole body felt weak from the energy she used in the spell. *Talk about out of practice.* She shook her head, then reached out to the wall and slowly stood, leaning against it. Once she felt steady, she began picking her way down the dimly lit tunnel, careful not to tread on the few mushrooms peppering the floor. Most of them were on the walls.

After several turns, she noticed a yellow tint to the light ahead. The mushrooms led around a sharp corner, and as she cleared it, she saw what had cast the yellow glow. The narrow tunnel suddenly opened up into a circular room with a domed roof. The mushrooms had stopped at the doorway, but the room was lit by candles placed along the wall, and several sat on a waist-high stone pedestal in the center.

Jade hesitated in the doorway with an eerie feeling of being watched on the edge of her mind. She strained her eyes, looking around the whole room. There was no one there. The walls and floor were smooth and unbroken. The ceiling, though barely visible, seemed solid. She placed her hands on opposite sides of the doorway and asked, "You sure I need to go in there? I mean, the mushrooms don't even want to go."

She felt a pulse under her hands, and a surge of confidence accompanied it.

"All right." She lowered her hands and looked forward. "Here goes nothing."

Gingerly stepping into the space, she approached the pedestal in the center, wary but determined. Five white pillar candles marked the edges, and in the center was a stone box. Jade reached between two candles and carefully lifted the lid of the box, revealing a black velvet pouch on a string. She picked up the pouch, realizing it was heavier than it looked, then opened it over her palm. A metal disk about the size of her palm slid out.

It was the dark gray color of aged silver, pitted and scratched. It had obviously seen much use. The edge of the circle was raised, as was a pentagram that spanned the entire surface. The depressed areas were much darker and rougher. Jade began to wonder if it was maybe iron instead of silver. She turned it over to find a mirror finish. Not a scar to be found, a perfect reflection of her puzzled face staring back at her.

"Hello, Earth Key," Jade said to her reflection. She replaced the disk back in the pouch and lifted the rope over her head, tucking the pouch under her shirt for safekeeping.

She turned around to face the doorway, but it wasn't there. She turned again, looking the whole way around the room. The entrance was gone.

What? Jade walked to where the entrance used to be. She felt along the wall, but it was just as solid as the rest looked.

The light dimmed and she turned quickly to find that all the candles spaced along the wall were gone. Now the only light was from the five candles on the pedestal. She shivered at the sudden change of tone simply lowering the light caused. She walked along the wall, thinking there had to be a door she missed, some way out.

When she felt she was back to where she'd started, she walked into the center and looked at the pedestal. *Wait a minute. Wasn't that farther from the wall?* She turned around to find the wall much closer. "Great, now the walls are closing in on me?"

The light dimmed again. She turned to look at the pedestal. It had shrunk to a narrow pillar with one candle perched on top. It barely lit the ceiling, which was now almost within her reach. She stepped to the wall and pushed, but it didn't move.

The last candle disappeared, sending her into complete darkness. She pushed her back against the wall and tried to slow her breathing. The wall was curving inward at the top now, causing her to be partly bent over. She reached out and found the opposite wall was right in front of her now. Dropping to her knees, she hit her head on the opposite wall. Once again, panic rose in her, but this time she took control.

Crouched into a ball, she struggled to pull the pouch out of her shirt. With no room left to move, she managed to get the disk out of its pouch and into her left hand before her arm got pinned beneath her. Her face was pressed up against the dirt floor, and she fought the panic, instead focusing on the energy she felt in her palm. It began to warm and glow softly, lighting what little space remained.

"I am Jade Cerridwen, and I will be High Priestess." She pushed her right elbow between her side and the dirt above her, pressing her hand upward. Pulling all the energy she could from the dirt surrounding her, she managed to voice one command: "Move!"

Her hand shot up through the dirt easily, as if it was getting out of her way. A moment later, someone grabbed her hand

and pulled her up out of the earth and into the light. She inhaled a deep breath as a second pair of hands pulled her the rest of the way free.

CHAPTER 17

"Jade! Thank goodness you're okay!" April hugged her so tightly she practically pulled Jade into her lap. "I was so worried." She shoved her to arm's length and looked intently into her eyes. "You are okay, right?"

Jade shivered as she looked down at her dirty clothes. Yes, I'm fine now, I just"—her voice wobbled—"I'm so grateful you're here."

April frowned, wiping her tears away. "Me too, but I'm still mad at you."

"Yeah, I know. I'm mad at me too."

April gave her a crooked grin. "Good."

"Did you find the Key?"

Jade glared up at Charlie. Even though the sunlight was blinding her, she managed a proper scowl. "Really? That's all you have to say?"

He stepped forward, blocking the sun from her face. "What? You said you were fine." His expression darkened as he looked her up and down, his brow furrowing for just a moment. "I'm glad you're okay too, but we don't have a ton of time, remember? What happened down there?"

Jade pried herself from April's embrace and stood on shaky legs. Her fear was quickly being replaced by her annoyance with Charlie. As she brushed the dirt off her clothes and out of her hair, she demanded, "I have the stupid Key. Just tell me where we are." She looked around as her eyes finished adjusting. They weren't in the chapel anymore or the forest surrounding it. At least, not the same forest. There were trees, but they were much farther apart and there was no underbrush, just wildflowers and grass—and headstones. Jade looked at the one right next to where she had come up: Ebony Rathbern.

"We're in the cemetery," Charlie said.

"I can see that now. How did that happen? It's on the other side of town. How did you even think to look here anyway?"

Charlie replied, "April figured it out. Once I explained how portals work, she knew you were underground."

April said, "Yeah, but he figured out exactly where. Without him and his little magical pendant, we could have searched forever."

April smiled at him and he smiled back. Jade raised an eyebrow. "That's it? You guys are friends now?"

They looked at each other and Charlie said, "No. Not friends, but we both want the best for you, so we're going to put our differences aside."

April said pointedly, "For now."

"So, what's next?" Jade held out her hand toward them and opened it, showing them the disk.

"Finally!" Charlie said excitedly and snatched it from her palm.

April frowned. "That's the Earth Key?"

"What's wrong?" Jade asked.

"I thought it would be more, I don't know, key-like." She looked at it as Charlie turned it over, examining the reflective back of the silver disk. "And earthy."

"Where did you find it? Was Andrew there? What about the other Keys?" Charlie asked.

"One question at a time. It was in a box, on a pedestal, inside this dome-shaped room. I didn't see him, but considering there were lit candles everywhere, I may have just missed him. There were no other Keys."

"Really? What about a clue? He wants you to find them, remember? You must have seen or heard something to guide you to the next one."

"I don't think so. I . . . wait a minute." She paced back and forth along the row of headstones, thinking over her time underground. "I think I'm missing something."

She stopped at the spot where she'd come up out of the ground. There was no hole or break in the grass, no clue that a person had passed through moments before. The headstone was calling to her in a way. Different from a vision, different from sensing energy. She leaned into the sensation and realized the pull was specifically from the name on the headstone. "Ebony Rathbern. Why does that sound so familiar?"

"Do you think it's a clue?" Charlie asked.

"I don't know but it's really bugging me. I feel like I should know who she is—was."

Charlie's eyes lit up. "Wait a minute, remember that girl in grade school . . . what was . . . Amy! Amy Rathbern."

"Who?"

"Don't you remember? She told you about Hidden Lake, and when you showed interest in it, she said you couldn't find it with a map. You were so determined to find it after that." He said to April, "Never tell her she can't do something."

"Oh, I know," April replied with a grin.

Jade rolled her eyes. "Can we discuss my character flaws later? Maybe Hidden Lake's the clue, but the next Key should be Air, not Water." Charlie was right though; Andrew did want her to find them, so it couldn't be too hard. *What else did he say?* "Didn't Andrew say something about the Witch's Pyramid?"

April shuddered. "Dare I ask what that is?"

Charlie said, "It's nothing bad. The Witch's Pyramid consists of four instructions. By following the four instructions, one can empower spells. By mastering them, one unlocks the power of the divine."

Jade glanced at him. "That doesn't sound recited in the least."

April asked, "So what are these instructions, and what do they have to do with the Keys?"

Jade said, "From what I remember, each instruction in the Witch's Pyramid corresponds to one of the four elements. Air, to know. Fire, to dare. Water, to will, and Earth, to be silent. They're usually practiced in that order. First, you learn the knowledge, the lessons. Then, you dare to practice magic. Then, you bend the elements to your will. Then, you silence your mind and it opens you to the final level of magic, divine."

"But we found the Earth Key first," April said.

Jade argued, "I don't think that was a coincidence. None of this is. Andrew's been planning this for a very long time."

Charlie said quietly, "What if there is no order? Or . . . no. What if the order is reversed? Widdershins!"

"Weird a . . . what?" April asked.

"Widdershins," Jade replied. "It just means to go counterclockwise." Her eyes lit up as she realized he was probably right. "So, if that's the case, it would go Earth, Water, Fire, and then Air last."

Charlie looked at the headstone. "So if Water is next, you think it's at Hidden Lake?"

"Yes. No. Maybe?" Jade shrugged.

Charlie nodded. "Right then. We have to start somewhere, might as well start there." He turned and walked away, Jade and April scrambling after him.

Jade said, "Are you telling me you know where Hidden Lake is?"

Charlie glanced at April. "After Amy dared Jade to find Hidden Lake, we looked for three whole days and never found it. We asked everybody in town, but no one could help. One day while she was off doing some spell training, I asked Mrs. Keepsake. Back then I thought she knew everything. She just laughed and said, 'You'll never find it until you stop looking for it.'"

Jade said, "Well, that's more than I ever got out of anyone."

Charlie said, "It makes so much sense now."

Jade asked, "Why's that?"

"Because, the Keepsake family crest is Water."

***

"Two visits in as many days?" Mrs. Keepsake cheered as she hugged Charlie. "How wonderful! Please come in. I've got a batch of chocolate chip cookies in the oven for tomorrow, but I bet you can talk me into letting you sample a few." She winked at April as she passed and gently rested her hand on Jade's shoulder before closing the door. She hurried past them toward the living room. "Make yourselves at home. I'll bring some tea, and y'all can tell me all about your subterranean adventures."

Jade tilted her head. "How do you know about that?" She spoke up as Mrs. Keepsake went through the swinging kitchen door. "We just came from there and haven't talked to anyone about it."

Between the clinking of china and pouring of water, Mrs. Keepsake's voice floated through the door. "Oh, I have little birdies everywhere, as they say." She reentered carrying a silver tray with a dish piled high with cookies, four flowered teacups, and a matching teapot. "What kind of gossip would I be if I didn't?"

She placed the tea service on the coffee table between them and perched on the edge of the high-backed chair at the end of the table. "Now, let's see." As she reached for the tiny silver sugar tongs, Jade noticed each teacup already had a teabag in it and the string was wrapped around the cup's handle. Mrs. Keepsake dropped two cubes of sugar into one of the teacups, filled it with steaming water, and looked to April. "Cranberry pomegranate for our guest?"

She handed the cup and matching saucer to a surprised April. "Thank you." April looked over at Jade with raised eyebrows. "My favorite."

Mrs. Keepsake poured water into the next cup, skipping the sugar. "Green tea for the returning heroine. Unsweetened, of course." After handing Jade her tea, she placed one sugar cube in the next cup. "Black tea for the gentleman." She served Charlie, then quickly placed two cubes into the last cup, and after hesitating, placed one more. As she poured, she said wistfully, "And chamomile for the high-strung hostess." She raised her cup and breathed in the steam a moment before taking a cautious sip. Holding her cup and saucer daintily at waist height, she asked with a smile, "So, how goes the quest?"

Charlie spoke up. "We were hoping you could help with that."

"Oh! How exciting! Anything you need." She leaned forward slightly.

Charlie explained, "You know we found the Earth Key."

"Of course, dear."

"Do you also know the next Key we need to find is Water?"

"Ah, and you think I can help with that?" She took a sip of her tea, but her eyes betrayed the smile behind her cup.

"Your family crest is Water after all." Charlie left the question hanging in the air between them. *Would she help?*

Mrs. Keepsake thought a moment. "Hmm. I suppose it could be in Hidden Lake. Oh, it was my favorite place to go as a kid."

"So, you've been there," Charlie said. "Great, you can tell us how to find it." He looked expectantly at Mrs. Keepsake. She looked calmly back. He frowned. "Well? Are you going to tell us?"

Mrs. Keepsake replied solemnly, "This is your trial, dear. I cannot interfere." She put her tea down slowly and stood. "However, I can point you in the right direction." She walked over to a door on the other side of the room and opened it. Looking back at them she said, "Well, come on then," and disappeared through the doorway.

CHAPTER 18

After glancing at each other, Jade, April, and Charlie all stood and walked over to the doorway Mrs. Keepsake had disappeared through. A carpeted stairway led down into the darkness. Suddenly a light came on, illuminating the basement.

They walked down the steps and into the cleanest basement Jade had ever seen. The ceiling had no wires or plumbing showing. It looked like the drywall ceiling in the rest of the house and was even regular ceiling height. Three of the walls were lined with regular wooden bookcases, their shelves filled with plastic containers and decorative cloth boxes. Only one wall was left mostly open. Against it was a sitting area with two comfortable chairs and an end table in between them. The wall behind it showed a large framed painting of a field of flowers with a snow-capped mountain overlooking a lake in the distance. The floor completed the illusion they were still upstairs somewhere, being made of the same hardwood with a large area rug.

Mrs. Keepsake walked over to Charlie, carrying two long, straight sticks, each with a ninety degree bend near one end. "These should come in handy." She handed them to him, then walked over to the sitting area.

"What's that?" April asked.

Charlie said, "Dowsing rods. People use them to find underground water for drilling wells. You walk slowly along, holding each stick by the short end, with the long end out in front of you parallel to the ground and each other." He demonstrated. "When you step over water the rods cross." He took one more step and they crossed, forming an X. "All by themselves."

April asked, "Magic?"

"No, that's the cool thing about it," Jade replied. "No one has been able to figure out how it works, but anyone can do it, magical or not. Now we just have to figure out where to start walking."

Mrs. Keepsake had been rearranging the furniture in the sitting area while they talked. She had moved the coffee table out and taken down the painting and was now standing between the chairs, leaning against the wall. Jade couldn't remember ever seeing her lean against anything.

She nodded solemnly at Jade and said, "Yes, sometimes knowing where to start is the most difficult part of any journey." She looked up to the right, then gave a huge exaggerated yawn and stretch.

As her right arm slowly came down, the wall seemed to ripple in its wake. As Jade looked closer, she noticed a faint glow visible, like something was lit behind it. She stepped close and glanced at Mrs. Keepsake for direction. The older woman nodded once. Jade hesitantly touched the rippling, glowing wall. It didn't feel wet. It didn't feel like anything. She pushed her hand forward and it passed through, disappearing up to her elbow. She could feel the air was colder on the other side.

April gasped. "Whoa, that was creepy. You should do that at the next company Halloween party." She smiled at Jade, then asked, "How did you do that anyway?"

Mrs. Keepsake replied, "It's a sacred space, dear. Like a . . . like a separate dimension. I made it during the coven battle. In case any of us needed a quick escape. It is spelled so only I can open and close the doorway. When it's closed it leaves no magical energy trace." She smiled proudly.

Jade asked, "The lake is through there?"

Mrs. Keepsake shrugged. "There's only one way to find out."

Charlie said, "If this is the only way there, and it's spelled for only you to use, maybe the Key isn't there, then. Andrew wouldn't be able to get there."

Mrs. Keepsake said, "I never said it was the only way there. While it is difficult to find, it's certainly not impossible." She looked at Jade. "Your mom and aunt used to go there quite often as children. It's certainly possible Andrew learned where it was from Joy. From what you've told me, I do think it's the most likely spot for the Key to be hidden."

Charlie stepped up and flicked his index finger at the wall like one would at a person's nose. The wall rippled, like a pebble thrown into a puddle, and Jade noticed the faint glow flicker. Charlie gave Mrs. Keepsake a quick hug and stepped through.

Mrs. Keepsake held out her hand to April, who warily stepped up to the wall. "If I don't make it through here, I'm gonna haunt you the rest of your life."

Mrs. Keepsake nodded solemnly. "I would expect no less."

April took a deep breath and stepped quickly through.

Jade was about to follow when Mrs. Keepsake took her hand in a gentle hold. "Be careful, Jade."

"Thank you. I will." Mrs. Keepsake let go and Jade turned, stepping quickly through the shimmering wall.

The area was cold and dark like the tunnels, but not quite as pitch-black. Light danced along a rocky wall, casting shadows of something moving. She turned toward the source of the light and saw the silhouette of a curtain of vines. She pushed them aside and stepped out of a cave into the afternoon sun.

Charlie was standing with his back to her and turned as she approached. "It's Hidden Lake!"

Jade stepped up next to him and squinted into the distance. Beyond the tree line was a large expanse of rough terrain, like a shallow canyon, dipping several feet down before returning to the same level on the other side. There was no water and nothing growing in the area, although a few dead skeletons of what used to be shrubs dotted the landscape.

"It's hidden all right. So well hidden I can't believe it's here." She rolled her eyes.

April said, "No, he's right, look." She pointed over to an old rowboat half-hidden under some bushes. "At least there used to be water here. Maybe it just dried up?" she asked.

The trio stood on the edge of the space, looking warily around.

Charlie reached out and grabbed Jade's hand. "You feel that?" He stood with his head tilted, as if he was listening for something.

Jade looked down at his hand on hers, then up at him. "Feel what?"

Charlie let go of her hand and shaded his eyes as he squinted out toward the valley. "There's something out there. Something warded."

"Warded?" April asked.

Jade looked around but didn't see anything out of place. "Wards are spells that protect an item against specific things or people. They can also be used to protect against everyone but a specific person." She asked Charlie, "Warded for what?"

"Can't you feel it?" Charlie asked in amazement. "I can feel its pull on you from here."

Jade frowned. Usually only the person being summoned by a ward could feel its pull. It must have been cast by a pretty strong Witch for Charlie to be able to feel it. "Great. That's not suspicious at all." She asked Charlie, "Do you still have the dowsing rods?"

He handed them to her. "Are you thinking the lake is underground? That would be a good reason why it's so hard to find."

Jade took them and lined them up, long ends facing out. "It's worth a try." As she took a slow step, April moved with her. "Um, I think you should stay here with Charlie. Better not to mess with a ward that strong."

"I get you're trying to be careful, but what's the worst that could happen?"

Charlie gave Jade a look and said, "You don't want to know."

April ignored him and told Jade, "Look, the whole reason I came here was to support you. So let me. If things start looking wonky, I promise to turn back."

"You've made up your mind, haven't you?"

"Yup."

"Well, I guess you're coming with me, then."

Charlie said, "This is a pretty good view of the whole area. Higher ground. I'll stay here and watch your backs in case Andrew shows up."

April followed Jade slowly down the hill, zigzagging around boulders and over gullies. Jade kept holding the dowsing rods out in front of her. She began to feel like she was being watched. At first, she assumed it was because Charlie was planted firmly at the valley's edge, scanning the area with that scowl of his. When they jumped down into a lower area and he was no longer in sight, she thought it was probably just April's curious gaze as she watched the rods expectantly. But as they reached the bottom, Jade realized this was something different. This was a presence. Like at the séance. Andrew was watching them. She looked around nervously, searching for any sign—a shimmer of light, a shadow that didn't belong.

April noticed and her posture straightened. "How we doing?" she asked pointedly. "Any sign yet?"

Jade felt the underlying question: *Are you all right?* But before she could answer, the rods in her hands crossed. "Looks like we're here."

Directly below the rods was a large flat stone. Jade put down the rods and squatted for a closer look. She still couldn't feel any ward or magic of any kind. She knelt and pushed the rock as hard as she could. It slowly slid and underneath was a shallow hole with a metal box about one foot square.

After a moment April asked, "Well? Is that what Charlie was sensing? Is it warded?"

"I don't know. Usually when you approach a warded thing or place you feel it pushing back on you, like magnets. I don't feel that here, but that could just be because I haven't connected to magic enough yet." She stood and walked to the other side, looking for any marking or break in the smooth dark gray surface.

April was standing with her arms crossed, looking between Jade and the box. After a moment she said, "Maybe you can't feel anything because there's nothing to feel. Andrew said he wanted you to find the Keys, so maybe this is an easy one. Maybe you just have to open the box." She took a step toward it and froze midstride. She looked down at her feet and back up to Jade. "Um. I think there's a problem. I can't move."

A circle gently glowed around April's feet. The swirls curving along the boundary looked like letters, but Jade couldn't make them out. She ran to April's side and grabbed her hand, trying to pull her away. Everything from her ankles up moved, but her feet were like part of the Earth itself.

April pointed behind Jade. "What . . . is that?"

She turned to see water flowing down the hillside. At least she thought it was water. It was black, though, so maybe it was oil. It moved like a flash flood, just an inch or so in depth. The black liquid ran over the dirt, tripping over dips and pushing small twigs with it, approaching them from all sides.

It reached them quickly, coming together at the box and splashing over it.

Jade tugged at April's legs, but they wouldn't budge. She shouted for Charlie, but there was no response. She looked up the slope they'd come down. They were in a deep gully, putting them just out of sight of the ridge where he stood.

"I had to say this would be easy, didn't I?" April joked but her voice wavered, betraying her fear.

"Don't worry. I'm sure Charlie can see what's happening, and he'll be here any second." The water had reached her knees. There was no time. "I'll go get him."

She turned to leave but April grabbed her hand in a panicked vise grip. "Don't leave me."

"Okay, I won't. I'm here. Ch-Charlie!" she tried to yell, but the frigid water was stealing her breath.

Jade could feel the current now pulling at her knees. She struggled to keep her balance. April was panting and frantically thrashing in a vain attempt to break free. "Aaah! Let me go!"

Jade took a step back and chanted, trying to connect to the water. She desperately reached out, trying to feel the water's energy but there was nothing. Nothing but the icy cold, like hundreds of needles digging into her legs from the knees down. April was beginning to shiver as she struggled to pull her feet free.

Jade shook out her hands and tried again. Closing her eyes, she thought, *I am Jade Cerridwen, High Priestess.* There was no response, no power responding to her as in the tunnels. The water was to her waist now, and Jade was struggling to stay in place against the mild current.

"I'm sorry, April, it's not working."

The level seemed to rise quicker suddenly and Jade was swimming, the current pulling her away. She gripped April's hands like a lifeline. "No! April. I—"

"It's not your fault," April said as the water rose to her throat. "Forgive yourself." The water covered her head, leaving nothing below its surface visible.

Jade was still desperately hanging on to April's hand. She struggled to think of a way out, a spell, an enchantment, anything to stop the rising water. She felt April's grip on her release. More than that, she could feel her fingers flexing. April was out of time. She struggled to keep hold, but suddenly April slipped out of her grasp, and Jade was swept away. "NO!"

A wave punched her in the face, sending water down her throat. She coughed it out as she flailed her arms, desperately trying to remain on the surface. She was spun in a circle by the opposing tides, then pushed under again. Completely turned around now, only pitch-black water in front of her face, she had no idea which way was up. She reached out in all directions, her lungs aching for a breath.

A hand clamped down hard on her arm and yanked her upward. It released her and she collapsed into a boat.

"Where's April?" Charlie demanded.

Jade was shaking and coughing but managed to say, "T-t-t-trapped under there! Some kind of spell bound her feet down. My magic didn't work. I tried."

He immediately turned and cast a spell, his hands rotating around each other as his voice competed with the crash of the waves. A whirlpool began to form, the surface of the water dipping lower and lower until April's limp body came into view, curled up on the lakebed floor. The box was still next to her. Charlie commanded, "Adducer!" *Bring.* Both the box and April lifted up and onto the boat.

"April!" Jade cried, shaking her shoulders, caressing her expressionless face. "No, no, no. Please no."

Jade was dimly aware of the slight bump when the boat reached the shoreline. Charlie pushed her back. Picking April up, he carried her onto the shore and laid her gently down. He cast a spell, pulling energy from the shoreline to April, then out to the lake, and back. With each pass, black water flowed out of April's nose and mouth. Charlie continued casting the spell, the liquid slowly beginning to ebb until it no longer flowed from her.

He knelt and placed his hands on her chest, head bowed, and muttered something. April bolted upright, gasping for breath.

Jade rushed to her side and held her tight while a coughing fit cast out the remainder of the lake water. "Thank you! Oh, thank you. I don't know what I would have done. I'm so sorry, April."

April's coughs subsided, and she croaked, "Well, that was fun. Let's never do it again sometime." She gave Jade a weak smile.

Jade pulled April to her, gripping her tightly. She'd almost lost her. Getting the Earth Key had been frightening, but this made her angry. Andrew coming after her was one thing, or Charlie even. They were going to be coven leaders. They were the ones who would have the power Andrew needed for his twisted plan. April was an innocent. *I can't let something like this happen again.*

Jade released her. "We need to get back to Mrs. Keepsake's. Can you walk?"

"Of course I can walk." She stood shakily but refused Jade's hand. "I'm fine, Jade. Really." Another wave of coughing overtook her.

Jade looked her over carefully. Her eyes were bloodshot, and her skin hadn't regained its color completely yet. "Charlie." Jade continued looking at April. "Is she really okay?"

"As well as can be expected. My spell wouldn't have worked if her spirit had left her body. There's a short time after death before the spirit leaves when they can, possibly, be brought back. Not always, but we were lucky. She's a real fighter."

April looked at Charlie. "What does—?" A new wave of coughing hit her.

Jade explained while she regained control, "If your spirit had crossed the veil between life and death, Charlie would have had to use dark magic to bring you back, and that . . . it would have left a mark on both your soul and his. Bringing the dead back is no easy feat, but it gets more difficult and dangerous the longer the spirit's gone."

"Well I'm glad you acted fast, then. Thank you, Charlie. Truly." She looked out toward the boat. What had been a black churning cauldron before was now a calm clear lake.

"You're taking it pretty well," Charlie remarked.

"What choice do I have? I'm a Citizen, I have to believe what my senses are telling me until they're disproved. Besides, nearly dying is a slightly bigger deal to me than magic right now. So, how do we get the Key now?"

"That won't be a problem." Charlie walked over to the boat and reached in. When he turned back, he was holding a small earthenware cup. "When I broke the binding spell on you, it freed up the box, and this was in it." He smiled triumphantly and handed Jade the chalice. "Two down, two to go."

Jade glared at it. About four inches tall, made of brown clay, its bowl section was covered with a green glaze, and the base had an inset tree of life. So small and simple, and yet her best friend had almost lost her life for it.

No, she corrected herself. *Andrew almost took her life.* Her throat tightened at the idea of how close she had come to losing her. She looked to Charlie with grim determination. "Fire trial is next, right?" She placed the chalice into her cloak's inner pocket, not surprised it fit easily.

Charlie nodded. "You have an idea where that will be?"

She looked over to the mouth of a cave, nearly overgrown with vines. "I think so, but I still don't know where we're at now. Do you think we need to go back the way we came?"

"That's probably safest," Charlie replied.

As they walked back to the mouth of the cave, April took Jade's arm in hers. "So, where are we going?"

She looked ahead at Charlie stepping through the vines. "First we're taking you back to Mrs. Keepsake. She can take care of you while Charlie and I go after the fire Key."

April stopped short. "What? Jade, I'm not some child who needs a babysitter. I'll be—"

"No, this is not up for discussion. I won't risk losing you again."

April straightened her posture and lifted her head at Jade. "I know you're scared, Jade. But you can't—" She coughed several times, then looked sheepishly at Jade.

"Like I said, you're going to Mrs. Keepsake's." She held back the vines for her. "Charlie and I are going back to where it all began."

CHAPTER 19

When Jade stepped back into Mrs. Keepsake's basement, she was still standing next to the doorway as if she hadn't moved. Charlie had already explained what had happened, and Mrs. Keepsake spent the next several minutes fussing over April, insisting that her special tea blend would help the cough she'd developed. Soon she was bundled up on the couch under a thick flowery quilt, and Mrs. Keepsake was handing her a steaming cup of tea.

While the two were chatting, Jade told Charlie, "I think we need to go to my parents' place."

He nodded. "It makes sense. You sure you're ready for that?"

Jade looked at April. She had no idea if she could ever be ready, but without April it would be much harder. "We need to keep April safe. I won't let her get close this time."

Mrs. Keepsake spoke up. "April will be fine here with me. I'll take her back to your place, Jade. Once she's warmed up and feeling better, of course."

April opened her mouth, then closed it as a shiver took over. When it passed, she gave a weak grin and said, "Sounds like a plan to me."

***

As Charlie drove, Jade gripped the Earth Key in her cloak pocket. The pentacle was a Witch's symbol of power and protection. Its solid metal form gave her some small comfort. She wished April had been carrying it at the lake. She doubted it would have helped, but you never know. Even Willow used to say, *Magic is a discipline of mysteries. No one Witch can ever learn them all.*

The fear of almost losing April was still tight in her chest, though. She couldn't believe how quickly it had happened. The first trial had been frightening, but the second had nearly killed April. It made her leery of what dangers may be waiting for them with the Fire Key.

When they pulled into the long winding drive, the cold pit in Jade's stomach started screaming at her to run. She gripped the edge of the seat, willing herself to stay put.

The house eventually appeared around the bend, like a monster waiting to ambush her. The black and gray of the burnt timbers nearly blended in with the stormy sky, the monster's attempt at camouflage. She could just make out its outline contrasted with the lighter gray of the clouds. The blackened and broken trace of what was once a grand wraparound porch seemed like a lower jaw grinning menacingly at her. The roof had collapsed in on itself, and the remaining burnt timbers that poked up reminded her of the rib bones of some colossal carcass. The entire upper stories were gone, except the stairs to the second floor could be seen rising into nothing.

Jade took a shuddering breath, steeling herself for the challenge ahead.

Charlie said quietly, "The house hasn't been touched since the night of the fire, other than to let the Lawkeepers comb over it for their investigation. They didn't find a cause for the fire, of course." He pulled up in front of the walkway and stopped the car.

Jade opened the car door. She stepped out and stood facing the ruins of her past. They were surrounded by woods, and most of the once maintained property was now covered in weeds and leaf debris, but the entire house and a three-foot radius surrounding it was scorched. Not a single vine or blade of grass had taken root in the rubble.

Jade asked, "This happened decades ago, where's all the overgrowth?"

"If the fire was lit with dark magic, like the shaman suggests, then no life will grow here again. At least, not without a strong blessing from the coven."

As Jade stared up at the black skeleton of a house, a shiver shook her whole body. She pulled her cloak tight around her.

Charlie looked worriedly at her for a moment. "Are you sure about this?" he asked gently.

The night her parents had died was much like this one, overcast skies threatening to rain, a chill in the air laced with foreboding energy. A light drizzle began to fall, and the wind picked up slightly. She pulled her hood up over her head and stood looking over her former home, dreading what was to come but fueled by wanting it over with. Andrew was playing games with her, manipulating her into doing what he wanted, and putting her friends' lives at risk in the process.

"I really fucked up that last trial, didn't I?"

"It wasn't your fault and you know it. Andrew's the asshole here, not you." His voice was as comforting as an embrace, though there was an edge to it when he said Andrew's name.

"Still, I'm not exactly casting spells with ease yet. What if something happens here too?"

"That's what you have me for." He leaned in and whispered in her ear, "I am the High Priest you know."

She raised one eyebrow at him, then shook her head with a smirk. "Oh good, I feel all safe now."

He waited as she took the first steps toward the porch, then fell in place behind her. Together they made their way up the steps and around the burnt holes in the floorboards. Jade kept her mind focused on finding her way safely, delaying thinking about what she was about to face.

The front door was gone, as was most of the doorframe. She couldn't count the number of times she'd run through there. The screen door would slam behind her, then again as Charlie finally caught up. They passed the entrance and began gingerly picking their way through the debris. They passed the broken stairs. The only broken bone she'd ever had was from challenging Charlie to see who could skip the most steps at the bottom. Moving down the blackened hall, Jade traced her fingers along the charred wall. She'd loved looking at the images of her ancestors on this wall. Pictures, paintings, and sketches; her family's history instead of wallpaper.

Jade smelled smoke. She reached out to brace herself as she stepped over a blackened timber, and she could swear the wood felt hot. She froze, her breathing quickening.

Charlie was right behind her and placed a hand gently on her shoulder. "I'm right here with you. Take your time."

Her breathing returned to normal and she moved forward again. As they entered the kitchen at the back of the house, Jade was a frightened little girl again. She didn't want to look to her left, she knew what she'd see. Standing still, she stared at the blackened floor in front of her, trembling as she fought the memory that haunted this place. It was there, waiting for her, she knew it.

She closed her eyes and took a slight step back. She leaned into the wall of Charlie's strength and calm.

"I'm here. What can I do?"

She turned to face him but couldn't open her eyes. "Do you see him, or the Key? Anything?"

He placed his hands on her shoulders. They were warm and she leaned against them as an anchor. After a moment he said, "No. There's nothing here. Let's go."

"No." She sighed and opened her eyes. "We can't leave until we get the Key." He looked so sad, or worried, like he didn't want to be here either. She felt silly then. There was nothing there that could hurt her. It was just a burnt-down house. She needed to get past it, and to do that she needed to face it. "It's time."

She turned and looked at the wall; the entire surface was burnt, black and scaly, like alligator skin, except for an eerie negative shadow. The lighter-colored wood was low to the ground and oblong, just large enough for two people to crouch within it.

This was where her parents had died.

This is where she had found them, when she was only twelve years old.

***

The morning had started as normal as could be. Jade had gone to the woods with Grandma Willow and Charlie, the boy who lived down the street. She called him her "little shadow" because as early as first grade he had become infatuated with Jade and followed her everywhere. While they had become best friends, Charlie was the least magical person she had ever known. He had never been able to master the heightened state Jade and Willow could during meditations. In fact, most times he fell asleep.

Today Grandma Willow had invited him along, and by the time they neared their mountain retreat they were all laughing and telling stories. They sat by the lakeside and practiced a group meditation she had experienced many times before. It always began the same. First was the settling of her mind as she gently told it to be quiet. Then she would focus for a moment on each distraction: the birds singing in the trees, the spring bubbling nearby, the pressure point in her right ankle, the itch on her nose. One by one she paid attention to them and then dismissed them until she was alone in her mind. She would reach out tentatively so as not to startle Grandma Willow's mind. She would search for the comfort and aged wisdom that was a constant cloak around her.

But this time, instead of finding Grandma Willow's amused reply of "I am here." she felt a scream. Felt it in her bones as if it was her own flesh that seared with pain. She tried to open her eyes, break her mind from the connection and tear herself back to the physical, but the feeling took hold of her. The death grip it had on her was frantic instinct, the desperate grasp of the dying. A moment later she recognized it. The High Priestess, Rose Cerridwen, her mother was dying.

At the moment of recognition, her mother pulled back, releasing her hold on her. The last thing she felt was love, still strong through the pain, sending her away. Protecting her.

Jade opened her eyes as she cried out, "No!" Blinking back tears, she looked to Grandma Willow, whose expression was one of complete knowing. She knew, *Jade thought to herself,* She knew before it happened, that's why we're here.

She glanced at Charlie but saw nothing more in his eyes than being startled by her sudden outcry. Jade dismissed the thought of him and demanded Grandma Willow take them home immediately. For a moment she looked like she might say no, but her face changed subtly to resignation, and she rose and headed for the car.

When they finally turned the corner into the drive and the house came into view, Jade couldn't believe her eyes. She jumped out of the car before it stopped and ran down the gravel driveway. When she reached the flagstone walkway, the blistering heat from the flaming structure forced her to stop.

As Jade stood before the raging inferno that used to be her home, the tears fell freely. She stifled the urge to rush in and instead struggled to think of a spell that would stop the towering flames roaring in the darkness. For a moment she just stood there in shock, tears rolling down her red cheeks, sobs wracking her whole body. She stared at the flames before her.

She felt Grandma Willow's presence. Her comforting touch calmed Jade's mind, and she was able to think clearly again. Jade took just a moment to appreciate that she was with her. She then raised her gaze skyward and closed her eyes in concentration. Her tears suddenly dried up as if the faucet was shut off, and rain began pouring from the sky. Bucketfuls slammed down on the once beautiful home. The flames made one last attempt to burst forth before being completely smothered.

She watched as rivers flowed over the now visible spires and slanted roof. Down they ran into the many gaping holes that were once the stained-glass windows of the upper floor. Soon all that was left was a smoking blackened skeleton that was once her home.

As the water slowly stopped, Jade ran through the charred opening where the front door had stood and past the collapsed stairs into the kitchen area at the back. She knew exactly where to find her parents. It wasn't a sound or a vision that told her, she just knew, the way she knew so many things coven members older than her had to struggle to remember.

She stopped inside the doorway, not wanting to look to her left where her mother and father lay wrapped in each other's arms. They had faced death together as they often said they would. Jade had not fully understood the look that passed between them in those moments until now. They had foreseen their own death. They had sent her away because they knew what was coming and wanted her safe.

A thousand questions raged inside Jade's mind: Why did this happen? Why didn't they stop it with a spell? They had made the fires dance to their will on many cold nights, why was this any different? Why didn't they run if they knew this would happen? And most importantly: Who did this to them?

A single thought struck like a bell in her heart. You can fix this. *It was both a question and a declaration. She answered it out loud, "This will not be." She turned to face her parents' remains. Two figures of blackened coal clung to each other, white ash hung where their clothing had been, swaying ever so slightly in the air currents.*

Jade closed her eyes and envisioned her parents healthy, happy, and alive. She knelt and placed both hands on the blackened floorboards. Keeping the vision of her parents clearly in mind, she felt down through the wood, past the cement foundation and into the Earth. Her spirit joined there with the pulsating essence of life. She pulled the essence up toward her parents' bodies, envisioning it entering them and repairing all the damage the flames had done, restoring them to their former selves, the vision she clung to in her mind.

She had used this magic before to rescue her neighbor's tomato plants from the frost. Plant or human, Jade knew it was all the same energy. She opened her eyes, confident that she had succeeded.

She stared blankly at the charred bodies still before her. She had in fact raised the energy, but as she stood there in shock, she watched it flow slowly back down to the Earth. Her anger bubbled to the surface. With a violent cry and a crashing of her fists, she slammed into them, pounding furiously as she screamed, "You lied! You lied! You lied!" Over and over she screamed the accusation as their remains disintegrated before her onslaught into coal-black powder, and small wisps of gray-white ash floated upward, released by her fury, as souls rising to heaven.

***

A wave of dizziness hit Jade, and she fell backward into Charlie. He caught her and they both sank to the floor. She closed her eyes and fell into a black abyss, where sorrow and pain were all that existed. It was too much to bear. She began to scream, and he rocked her, holding her tightly while each breath cut her lungs and throat. The tears flowed as freely as they had that day. Her world collapsed around her, and she was powerless to stop it. The sorrow engulfed her. Burying her. Drowning her. Leaving her alone in its cold darkness. She was losing herself.

It's not fair. A voice in the dark. A spark of anger accompanied it.

It's not your fault your parents were taken from you. She grasped the anger, a lifeline in the void.

All this sorrow, all this pain, because of him. The thought of Andrew burned inside her, and she snapped back into consciousness.

A sharp pain passed through her, like a flame, burning a path through her chest. She opened her eyes and felt the determination in its wake. This was all because of Andrew, and she would make him pay for it. Charlie's arms were still around her and she smiled as she pulled them open and turned to look at him.

His face was ghost white, his eyes too wide, and his mouth hung open, frozen in a silent scream.

"Charlie! What happened? Are you all right?" She held his face. He was hot. Too hot. His skin felt hotter than if he had a fever. She looked around as she pulled him close, wrapping her arms around him and trying to pour what she hoped was healing energy toward him. It was her turn to rock him. "Shh, Charlie. It's okay, you're okay."

Cradled in her arms, his fiery skin slowly began to cool. Sweat beaded and rolled down his forehead and arms. His skin slowly became pink.

Soon she heard him mumble something. She pushed him slightly away to look into his face. "What?"

He whispered, "I felt it. I felt everything." He was shaking now.

"What do you mean?"

"Pinpricks . . . little . . . pain . . . " He looked up into her eyes. "I became her. I felt it all. The flames . . . they—"

"What flames, Charlie? Became who? What are you talking about?"

He looked behind her, to the shadow on the wall.

A shock ran through her, like cold electricity. "No." It couldn't be.

"The flames were blinding, all around us . . . around them." It was like he was struggling to remember who he was. "Her skin . . . the flames were searing my skin . . . my . . . burning their way through me. I was on fire. I . . . Goddess."

No. Jade pulled him close again. "No," she sobbed. "I'm so sorry."

He continued as if he hadn't heard her, staring through her to the spot on the wall. His face changed from horrified to sad. "I clung . . . she . . . clung to him. She tried to protect him, shelter him with herself. But . . ." He broke down into huge gut-wrenching sobs that left no room for breath.

Jade cried as she rocked him. She cried for his pain, for what she had unintentionally done to him. He had experienced her entire memory. The moment of contact Jade had with her mom had transmitted everything her mother had felt. It had been too much for young Jade, so her mind had blocked it. In this place, Charlie had somehow experienced the part of the memory Jade had blocked, even now.

After a time, his crying stopped. He pulled away from her and sat up straight. "I knew. Not what I would feel exactly, but I knew I would experience whatever you had that night." He looked at her with sad, tired eyes. "I welcomed it. I wanted to know what you had gone through, to share your burden and lessen it if I could."

He looked down at his hands as if they were strange to him. "I hadn't even guessed it would be like that. No wonder you shut down." He looked at her again. "I understand why you left town now. You had to."

Jade looked at his tear-stained face, now hot pink as the shock was wearing off. "I'm so sorry, Charlie."

"No need to be sorry. I'm fine. I will be fine. It's over now, the memory's fading already," he said shakily, giving her a weak smile. "Any sign of the Key? I'd hate to have gone through that for nothing."

Jade looked around but saw nothing suggesting a hidden Key. No box, no visions. "You were right, there's nothing here. Let's go."

Jade stood shakily and helped Charlie up. She felt something then. A very faint warmth, like a campfire from a distance. She turned toward it, but there was only blackened wood, burnt out long ago. "Can you walk okay?"

"I think so. You have an idea?"

"Kind of." They made their way back out of the house. When they were almost to the door, she felt a tingling in her left hand. She looked at her palm, and a memory floated to the surface. A time when she didn't fear fire or magic. A time when it bowed to her will.

"The fire side of the pyramid is 'to will,' right?"

"Yes. Why?"

She raised her hand out in front of her. "Because I'm damn tired of being at the mercy of Andrew's will." She closed her eyes for a moment, trying to remember her Latin training. She opened her eyes and commanded, "Inveniet." *Find.*

A faintly glowing golden ring of fire encircled her wrist. She repeated the searching spell over and over. Each time the ring grew in brightness, and soon sparks flew out from it like fireflies. She felt it pulling her back into the structure, and she followed.

It led her into what was once the library. It was really just an oversized living room, but they had divided up the space so on the right of the fireplace was a small seating area and on the left was the library. The three walls that made up this end of the room had been packed floor to ceiling with books. Jade looked around at the debris field of black and gray timbers and bookshelves, twisted and broken like a giant's matchsticks. She closed her eyes and whispered, "Inveniet."

She opened her eyes and held her left hand out to her side. Slowly waving it back and forth, she stepped forward into the space. Wood beams were lifted by unseen hands and tossed aside to allow her passage. She felt a pull in her hand as the spell called out to the Key.

The glowing ring around her wrist suddenly shot forward and under a beam. There was a glow emanating from where it had gone, and after a moment the beam began to shake. The glow became brighter just as the beam exploded, sending splinters flying everywhere, except where Jade and Charlie stood.

She felt the energy of the spell leave her and a new excitement replace it as she knelt and picked up the athame. The dull silver double-sided blade was about six inches long, ending in a black leather handle. She had done it. She had successfully used a spell with intention. Not out of fear or anger, she had done it calmly, as all magic should be done. Instead of feeling drained or weak, she felt powerful.

She turned and threw her arms around a smiling Charlie. "I did it!"

He hugged her tightly. "You sure did." When neither of them pulled away immediately, he whispered, "I knew you would."

She backed up from him then. "Well, don't get cocky. We still have a last Key to find." She turned and walked out, a small smile tugging at her mouth.

CHAPTER 20

As Jade and Charlie walked down what was left of the porch steps, she thought about how far she'd come. She had started not wanting anything to do with magic, not even wanting to think about her past. The night her parents had died, she'd felt so betrayed by their loss and wondered if she'd ever feel normal again. Now here she was casting spells, and she had to admit, it felt good.

As Charlie drove off the property, he said, "Think April made it to your house yet?"

"Probably," Jade mumbled. She was looking into the side mirror as the remnants of the house disappeared behind her. That's all it was to her now. Not a monster, not some dark thing waiting to get her, just a broken house.

"You okay?" Charlie glanced at her, worry apparent in his face.

"It was just hard is all." She looked down at the athame in her hand. She could see now that the blade wasn't made of metal. It was hard like stone and the edge was very dull. The cross brace between the handle and blade was inscribed. *Cast in Peace, Cut in War.* She turned it over. The opposite side had Celtic knotwork instead of words. In the center of the handle, a narrow band of bone was inset between the leather wrappings.

"Trials," Charlie said.

"What?"

"The Fire trial, it was different from Earth and Water. Those were physical dangers. In fact, being buried alive and drowning are both similar to the Witch's trials from the Lost Years."

Jade definitely remembered this part of her training; she hated it. Long before the Accords, there was a time when Witches were hunted. The trials were designed so that a Witch could easily escape, thereby confirming the charge against them, and they were then executed. However, if they were "innocent," they died failing to escape. Jade had been horrified when she'd learned this, and even now it saddened her to think about it.

"What's your point?"

"My point is, these trials started out dangerous, but this last one wasn't even physical or dangerous at all. It was all mental."

"So, what, you think Andrew's going easy on me now?"

"No. I wouldn't call it easy, but it is odd." He thought for a moment. "Willow needs to know what's happened. Maybe she'll have an idea how to proceed."

When they arrived, April was sitting on the couch in front of the fire, and Mrs. Keepsake had just entered the room with a quilt. "You're back. Wonderful."

April jumped up and hugged Jade tightly. "I'm so glad you're back. How did it go? Was it dangerous? Did you get the Key?"

"I'm fine, and yes, we got it." She held it out for April to see.

Mrs. Keepsake put the quilt on the couch and picked up her bag. "Well, my dears, it's been a long day, and I must be off to bed. There's much to do tomorrow, and I need to be up early for it. Willow's gone to bed, and she asked me to tell you, 'Whatever it is can wait until morning. Thank you for not waking me.'" She chuckled. "Right to the point, that one."

She hugged Jade gently. "I'm glad it worked out, dear. Get some rest and we'll tackle the morning together." She patted Charlie's shoulder and left.

April handed the knife back to Jade. "Do you feel like talking about it?"

She had missed April, but she was exhausted. They all needed sleep if they were going to have any chance of "tackling the morning," as Mrs. Keepsake had put it. "Yes, but not right now. We all need some sleep." Charlie turned toward the door but Jade stopped him. "I think you should stay." She could feel April's eyes on her and quickly explained, "I mean, we have extra rooms, and that way you're close . . . if something happens. And we can get an early start tomorrow." Her face was getting hot, and she only hoped he couldn't see her blush in the dim lighting.

"Sure. Sounds like a good idea." He smiled at her and turned toward the stairs.

***

There was no dream or vision that woke Jade. No sound or movement in the large house that she could tell, she simply opened her eyes. The room was still dark, and she turned over to look at the clock on her nightstand. 4:03 stared back at her. *It's practically morning.* She felt surprisingly good, considering what she'd been through.

Deciding to take a walk in the garden, she threw her hair in a messy ponytail and put on her cloak, then tried to sneak out of her bedroom door, closing it quietly to not wake anyone. She turned around to walk down the hall and was confronted by Charlie. A fresh out of the shower and still in a towel Charlie.

"Where are you going?" His arms were crossed, and he looked down at her with one eyebrow raised, seemingly unaware of his half-naked appearance.

"I . . . uh, I . . . I was go . . . you know." Full stop. She couldn't think.

"Yeah, yesterday was pretty rough. I couldn't sleep anymore either." Relaxing his posture, he placed his hands on his hips.

There was barely any space between them, and she could feel his body heat radiating at her. Jade had the distinct impression he was watching her for a reaction. She forced herself not to look at his muscled arms and chest and focused on his eyes. "I just wish Willow had been up when we got back. You know, to tell us what to do."

"You never were very patient." He smirked at her. "Maybe it's for the best though. You've been through a lot lately. You needed some rest." He reached out and gently moved a curl that was hanging down her cheek, tucking it behind her ear.

She felt her cheeks flush and ducked her head, turning away from him. "I guess." She slowly started walking down the hall. "I'll just be glad when this whole thing is over and we don't have to worry about Andrew anymore."

He walked beside her, barely an inch of space between them. "Me too. But I have faith it'll work out all right." He stopped at the top of the stairs and smiled at her warmly. "You still haven't said where you're going."

"I just need to clear my head. I was thinking of taking a walk in the garden."

"Do you—I mean, would you like some company?" He looked expectantly at her, and for a moment she considered saying yes.

"No. I mean, thank you but—"

He took a step back. "Yeah, I'm not exactly dressed for a stroll." He gave her a sheepish grin.

She glanced downward and immediately brought her eyes back up to meet his. "Yes. Good point. I'll just . . ." She almost fell backward down the stairs, catching onto the railing at the last second. "Go then, he-he." *Was that a giggle?* Mortified, she turned and ran downstairs as quickly as she could without looking like she was actually running away from him.

She turned the corner into the front living room and nearly collided with April. "Ah! What is this, Grand Central Station?"

"What?" April asked.

It wasn't April's fault Charlie had gotten her all flustered. Jade hated being embarrassed, so much so that it usually turned into anger quickly. April just happened to be the closest target at the moment. "Sorry. I just ran into Charlie upstairs and now you. Felt kinda crowded for a moment." She gave a halfhearted smile. "How are you feeling?"

"Better. I think. Still a bit cold though. I came down to grab the quilt." April looked at her clothes and asked, "You going somewhere?"

"For a walk in the garden. I can't sleep anymore, so I thought some fresh air might help clear my head."

"Could I come with you? Maybe I just need to move some."

"Sure." Jade would agree to anything to get her mind off Charlie. He was one complication she did not need. At least, not until this whole thing with Andrew was settled. She waited while April went up to grab her shoes and jacket.

They went out the side door, and Jade shivered at the eerily silent garden. The nearly full moon was huge, resting near on the horizon, a hunter's moon. It cast a slightly orange light on everything but illuminated the path enough for them to walk easily.

The garden paths were edged with two levels of stone terrace. On each level were plants of various colors and sizes, all of them edible. The path itself was made of rounded pebbles set in swirling patterns and the design changed throughout the garden; some areas had spirals; others had Witch's symbols. One small patch was random colors with no apparent pattern at all. That was Jade's section. She smiled down at it as they walked over it. As a kid, she'd helped her aunt extend the path for a while but had soon grown bored and asked to be excused.

April stopped to look closer at a plant with spindly purple flowers. "Is this lavender? It kind of smells like it but looks different."

"That's because you're used to the kind they ship into Sun City from Marshfield. That lavender is originally from overseas, but they grow it for the cities because the smell is stronger and more consistent. This is wild lavender. It's native to this area, and each season the smell is slightly different."

"Isn't it late in the season for blooming flowers?"

"Yes, but my aunt often spelled her garden to extend the growing season. Now that she's gone, they'll probably only last a few more days."

April nodded and continued on the path.

There was something about the way she was wandering slowly along, stopping to smell and touch plants, looking up at the night sky. She seemed carefree. Jade caught up to her and asked, "What's got into you?"

"What do you mean?"

"We've been trying to talk out this coven leader situation for a while now, and every time we start to, something comes up. Now is the perfect time and you don't seem to care."

April turned to face her. "Of course I care. It's just . . . I had a talk with Mrs. Keepsake while you two were off getting the Fire Key. She explained how important the coven is to the township, how it not only regulates things and protects the Witches who live here, but it's also important to the people in an emotional sense. It's kind of the township's heart.."

They had nearly reached the center of the garden, and April led Jade over to one of the benches that ringed the open space. As they sat down, she said, "I get it now, Jade. I'm gonna miss you like crazy, but this is bigger than the two of us. The town needs you." She squinted at her. "I'm still pissed you tried to hide it from me. But what's done is done. I'll get over that eventually. Just promise never to hide things from me again." She held her hand up between them, pinkie finger high in the air.

Jade said, "I promise." She looped her pinkie around April's. "No more secrets."

A voice came from across the clearing. "Great, now that it's settled, we can get down to business."

A hooded figure appeared in the shadows. At first Jade thought it was a ghostly apparition, but as it drew closer, she realized it was an actual person. As he stepped forward into the moonlight, she saw his face. "Richard?" He smiled warmly at her.

She ran to him and hugged him. "I'm so happy to see you!" She pulled away to look at his face. "What are you doing here? Did you come for Joy's funeral? I didn't see you there."

"No, Jade. I came here for you."

There was something in his tone that seemed off. She took a step back. His normally neatly trimmed beard was a scraggly mess, his suit was crumpled and dirty, and he was wearing boots instead of his usual loafers. The most drastic change of all was a cloak. It was black and floor-length, with a hood and a penannular brooch at the collar. A Witch's cloak.

CHAPTER 21

"No." Jade backed away from Mr. Whetstone to where April stood. Her brain was in denial, going in circles, trying to find a logical explanation for why he was here. "No. It's not possible." She shook her head. "You can't be Andrew. Why are you here? Give me a reason I can live with."

Mr. Whetstone took a step closer, and the sun peeked over the horizon, lighting his face and revealing how sunken his eyes were, how pale his skin was. He looked more than just tired. Jade raised her hand toward him. He stopped and looked at her with head bowed, hands spread in front of him. "Jade, honey. You're doing so well. I've been so proud of you these last few days. You only have one more Key to connect with."

"You're Andrew?" April glared at him, pointing her finger. "You're the one behind all this? You almost killed me!" She tried to charge him, but Jade held her back.

Jade understood April's fury, she felt it to, but considering all he'd put them through, she had no doubt April would be the one hurt in a confrontation between them. He may look like hell, but she could feel the power emanating from him. Besides, she needed answers first. "How could you lie all those years? Pretending that you knew nothing of magic, nothing of what I was going through. You lied to me." She turned to face him. "Just like my parents." She could feel the tingling as angry static pooled in her palms. She clenched her fists, fighting to keep control. "You killed my aunt too, didn't you?"

Mr. Whetstone raised his hands in front of him, palms out. "Your parents were an accident, and I had nothing to do with your aunt's death. I would never harm her in any way. She was my wife. I loved her."

Jade glared at him. All the anger, all the sorrow over the past years, the danger April had been in, it had all been his fault. The building energy was becoming too much to contain.

He was smiling back at her now, his posture relaxed. *Perfect, stay just like that.* She focused within her, pulling more energy from the elements around her: the solidity of earth beneath her feet, the tiny droplets of icy cold rainwater against her cheeks, and the anger burning like a fire within her. "You liar!" She flung everything she felt toward him. It morphed as it left her fingertips, becoming pure energy.

The electricity shot from her hands like lightning bolts. They ricocheted inches before hitting his palms, deflected by the barrier he had raised. It crackled as mini shocks ran over its surface, an arching wall in front of him.

One lightning bolt hit the fountain in the center of the clearing, destroying it and sending water spraying everywhere. The other crashed into a nearby tree, making it explode in a shower of sparks and wood splinters. A splintered branch was heading straight for her. It burst into flames, then disintegrated into nothing just before reaching her face. April screamed and Jade turned to see her clutching her arm, a shard of wood sticking out it. She raced to her side.

The splinter was only an inch long and not very wide. April pulled it out angrily and tossed it aside. A small amount of blood seeped out. "I'm okay," she said, as she placed her hand over it.

Jade turned to face Richard. "That's the second time you've hurt her. There won't be a third. You want me to find the Keys? Tell me where they are." She stalked toward him, hands at her side, head dipped low.

"Now, Jade." Mr. Whetstone shifted his stance, raising one finger warningly.

She stopped her approach, or rather something stopped her. She couldn't take a step. She pulled at her back leg, but her foot wouldn't budge. "Let me go," she commanded.

Mr. Whetstone shook his head and sighed. "Jade, my dear. I'm happy to see your powers are returning so quickly, but you really must control your anger."

She glanced behind her. April was trying to move her feet, but they wouldn't budge.

"Not again," April moaned, fear evident in her voice. She looked up at Jade, tears in her eyes.

Jade turned back toward Richard, who had closed the distance between them. "We have so much to accomplish together, don't you see?"

"No. All I see is Andrew, the man who killed my family. Richard is dead."

"No, Jade, don't say that." Andrew spun away from her and began pacing, mumbling to himself. "Ugh, you don't understand. What I'm doing, it's not just for me. I'm also doing this for you."

Jade stopped struggling. "How could this possibly be for me?"

"Because once we bring my daughter back, we can bring back your parents, your aunt, whoever you want. You want that, don't you?"

Jade felt like the wind had been knocked out of her. She wanted that more than anything, to have her parents back, her aunt. But it couldn't happen. People raised from the dead came back wrong. She didn't realize that when she was a kid, or didn't care, but now she knew better. She wouldn't do that to her family, no matter how bad she wanted them back. She glared at him, hating him even more for taunting her like that.

"Did I ever tell you I was married before Joy?"

Jade blinked and shook her head. "What the hell does that have to do wi—"

"You would have liked her, Jade." Andrew was looking off into space. "Raven was so beautiful, smart . . . powerful." He turned back to her. "Like you will be. It's too bad you never met her, she died before you were born." A shadow crossed over his face. He frowned at the ground between them. "If only I could tell you everything." He looked at her sadly. "Jade you have to trust me; this isn't for nothing. Your parents, your aunt, it's all part of the plan."

"What plan?"

"I can't tell you, but it's bigger than you or me. Please trust me, Jade. She wouldn't have done all this for nothin—" He stopped suddenly.

"She?" Jade asked. "She who?"

He seemed caught, eyeing the woods to his right. Then he deflated and stepped back, frowning at the ground between them. "Find the last Key. Become High Priestess." He looked pleadingly at her. "Then, I promise, you'll see." He walked away, back into the shadows.

Jade struggled as hard as she could, but her feet would not budge. Only after he was completely gone was she able to move.

From the moment the power had left her hands, she'd felt drained. She fought against the weakness, her anger fueling her to some extent. Now that he was gone and his spell was no longer keeping her in place, she struggled to keep to her feet.

She looked behind her. Charlie and Willow had come out of the house and stood on either side of April, who was visibly shaking as she stared wide-eyed at the demolished tree next to her. Willow was examining April's arm. Jade approached with arms outstretched. "April, are you okay?"

April jumped backward and stood eyeing the ground in front of Jade. "I'm fine."

Jade looked to Willow, who replied, "She wasn't badly injured. She just—"

"Could you not talk about me like I'm not here?" She glared at Jade. "Richard is Andrew? Really? And all this talk about magic . . . I didn't know you could do *that*." She gestured emphatically at the debris around them. "I just need a minute to—I need a minute. Okay?" She kept looking at Jade's hands as if they were a snake that could strike at any moment.

Jade put them into her cloak's pockets. "Sure. It's all good. Take all the minutes you need."

Charlie said, "Jade, we don't have—"

"No. April said she needs a minute. We have time for that. Then we find the Air Key, perform the Ascension ritual, and once I'm High Priestess"—Jade glared off the way Andrew had left—"we make him pay." She looked back at April, shoulders slumped, turned away, wringing her hands. *We make him pay for everything.*

Willow said, "Charlie, thank you for raising the protection spell on the property." He nodded and headed toward the front of the house. She gently took April's arm again and began leading her toward the house. "We'll make a nice cup of chamomile tea and a comfrey bandage, and you'll feel better in no time."

As they walked back to the house, Jade brought Willow up to date on what had happened the day before and just then in the garden. Willow didn't seem fazed by any of the trials, but when she told her who Andrew really was and what he had said, her posture stiffened.

"You sure he mentioned Raven?"

"Yeah, it was weird. Said he wished I'd met her. Who was she?"

Willow examined her for a moment before answering. "She was a very powerful Witch, and toward the end of her life she had no qualms about working with dark magic. Richard and she—"

"Andrew." Jade corrected with fire in her voice. She wanted to make sure she was reminded of all the years he'd lied to her face.

"Andrew," Willow acknowledged, "would have done anything for her at one point."

"So, what do we do about it?" Jade asked.

"Nothing. Your focus should be on finding the last Key and performing the Ascension ritual. Once you and Charlie are confirmed coven leaders, you'll have the full power of not only the coven but, Goddess willing, the divine spirit. Andrew will have no sway over you or anyone else then."

April said, "But that's exactly what he wants, for Jade to become High Priestess. Why are we doing what he says?"

Willow placed her hand gently on April's back. "Because the coven's magic is failing, and the only way to save it, and protect everyone within, is to make her High Priestess. Once that is done, she'll have the power to stand up to Andrew and anyone else who threatens this coven, if need be."

As the rain began to fall heavily, they hurried in the back door

CHAPTER 22

When Willow, Jade, and April entered the kitchen, Mrs. Keepsake was at the stove stirring a large pot, and two other ladies were gathered around the kitchen island. Jade recognized one of them as having been at the Crossing Over ceremony, opening the east quarter gateway. Her hair was still braided up, but steel-gray and white ribbons were woven through it, replacing the flowers she'd worn earlier. There were several rows of white pillar candles on the island in front of her. She was carving symbols into the side of a pillar candle. When she was finished, she added her candle to the end of a row of some that were already done.

The other lady sat at the end of the counter, tying bundles of herbs. Her white hair was pulled into a loose bun, fastened by what looked like black clock hands.

Mrs. Keepsake looked up from the stove. "Ah! There you are. We started without you. Much to do, you know."

Willow introduced them as she went to snip some of the comfrey plant on the windowsill. "Madame Belle, Sophia, this is Jade Cerridwen and her friend April. Ladies, meet the crones of Sugar Hill."

"Crones?" April asked.

The tiny woman sitting next to Madame Belle waved a sprig of herbs at her. "A crone is just an older woman."

"And wiser, Sophie," Madame Belle corrected with a thick French accent. "I suffered many failures to earn that title. Do not take it from me now, š'il vous plaît." She giggled and Sophia nodded sagely.

As Willow pulled a strip of cloth out of a drawer, she announced, "They have retrieved the Earth, Water, and Fire Keys, but there's some news: Andrew is back."

Mrs. Keepsake continued to stir but looked up as Willow walked past her to April's side. "Really? He finally showed his fa—" Willow placed the chewed comfrey on April's arm. "My dear, what happened?"

April didn't respond, staring at her arm as Willow wrapped it. Willow said, "Sophia, would you please make some chamomile tea for April? Thank you."

Jade said, "I tried to attack Andrew and . . . April got hit in the crossfire."

"He's an asshole," April muttered.

Jade looked at her, but she turned her head away.

Sophia took a glass jar of tiny cheesecloth bundles off one of the kitchen shelves. "Andrew's back?"

Willow said, "Yes. He's been living in Sun City and calling himself Richard. He's CEO of the company Jade and April worked in."

For a moment, the only sound was the pouring rain and distant thunder, then everyone reacted at once.

Sophia nodded. "It all makes sense now."

Mrs. Keepsake pointed at Madame Belle. "I told you!"

Madame Belle responded by shaking her head. "No, madame, you said nothing about Sun City specifically."

This went on for several moments—Sophia speaking to herself as she filled a large mug with water, Mrs. Keepsake and Madame Belle arguing over how accurate Mrs. Keepsake was, and Willow, who had taken the ladle from Mrs. Keepsake, silently stirring the pot as if she was the only one in the room.

When it became quiet for a moment, Jade addressed the room. "Did you know?" *There's no way they let him be in my life all these years if they knew. They better not have.*

Mrs. Keepsake said gently, "Jade, dear—"

"Don't 'dear' me," Jade warned, "just tell me the truth."

Willow raised an eyebrow at her. "Child, I know you are hurt and angry by what you have learned. You have every right to be. That does not give you the right to disrespect your elders. Are we clear?"

Jade went cold. The power emanating from Willow was sending a clear warning, contrary to her light tone of voice. Jade took a calming breath and replied, "Yes, ma'am. I'm sorry, Mrs. Keepsake."

Mrs. Keepsake patted Jade's hand. "No harm done, love."

Willow looked deep into the pot. "Just about done. Belle?"

Madame Belle scurried around the counter with a small pot and positioned herself next to Willow. Willow continued looking and stirring. "Now." She pulled the pot off the stove and tipped it over the smaller pot. Nothing appeared to pour out, but the smaller pot slowly filled with a golden amber liquid. By the time the large pot was completely upended, the smaller pot was filled nearly to the brim.

Willow placed the large empty pot in the sink and ran the faucet. Thick blue and gold steam billowed out for a moment, then dissipated. "That's the last of it," she said to the room.

Madame Belle placed the small pot back on the trivet next to the empty bottles. "Thank goodness. We are almost out of bottles."

"What's all this is for?" Jade asked.

Sophia said, "It's for the Ascension ritual. An awful lot of power is raised during the ritual, and all this is to help contain it." She waved her hands over the mug, mumbling a spell.

Willow said, "Since that needs to cool a bit, why don't we all go into the living room and have ourselves a nice little chat, shall we?"

Madame Belle and Mrs. Keepsake left with April. Sophia called to Willow, "Willow, it's happening again."

Willow went over to where Sophia was frowning down at the mug. "You don't seem to be in pain this time."

"No. But it is a pretty small spell, one I do every day." She looked at Willow worriedly. "If it's starting to affect our daily magic—"

She patted Sophia's shoulder. "I know. But we've been through difficult times before. Once the Ascension is complete, things should return to normal." She pointed to the tea kettle sitting on the back of the stove. "Until then, we make do."

As Willow approached, Jade asked, "What was that about?"

"I asked Sophia to make a cup of chamomile tea for April, but her spell backfired. Nothing to be done about it right now." She motioned toward the door and Jade went through.

Charlie had just come in the front door. He was completely drenched. As he took his coat off and stood by the fireplace, he said, "It's really coming down out there but the protection spell is up."

They all found a place to sit at the dining room table. Jade was disheartened to see April slide away from her on the bench. It wasn't a huge gesture, but Jade got the hint. Apparently, her minute to sort things out would take a bit longer than that.

Willow said, "First of all, no, we didn't know Andrew and Richard were the same person. We all knew to some extent that something was not right in your little corner of the world, but the signs were all very vague."

"Why didn't you tell me?" She regretted asking the minute she said it.

Willow tilted her head at Jade. "For one thing, you were determined to have no contact with us, remember? I wasted whole reams of paper, trying to keep in touch with you over the years. Do not try to place blame on us, child."

Madame Belle clicked her tongue at Willow. "Madame, let the past be." She turned toward Jade. "You weren't in any immediate danger, ma chère. And what would it benefit to worry you when we had no . . . specifics?"

Willow said, "In any case, finding the final Key is now our top priority. Andrew may have taken the Keys and think he's in charge, but magic has a life of its own. I don't believe the Keys would bow blindly to his will. Their purpose, after all, is to bind to the coven leaders in order to assist them with coven business. Andrew may want them focused on Jade, but from what you've told me of the last two trials, it seems they are now connecting with Charlie too."

Charlie said, "But I'd already connected with them. I mean, I've used them in ritual, and I've been High Priest for a long time now."

"Yes, but it's different now. Jade is here. Just by being present she changes your energy. The Keys need to adjust to that. With the last trial affecting you more than Jade, I believe the next trial will need you both to complete it. The Keys are calling to you both now."

Sophia entered from the kitchen carrying a steaming cup. She brought it to April. "Here you are, dear. Chamomile tea with honey. Sorry it took so long to make."

"No problem at all. Thank you." She took the cup and placed it in front of her, wrapping her hands around it.

Jade said, "So, if the Keys are trying to connect to us both, how do we find them? There was no clue in the last trial."

Sophia said, "What clues have you gotten?"

Charlie told them all about the trials and what their theory was about them being similar to the Lost Years' trials.

Sophia said, "I have a suggestion. Since the first two trials were different from the last one, and it was personal because

Jade had a personal connection to Fire, because . . ." She looked at Jade. "Because of the way your parents died. I think the final Key will be personal too."

"But I don't have a personal connection to Air. At least, not that I know of."

"Ah, but you do, ma chère." Madame Belle smiled at her. "Me."

Charlie said, "I know your family crest is Air and Jade knows you, but I'm not sure that's enough of a connection."

Madame Belle said, "Oh, it's more than that. Whenever Jade was upset, she would come to my house and spend some time. Ah, we had such fun, Jade and I. The fairies would join us and play games in our yard. We would practice Air magic and then watch the stars dance."

Jade smiled at the memories. Every Witch was better at working with one element, their primary. Madame Belle's primary element was Air. She could make the stars appear to float down and dance around. Whole galaxies even. It was beautiful.

Jade frowned and looked around. "It's a shame I haven't seen any fairies around since we arrived."

Sophia said, "Yes, I'm afraid they are the first to go when a coven begins to lose its magic."

Jade was disheartened. She had been hoping for a different explanation. They could often be such sensitive creatures, almost anything could make them go into hiding. They often returned quickly, so she hadn't worried about them too much. But if they'd left because the magic was failing, that was more serious. "Could Andrew be causing the magic to fail?"

"I doubt it," Willow replied. "He needs the full coven's power to raise his daughter. This is most likely something else, the result of Joy's death and being without a High Priestess to immediately replace her. The magic is turning dark, like a sickness, and leaving us little by little. It may be why Andrew is taking it easy on you now, as you said. He needs you to become coven leader before all the magic is gone and our coven disbands."

"Which means he's in a hurry," Mrs. Keepsake said. "So, we should probably figure out if your connection"—she pointed to Jade and Madame Belle—"fits into the last trial."

"Great," April said. "Let's get going."

Jade was so happy to hear from April again; it took a moment to realize what she meant. "Oh no. You're staying here. I made the mistake of letting you go with us for the Water trial and you almost got killed. I'm not about to make that mistake again. You'll stay with Willow in the house, where it's safe."

"Spell me."

"What?"

"Charlie put a protection spell on the property, right? Why can't he put a protection spell on me? That way I can go with you, but I'll be safe. In fact, you should put a protection spell on yourself while you're at it. Can't be too careful."

Charlie said, "It's not a bad idea."

Jade said, "What? Yes, it is. It's a very, very bad idea. Especially with the coven's magic failing. Willow tell them, please."

"There's no question casting a protection spell on all three of you is prudent, and I will be happy to do so. As for whether April accompanies you to find the next Key . . ." Willow twisted the ring on her right hand. She looked at April for several moments, then back to Jade. Finally, she spoke, "I see the merits to both. Staying here would be safer. However, it's vital Jade complete this final trial successfully, and having April's support could be needed. I believe we should consult the Goddess on this matter."

Charlie said, "Respectfully, I don't know if there's time for that."

"Well, you're not sure where the final Key is anyway. A tarot reading might also solve that problem at the same time." She turned to Madame Belle. "Belle, would you be so kind?"

"Of course, ma chère. My cards are at home."

Jade wished Willow had simply agreed with her, but at least a tarot reading wasn't dangerous, and she didn't believe the Goddess would put her best friend in danger.

Charlie stood and pulled his car keys out of his pocket.

"Mon chère, while I value the horsepower of your automobile, I believe mine is much better suited to finding its way safely in a storm like this." A thunderbolt crashed, emphasizing her point. "You see? Mother Nature agrees." She put on her coat and headed for the door. "I will happily return you to your behemoth when we are finished."

***

Madame Belle was the only person in town with a bright red convertible sports car, and she drove it with the top down every single day. Even now, the rain was pouring down, but no water was entering the vehicle. It was stopping just shy of where the roof would have been and sheeting off as if there were an invisible barrier. Madame Belle drove along, humming happily to herself.

Jade looked at April in the front seat. She turned back to Jade and mouthed, *No roof?* while pointing up.

Madame Belle said, "Ma chère, it is but one of the many perks of mastering Air magic."

They arrived at Madame Belle's cottage at the end of Main Street, a quaint little cottage with a carport to the right side. As they drove under the covered parking, it was as if someone had turned off the volume. Jade looked behind her. The rain was pouring down as before, but she couldn't hear it. She looked forward again and all was calm. Madame Belle had already exited and was heading for an overgrown arched gateway along an equally overgrown path, waving them to follow. They got out of the car and followed her into the backyard.

As Jade passed through the arched doorway into Madame Belle's backyard, it was like stepping into a fairy land. There were flowers blooming everywhere and green leaves of every shape and shade. The branches swayed slightly, brushing against them as they passed. It was as if they were reaching out to them and siphoning off the residue of darkness that clung to them from their earlier encounters. The air smelled clean and fresh, and breathing it in made her feel lighter somehow. By the time they stepped into the open grassy area of the backyard, she felt measurably better.

Naturally shaped pavers led from the side of the house into the middle of the backyard in a loose, crooked pattern, ending in a spiral with a stone birdbath at its center. The back half of the yard was covered in thick moss and at a slight angle, forming a kind of amphitheater with the birdbath and house as the stage. The edge of the glen was surrounded by tall trees and thick underbrush of various plants and flowers, blocking everything beyond from view.

Jade looked up as some lightning flashed, silhouetting the circle of open sky where the tree branches had naturally grown to frame it. Above them the rain continued, but just like with her convertible, the trees and air beneath remained untouched.

Madame Belle stopped in the center of the glade and placed her hands on either side of the birdbath. She raised her head and softly spoke a chant. Jade felt a change in the air, like a window or door had closed and the breeze that had been present stopped.

Madame Belle turned to face them. "We may talk freely now. I have raised a Sacred Circle."

Perplexed, Jade asked, "Didn't you already have a circle raised? I mean the rain—"

"Ah, my little spell was to keep out the storm and cold." She walked over to a flower bed near the back porch. "And of course delay my lovely summer blooms' demise." She caressed a carnation lovingly before walking up the porch steps. As she approached, lights sprang to life on the steps, railing, and sconces along the house wall. As she motioned to the porch swing, a few of the lights flickered out. Frowning, she stomped her foot several times and they relit. She eyed them suspiciously as she removed her white driving gloves.

"Charlie, April?" She motioned again to the porch swing. As they sat, she explained, "The Sacred Circle is to protect us from that horrible man eavesdropping, or anyone else, of course." She sat at a small round table by the railing and pointed to the chair opposite her. "Jade, š'il vous plaît, sit." She pulled a large deck of cards out of her pocket and began shuffling. Once Jade was seated, she placed the deck facedown in front of Jade.

"Please, focus on what you want and cut the deck three times."

Jade wanted a lot of things at the moment, but she focused on the two most urgent things: keeping April safe and finding the Air Key. She reached out and lifted part of the deck, placing it next to the first pile, then did it twice more so there were four piles in front of her.

Madame Belle took the piles and placed them together in a different order. "First you, ma petit, the querent." She dealt the top card faceup in the center of the table between them. The image had a giant sun with rays streaming out in all directions. Below it was a countryside of rolling green hills with farmland, scattered cottages, and a low stone wall with a gate.

April leaned forward, looking at the card. "That looks like the outskirts of town, only it wasn't that sunny. Is it supposed to be Sugar Hill?"

Madame Belle nodded. "In a way. The sun rising over the countryside represents your arrival in Sugar Hill. The prodigal daughter returns to cast out the darkness."

She placed another card directly over it, perpendicular to the first one. It showed a king on a throne, dressed in golden robes. On his left side lay a green valley, much like the other card had shown. On his right side was a shining city with gold and glass towers rising in the distance.

Jade knew immediately what that card represented. "Andrew."

"Oui." Madame Belle scowled at the card. "A cold and calculating man, torn between two worlds. He expects to have it all and will use his considerable powers to stop anyone who gets in his way. He is what is stopping you. Your love for him, your respect—"

"No. He lost my love and respect the moment I found out he killed my parents."

"Bien, ma petit. You will need that fire to defeat him."

She turned over another card and placed it next to the first two. A young man sat lounging in a field, dressed in armor, his sword lying by his side. In the background were two mountain ranges, separated by a deep valley. A raven circled overhead.

"Hmm . . ." Madame Belle considered the imagery. "This card should represent your immediate future. It is usually a location, but this is the Page of Wands. This is a person card." She looked at Jade. "What do *you* see, ma petit?"

Jade looked at the man on the card. His hair was dark and curly, like Charlie's. As she stared, the tiny image shifted. He looked straight at her and smiled—the same damn crooked smile Charlie had. Without breaking eye contact, he pointed with his left hand behind him, straight to the meeting of the mountain ranges in the distance.

Jade refocused her attention where he was pointing. The line of pine trees framing the edge of the field stopped where the mountain reached the valley. She squinted at it and noticed a tiny cabin tucked up under the branches of the last tree, blue-gray smoke curling up from the chimney.

"Well, that's Charlie," she admitted, "and he's pointing to a cabin in the distance, in the valley between the mountains." She looked at Charlie. "Could it be your house?"

"No, I don't live in a valley." He thought for a moment, then said, "What about the lake cabin? They're near some cliffs, aren't they?"

"Oh yeah. About a mile north of the property there's this huge cliff face, probably about three hundred feet high or so. You can see for miles from the top." Jade looked at the card again. "I don't know, though. I don't see a cliff face, just a valley."

"Ah, but ma chère, the cards are not precise. They merely represent what you need to know." She paused a moment. "And now for the question of April. This next card usually represents what you will find along the way, or another translation: what will be of value. I believe that should give us an answer, yes?"

She placed the next card below the last one. There was a calm lake with hills in the distance. As Jade stared at the card, a woman rose out of the lake. She had long blonde hair and pale blue eyes. Her slim figure was dressed in a flowing white gown, and she held an ornate chalice in one hand. Her posture was tall and regal. There was no doubt in Jade's mind it was April.

A cold shock flowed through Jade. *No.* She sat back and crossed her arms. "That doesn't mean anything. Cards are open to interpretation."

Madame Belle looked at her sideways. "Oui. And this is in fact, the card of intuition. So, ma chère, what is your intuition telling you?"

The location on the card was a stark reminder of what had happened at Hidden Lake. But she looked strong, standing there above the water's surface. Her clothes were dry. She looked safe. Was the card telling her April had survived, and she would survive the next trial?

She looked at Charlie. He was calmly waiting with a blank expression. Probably not wanting to influence her either way. Readings were usually done in private to avoid confusion in the results. He sat tall though, and Jade felt strength and confidence emanating from him.

She looked to April. "Are you sure you want to come with us? We've no idea what will happen." She almost said "to you" but stopped herself.

April looked the card over, then looked to Jade with a smile. "We've been through some things, haven't we? But you've never abandoned me, and I won't abandon you now. If you need me, I'll be with you."

Jade always needed her. Just having her around made her feel strong and capable. As long as she was safe. Willow had spelled her at the house just before they left. *The most powerful Witch in the coven, Shouldn't that be enough to protect her?*

"Okay, fine." She looked back at the card. "April will come with us." She felt stronger saying it out loud.

Madame Belle said, "Bien. Now for the final outcome." She placed another card below the last.

At first Jade only saw forest. Branches and leaves, some berries and pinecones. "What is this supposed to represent?"

"This is The Green Man. The primal force of nature."

"But that doesn't make sense. The last trial should be Air, not Earth." She looked at the card again, and after a moment she could see the man. He was covered head to toe in plants, camouflaging him with the wild around him. She continued staring at it for several seconds, hoping it would move like the other card had and give her a clue. Nothing happened. She sat back, crossing her arms.

"Perhaps you will realize its meaning later." Madame Belle stood and hurried into the house, returning with a small mason jar. "Please take this, ma chère. The smudge stick contains herbs from my garden. It should fit in nicely with your Ascension ritual preparations." She smiled as Jade took the jar.

Jade looked over the small bundle of dried herbs inside, then opened the jar and smelled. "Lavender and sage? This is perfect. Thank you, Madame Belle."

"Of course. Now let me walk you to my car so I may transfer its spell to Charlie."

Charlie looked shocked. "You're going to let me drive it?"

"Oui." She looked at him innocently. "Is there some reason I should not?"

"No, I just . . . you love that car. And I've never seen you let anyone else drive it."

"As you said, time is of the essence. We would have to backtrack out of our way to retrieve your car. This way you may go straight to the cabin. I have things to do here and won't be needing it for a while."

They said their goodbyes and left.

CHAPTER 23

Charlie's hands gripped the wheel just a bit tighter, and he drove a few miles an hour slower than Madame Belle had. The rain still refused to touch them though. They turned right off Main Street and began the steep climb on Sugar Hill Road. There was only one house, which lay at the top of the hill. The mansion had a spectacular view, overlooking the whole town and part of the countryside beyond. Whoever lived there wasn't really a mayor, but the Accords required all townships to have one as a liaison between them and the capital. So, the house had been built for the figurehead mayor to use as needed.

Just past the mayor's mansion, Sugar Hill Road turned into a dirt road and continued north, zigzagging at a steep incline. When they reached the end of the pavement, Charlie slowed down and considered stopping. He needn't have, because they lifted several inches and the ride continued as smoothly as before.

The road dead-ended in front of the cabin. It looked just like Jade remembered it. Perhaps a little smaller. The rain had completely stopped and scattered clouds filled the sky as they got out of the car.

"So, where's this cliff?" April asked.

Charlie led them around the cabin and north through the woods. They came out into a clearing. Several feet away the ground just stopped. The sun lit up the valley and hills beyond, while behind them dark storm clouds were gathering. It was a breathtaking contrast of darkness and light.

"Now what?" Jade asked.

Charlie said, "Well, this is the last Key, and if Andrew really wants you to finish, he might have taken the cloaking spell off it. I think doing a locator spell is worth a try."

April asked, "So how do you do a locator spell anyway? Please tell me it doesn't involve exploding trees."

Charlie replied, "Not at all. Young Witches use trinkets. Physical items they hold or wear, which connect them with the element they're working on. When I was young, I figured since I wasn't a Natural Witch, I should keep the elements on me at all times. So, I made jewelry for myself connected to each element." He pulled his right sleeve back, exposing a blue beaded bracelet. Jade also noticed the iron band on his index finger. "Bracelet for Water, ring for Earth, earing for Air, and necklace for Fire. I rarely use them these days, but I've kind of gotten used to wearing them. Since Jade has only just started practicing again, I'm thinking it wouldn't hurt to use one."

"So, you're saying I should borrow your earring?" Jade pursed her lips and raised one eyebrow at him.

"No, these trinkets are bound to me. They wouldn't work well for you. What I'm saying is—" He looked around at the ground and walked over to a tree. He bent down, then came back, holding up a black feather. "I'm saying you should use this. The most powerful trinkets come from nature."

Jade shrugged and took it. "Worth a try." She held the feather in her open palm and closed her eyes, focusing on how light it was. The energy emanating from it was so faint. She turned her attention to that. At first, she thought she couldn't feel it clearly because of being out of practice, but then she realized she could feel the Earth's energy very strongly in contrast. Taking a deep breath, she focused on the feather, its energy just a wisp surrounding her palm. It tickled, barely brushing against her. She opened her eyes, half expecting to see tendrils emanating from it. She whispered to it, "Inveniet." *Find.*

It rose about an inch up and began slowly spinning in her palm. She asked Charlie, "What does it look like?"

"It's a small raw branch of aspen, not carved, with an amethyst crystal in the tip."

Jade focused her mind on his description, picturing it as clearly as possible. After a moment the feather stopped spinning and pointed straight ahead, into the woods. "I guess it's not near the cliff after all." She began walking, and the feather swiveled back and forth. She turned back to Charlie and April, who were behind her, and the feather turned and stopped, now parallel in her palm. "Um . . . okay." She slowly turned toward the cliff, and the feather turned with her until it was pointing straight out from her again. She took a couple of steps, and it stayed firm in its position.

She walked slowly forward and when she was only a foot from the edge, the feather lowered back down to touching her palm and became much heavier than it should be. "Oh, great. It's down on the cliff face somewhere."

They all carefully peeked over the edge of the cliff. It was nearly vertical with small roots protruding from the surface. Jade doubted any of them would support her weight for long. She turned to Charlie. "I guess you'll have to levitate me while I look for it."

His eyes widened. "Maybe we should go get some rope or something."

"What are you saying? I thought you had mad magical skills."

He straightened his posture, the self-assured expression slipping back into place. "I do. It's just"—he looked between them and the cliff—"levitation's a pretty advanced spell, and with magic being so iffy lately—"

Jade stage-whispered to April. "Sounds like an excuse to me." April grinned back, and Jade felt a wave of relief. She could tell April had been trying to relax, but it wasn't going as well as she'd like. This was a good sign.

Charlie countered, "Look, lifting someone up is simple, you only need to move them one direction. Holding someone steady in the air—"

"We get it, easier said than done. But I can't do both spells. It's hard enough for me to do this one." She placed her hand on his shoulder. "Without you, we wouldn't have made it out of the Water trial alive. You can do this."

He looked into her eyes, and for the first time Jade noticed that one eye was darker blue than the other. One side of his mouth rose, a crooked smile she was starting to like seeing on him.

Just as it started to feel weird, he broke the silence. "Okay then. Let's get to work." He reached into his jacket pocket and pulled out the jewelry box he'd gotten at the will reading. It seemed like a lifetime ago.

He opened the box. Two chains—one silver, one gold—came together in the center of the box, attached to a perfect circle of wire with a tree of life in the middle. The tree trunk curved through the center in a slight *S* shape. The branches and one side of the trunk were gold with tiny amethyst crystals twisted into the branches as leaves. The other side of the trunk and bottom roots were silver, on a background of jet stone.

"These are the High Priestess and High Priest pendants." Charlie lifted the gold chain out of the box, pulling the gold half of the pendant with it. He let it dangle, spinning in the air between them. "This one is mine. It has elements and symbology corresponding to the High Priest. The other one is yours, with elements and symbology corresponding to the High Priestess."

Jade lifted the silver chain and watched the tear-shaped pendant spin in front of her.

Charlie continued, "Most coven leaders only wear them during special ceremonies, but their properties may be helpful now. Their energies are entwined. By wearing them we will have another link between us."

Jade felt slightly better they had an extra boost of magic to keep her connected to the top of the cliff, but she tried not to show it. "I told you, you got this."

He mirrored her nervous grin. "*We* got this." He put his necklace on and took several steps away toward the cliff.

Jade placed the chain over her head and stepped to the edge. The wand was there somewhere. She could feel its energy like a warm breeze. She only needed to pinpoint its location. She scanned the rough wall below her and saw a few tufts of grass and exposed roots, but nothing out of the ordinary. The ground at the base looked covered with tiny pebbles from this height, but they were probably boulders. She felt a wave of dizziness and stepped back quickly.

April asked, "Are you sure about this?" She glanced at Charlie, waving his hands over the ground nearby.

"Not really, but I trust him."

He was in a defensive stance facing the cliff: one foot forward, one back, feet spread shoulder width. His feet were slightly dug into the earth, but it wasn't like he dug down with them. It was as if the earth had grown up around his feet, covering the bottom half up to his ankles.

Jade told April, "I'm gonna be fine, you know." April nodded and frowned at Charlie. Jade hated to see her like this. "Hey. Just in case, you should think light thoughts for me." She wrinkled her nose at April.

April gave a slight smile. "Like cotton candy and hot-air balloons?"

"Lighter. Like clouds and the space between Charlie's ears."

He raised an eyebrow. "I heard that."

"You were meant to," Jade told him. She looked at April and whispered, "See you soon."

April whispered back, "See you soon."

Charlie ran his hands over each other in circles, like he was knitting without needles. He closed his eyes and tilted his head down. Making a fist with each hand, he tucked his elbows into his sides and rotated his fists palms up and outward in a V-shape from his body.

After several moments in that position, he threw his hands toward Jade with a clap and raised his head, looking at her intently. Jade felt a warm energy surround her and squeeze in slightly. Then she lifted about three feet off the ground. She couldn't tell where the lift was coming from. It wasn't the pressure of the energy Charlie had thrown at her. That felt like it was just gently holding her still. It was more like every atom in her body was slowly falling upward. It felt as natural as breathing.

The distraction over being lifted had been enough to break her locator spell, and the feather was resting normally on her palm. She whispered, "Inveniet" at it again, and it resumed its elevated position.

"Ready?" Charlie asked.

"Ready."

As Charlie moved her over the edge of the cliff, she struggled to control her breathing. She also tried hard not to look down. Instead, she focused on the feather in her palm and the idea of the wand.

The feather swiveled slightly back and forth as Jade drifted over the edge of the cliff. She rotated until she was facing April and Charlie. The feather settled, pointing slightly to the right, its weight pressing her palm. "Down and to the right," she said quietly.

Charlie lowered her slowly. Jade looked up at April just before she and Charlie went out of sight. The smooth dirt slid past about a foot from her hand. She fought the urge to reach out and grab hold of the occasional root sticking out.

The feather swiveled nearly continuously. Jade closed her eyes to refocus on the wand. She remembered how she would use one to aim spells when casting them over a distance, or how her mom would use one to guide her power while raising a Sacred Circle in ritual. The thought of her mom brought a pain to her heart. She opened her eyes to remind her of the here and now. The feather had stopped spinning.

"Wait," she called above. She stopped moving. The pressure had left her palm. "Go up a little." As she rose the feather pressed down again. "Stop."

She moved her hand back and forth in front of her, pinpointing the spot where the feather was pointing to. There was a root sticking out. Looking closer, she realized it was too smooth to be a root. It must be the wand. She reached forward and just barely grabbed it with the tips of her fingers, then pulled gently. At first it didn't budge, but then it slowly started to move, bits of dirt and pebbles falling away.

She was falling! She screamed and grabbed for the cliff, but it was just out of reach. She grabbed her necklace free-falling in front of her and jerked to a stop. The feather continued downward without her in a gentle spiral.

She felt Charlie's presence then, as if he were standing next to her. She asked, "What happened?"

His voice seemed to come from right beside her. "I don't know. Are you all right?"

"Not sure." She panted heavily. "I'm not falling anymore, but I'd really like to come back up now, if that's all right with you."

"Hang on."

His presence faded from her slightly, like he'd turned away. She felt a grip around her waist then, like a large rope had tightened around her. It was much less comfortable than before. The invisible rope was lifting her in fits and starts, digging into her painfully with each tug.

As she neared the spot where the wand was still sticking partway out, she called, "Wait. I need to be closer."

Charlie's strained voice floated down to her. "Make it quick. I can't hold on forever."

She swung closer and was able to grab the wand. Pouring her energy into it, she commanded, "Dimittas!" *Let go.*

Her energy rebounded from the wand, through her whole body. She flew upward, faster than before. Passing the surface, she fell back down onto it, as if she'd been tossed up by some monster from below.

She landed on her stomach but luckily not from a great height. She rolled over and got her first good look at the wand in her hand. It was about a foot long, made of a raw branch of aspen. An amethyst crystal was tied to the end with thin copper wire. This wire wrapped around it in an intricate pattern, one inch in from the end, where it disappeared under black leather wrapping that formed a Celtic knot pattern up the shaft about a hand's width.

Charlie ran to her. "Are you all right?"

"Yeah, I'm fine. Did you see that? I was flying!"

He pulled her up and into a tight embrace. "I thought I'd lost you." She barely had time to enjoy the hug before he pushed her away, looking into her eyes. "I dropped you, Jade. You just . . . slipped through my fingers." He swallowed hard, looking back at the cliff.

Jade reached out and gently pulled his chin back toward her, forcing his eyes to find hers. "I'm fine. We got the wand. It's all good." He nodded and breathed a sigh of relief. "What do you think, April? Should—" She wasn't in sight. Jade took several steps toward the tree line. "April! We got it."

Only a distant bird call answered her. She turned on Charlie. "Where is she? Did you send her for rope or something?"

"No. She was right here. Maybe she decided to go try to find some at the cabin. Let's go look."

They walked back slowly, several feet apart and yelling as they went. "April! April! Where'd you go? We don't need the rope now, we got it!"

When they arrived at the cabin, the car was still where they'd left it.

"April!" Jade headed up the porch steps.

"I'll check the shed." Charlie walked briskly toward the small wooden structure on the side of the house.

Jade burst through the front door. Not in the living room, kitchen, or bedroom. She peeked behind the shower curtain in the bathroom for good measure. The tiny cabin wasn't hiding her. She ran out the front door, confronting Charlie on his way back. "No luck?"

"No. Where could—" He walked over to the car windshield. Jade hadn't noticed the small rectangle of white tucked under the wiper blade until Charlie picked it up. He read it, flipped it over, then handed it to Jade. "Damn it!"

Jade read the block lettering: *SHE'S MY INSURANCE.* The other side of the card had a typed name in gold embossed lettering: *Richard A. Whetstone, CEO*. "What the hell! How did you let this happen?"

Charlie's eyebrows rose and he pointed at himself. "This is my fault? How do you figure?"

"She was standing right beside you. You didn't even notice her disappear?"

"I was a little busy trying to keep you from falling to your death!"

"Yeah, and I was hanging off the side of a cliff, trying to find a Key, and completely out of sight. Why didn't the protection spell work?"

"It did! Look, she's not hurt, she's just not here."

"You promised she'd be safe. You promised." She couldn't yell anymore. "Let's just go get the Book of Shadows. The sooner we get this ritual done, the sooner I can get April back."

CHAPTER 24

Charlie glared straight ahead the whole ride home. At first, Jade was fine with it. He had promised he'd keep her safe after all. But the more she thought about it, the more she came back to one fact: without Andrew, none of it would have happened. *He's the asshole, not Charlie.*

She glanced over at him. He was gripping the wheel so tightly his knuckles were white. His lips were pressed into a thin line. They pulled up to the front gate and waited while it opened.

Jade reached out and placed her hand on Charlie's arm. "I'm sorry. It's not your fault and it was wrong of me to make it seem like it was."

He didn't let go of the wheel, but he dipped his head, looking toward her. "I promised you she'd be safe." He lifted his head. "That's a promise I intend to keep." The gate had opened by then and he drove through it.

Willow was waiting for them on the porch. As Jade came up the steps, she opened her arms wide. Jade gratefully accepted the hug, allowing her anger and sorrow over April's disappearance to flow into her.

Willow said quietly, "I sensed your pain coming a mile away. What happened?" They explained everything to her. "I see. Well, now is not the time for tears. Charlie is right, she's not hurt. Andrew's proven he's capable of a lot, but he's not strong enough to break through one of my spells."

Looking into Willow's eyes, Jade felt her strength and power. She was right. Jade set her mind to the task at hand. "We have all four Keys, where is the Book of Shadows?"

"It's in the vault, in the study. Charlie, thank you for showing Jade how to retrieve it." She began walking down the hall. "I have preparations to make."

***

The walls of the small dark study were completely covered from floor to ceiling with bookshelves. The only spot not covered, besides the door, was the wall behind a large mahogany desk, which held a framed mirror. In front of the desk was a round table with five chairs.

Jade breathed in the once familiar smell of dust, paper, and old leather. Sun City may be a technological marvel, but Jade had to admit, *There's nothing like the smell of old books.*

Charlie said, "It's been a long time since you've been in here. Do you remember how this works?"

Jade stepped away from him, trailing her fingers along the books on the nearest shelf. "Kind of. First is puzzling out exactly where the safe is. Second is facing the guardian.

That's as far as I got. I guess it didn't like that a nine-year-old was trying to take the Book of Shadows without permission."

"Yeah, that's a bad idea. The guardian can sense your intent. You'll need to keep firmly in mind why you need in the safe to get past it, and it better be a good reason. The third lock is the test of blood." When Jade cringed, Charlie continued, "No actual blood is drawn. Only certain people are allowed access, and a simple spell will test to see if you're one of them. Finally, the safe will be revealed, and you must enter the right combination into the physical lock."

"All right, so first we find the safe." She looked around the crowded space. "Any ideas?"

"Well, every time the safe is accessed, it moves to a random place. I've only had to use the safe a handful of times, but I've always found this to be the most difficult part."

The bookcase to the right of the desk was pulling at Jade's attention. She smiled smugly. "I got this." She pointed at the area. "It's kind of, I don't know, prettier than the rest of the room?"

"If you say so. Now we just have to activate it."

She looked the bookcase over. Nothing seemed out of place. The books were a bit dusty, different sizes and colors. She noticed a bright red one on the left side of the shelf at eye level, which seemed out of place somehow. She reached out to touch the binding and felt a hum as she drew closer. Tilting her head, she stepped back and looked over the rest of the books. A thick blue one stood out on the bottom shelf, below the first, and a thin green one on the same shelf as the blue one, on the right side.

"Charlie, do you see anything strange about the books?"

He stepped next to her. "Strange how?"

"Do any of them stand out to you as different?"

He stared at them for a moment. "Nope. Just a bunch of dusty books."

"Hmm. I wonder." Jade took the green book out and over to the left, trading it with the blue book. She switched the blue book with the red one above it, then looked over the right side of the bookcase. "It must be here somewhere." A gold spine caught her eye. "Well, it's kind of yellow." She switched it with the red book and put the gold one back into the space left by the green one.

She stood back and waited. After a moment Charlie remarked, "Oh! I see it now. It's a pentagram."

"Almost," Jade corrected. "There's something missing for the top point."

"I got this." Charlie walked up and placed his hand on the dull silver spine of a book. He tilted it forward, then let it fall back into place.

As Charlie stepped back, all five books began to glow, and a soft white line connected them. The glowing pentagram pulled away from the bookcase and hung in the air. It began spinning, faster and faster until it was sphere of energy. The energy coalesced into the form of a lion.

Jade looked up into its glowing amber eyes. It sat back on its haunches and asked in a deep rumbling voice, "What is your intent?"

Charlie replied, "We request our coven's Book of Shadows so that we may perform the Ascension ritual and protect the coven."

"You may pass." The lion changed shape again, becoming a glowing doorway.

"Almost there," Charlie said as he crossed the threshold. The moment he was through, he dropped to his knees, screaming in agony.

Jade yelled, "What's happening?"

He writhed on the ground, barely able to speak through gritted teeth. "Don't know. Aaah! Shouldn't—"

Jade tried to go around, but when she stepped to the side he disappeared. She ran to the space on the other side of the doorway, where he should be, but there was nothing. She ran back to the other side and there he was. He had stopped moving. *No!* She jumped through the doorway.

The pain was intense. She'd never felt anything like it. It was blinding. It stole her breath. Then, it stopped.

The lion's voice said, "Accepted."

Jade looked around. The doorway was gone. All was silent. She reached over to Charlie. He was breathing but unconscious. "Hey." She shook him gently. "Charlie?"

He replied with a groan and opened his eyes. "What happened?"

"You fainted. Like a little girl." Jade smirked at him.

"Nice. Always wanted to try that." He sat up slowly.

"I'm guessing something went wrong with the test of blood?"

"Yeah, you could say that." They got to their feet. "It must be because of the waning power. Long-lasting spells have been having the most issues lately."

A rumbling could be heard coming from the bookcase, then it slowly opened like a set of double doors, revealing a combination safe in the wall behind it.

Charlie said, "Lastly, the code." He stepped up and put in a combination. The safe opened, revealing a large black leather-bound book.

He took it out and Jade peeked inside the safe. It was just an empty box. "That's it? I thought Ms. Scrivener was going to put the deed in here too."

"She did. We're only allowed access to the items of our intention. When you want the deed, you'll have to ask for that specifically."

"Wow, sounds like you should have kept the Keys here instead of at the altar."

"The safeguards there were just as thorough." He closed the safe.

"Then how did Andrew get past them?"

"I have no idea," Charlie shot back. "Next time we see him, maybe you should ask him." He dropped his head, shaking it sadly. "I'm sorry."

"It's all right. We're both under a lot of pressure. Let's tell Willow we're ready to get started."

CHAPTER 25

Jade and Charlie entered the kitchen as Willow and Madame Belle were packing up the last of the bottles and herbs they'd prepared earlier.

Willow looked up as Charlie approached her with the Book of Shadows. "Ah, good." She took the book reverently from him. "I believe we have everything we need now. Charlie, I appreciate you meeting us at the circle. I'll send word to the coven to have everything prepared for when you and Jade arrive."

Madame Belle said, "Mon chère, would you mind dropping these off at Sophia's on your way?"

"Of course." He picked up one of the baskets filled with bottles while she took the other and nodded at Jade as they passed her. "I'll see you soon."

Willow and Jade followed them to the foyer. "I laid out your dress on the end of your bed and prepared your ritual bath.

I'll escort you to the circle when you're finished. All you have to do is follow Charlie's lead." She smiled kindly at her.

Jade felt she was about to cross over into a new world or at least a new phase of her life. Crossroads, her mother had called them. Moments that were definite turning points when you looked back on them, but at the time you usually just thought they were another simple choice. This one she could feel, like a knot in her stomach, warning her to tread carefully. She nodded and turned to climb the stairs.

"One more thing, Jade." Willow pulled a folded envelope out of her robes. "Charlie wrote you every day for years after you left, until one day he couldn't bring himself to anymore. A couple of years ago, he wrote you another letter and asked that I find a way to make sure you received it. I knew you weren't ready then, but I think today you might be." She held it out to Jade.

"Thank you." She slowly took it from Willow, then went upstairs to her room. On the foot of her bed was her ritual dress as Willow had promised. She put the envelope down and lifted the dress by its neckline. The pure white fabric flowed to the floor, and the silver and crystal neckline sparkled. She laid it back down and looked at the leather pouch lying next to it. It was just large enough for the chalice and disk Keys. She placed her hand over her cloak pocket. They had gone through so much to get these Keys. She dared not let them out of her possession now.

Jade stared at the envelope on the bed. Her name was written in block letters on the front. She wondered what could have happened a couple of years ago that would have made him try to contact her again. As soon as the Ascension was over and they'd dealt with Andrew, she would open it, but now she needed to focus.

This private ritual was meant to cleanse not just her body but her energy and spirit as well. Most spells could be performed without it, but certain rites of passage required it. Though it had been decades since she'd had need of the cleansing ritual, she remembered it clearly.

She went into her small bathroom. It was already set up for a ritual bath. Small white candles were placed around the tub and sink, giving the cold room a soft warm glow. On the edge of the tub, a shallow wood tray held two small vials of oil and a small dish of incense, and a fluffy white towel and washcloth hung from the hook next to the tub.

As she closed the door, she felt some of the tension begin to leave. She was looking forward to sinking into the tub of steaming water. She released three drops each of rosemary and sandalwood oil into the bath, then lit the lavender smudge stick Madame Belle had given her and placed it in the dish. Undressing quickly, she hung her cloak on the hook on the back of the door and folded her clothes neatly onto the sink ledge. She slipped into the water gingerly, its heat seeping into her sore muscles. She hadn't been aware they were aching until just then.

Lying back, she breathed in slowly, the scents of sandalwood, rosemary, and lavender working in harmony to pull negativity and dark thoughts to the surface. Holding her breath for a moment, she focused on the most pressing thought. *April's in danger.* As she released her breath slowly, she countered the thought. *Becoming High Priestess will grant me the power to save her.* Another slow scented inhale and a pause. *What if I don't pass the Elementals' tests?* Breathing out, she didn't have an answer, so she simply let it go, and focused on her breath.

This process continued for several minutes as she focused on each negative emotion and either countered them or released them. It was a relaxing ritual, but it was tinged with darkness as the thought of April in danger kept returning to her. She persisted though, and eventually she did feel much calmer, her mind quieter and more hopeful. She stepped out, dried herself off, and anointed herself with the sandalwood oil, speaking the cleansing blessing from memory.

She entered the bedroom and put on the ritual dress, then stood at the picture window, looking out at the skyline. The gentle rain from before had upgraded to a full-fledged storm. Rain and leaf debris hit the window with such force Jade took a step back instinctively, thinking it might break. "So much for my calm," she complained to the empty room. Lightning flashed and the thunder happened in sync, shaking the room in answer. The trees outside thrashed like they were battling against the wind. Nature seemed at war with herself.

Jade grabbed the leather pouch off the bed and wrapped the straps around her waist, tying them so the pouch hung against her right thigh. She transferred the chalice and disk from her cloak into the pouch, then put on her silver tree of life pendant under the neckline of her dress. Feeling the cool metal against her skin and knowing Charlie felt the same thing with his half made her feel connected to him.

She was grateful he was here. They'd had their differences, but she knew he meant well. They'd complete the ritual, then she had no doubt they would get April back, together. She slipped on the thin leather sandals and grabbed her cloak. Giving the envelope one last glance, she turned and headed downstairs.

Willow and Madame Belle were waiting for her in the foyer. They looked up as she came down the staircase, and she tried to ignore the fact that they were both staring at her. *I feel naked.* The fabric was very lightweight, one solid piece from neckline to hem. "I feel like I'm wearing a sheet," she said, as she reached the bottom step. She quickly put on the cloak, wrapping it around her like a safety blanket.

"You look lovely." Willow beamed.

"Charlie is going to lose his mind, ma chère," Madame Belle said with glee.

Jade smiled back. A thunderclap startled her, and she looked out the front windows. "This storm is looking pretty dangerous."

"Nonsense," Grandma Willow assured her. "What kind of Witch would I be if I couldn't run a little interference with the weather? Watch and learn."

She turned toward the door and opened it calmly, then stood facing the storm, arms outstretched like she was holding on to something. She spoke words that didn't sound like Latin but were clearly not any common language. At first, leaves entered the open doorway and swirled around, but as Willow spoke, the wind began to settle. She took two steps forward until she was just on the other side of the doorway. Arms still raised, she turned her head slightly and told them, "Follow me."

They followed her out and into the wild night. Willow walked with both hands held up, like she was pushing back a curtain. Inside the area of safety around them there was no wind, no rain, not a leaf dared break the barrier Willow was creating around them. When Madame Belle had done this earlier in her car, it had been lighthearted. Now it felt eerie, as if nature was displeased with being controlled.

Just as they reached the car, Willow gave a final wave of her hands, and the safety bubble expanded, encompassing the entire car. They all piled in, and as she started the engine the rain suddenly began pounding on the roof and windows of the car.

When they reached the cemetery, there were cars lined down the block from the gate. There were more inside, as if everyone from the entire state had come.

Great, Jade thought, *I needed more pressure about now.* She asked Willow, "Is it typical for this many people to show up for an Ascension ritual?"

"Quite a few usually, but not this many. The entire coven always comes of course, and a few key others, Witches and nonmagical people of importance from town. But you see, this one is special." She wove through the parked cars to the gate, where one spot had been left open for them. She pulled in and parked. "It's nearly unheard of for a High Priestess to be murdered, and with the growing issues of our magic weakening, everyone is looking forward to having two permanent coven leaders again." She turned forward and flashed the lights on the car. The rain stopped. Looking through the front window, Jade realized she could see straight ahead, all the way to the east edge of the clearing, where a handful of people were gathered.

Willow told them, "The coven has raised the circle already and provided a safe path for us to get there." They got out of the car and began the walk to the clearing. It was just like outside the house, only the barrier was higher and wider. This time Jade could see it glowing faintly.

She asked Willow, "Why did they raise the circle already? I thought the coven leaders are supposed to do that together. Is it because of the storm?" Most spells and rituals could be easily done with changes from the norm, but she figured this one was too important to be messed with.

Willow replied, "Partly. With everything that's happened lately, we thought it best to have the coven raise the circle early so that you and Charlie could focus on the ritual. You'll be channeling pure energy from the divine. You must avoid any distraction so that you can control it properly."

When they arrived at the clearing, she could see the Sacred Circle covered the area like a giant faintly shimmering dome. The tunnel they had been walking through ended at the Sacred Circle, where Ms. Scrivener, Mrs. Keepsake, and Charlie were gathered, talking. She expected to see crowds of townsfolk within the clearing, but it looked empty. Through the swirling light, she could plainly see the clearing and five crypts.

She asked Willow, "Where is everybody?"

Willow pointed toward the circle. "They're waiting for us inside. Ascension circles don't just block negative energy, they cloak the area."

Ms. Scrivener approached them. "Jade, it's so nice to see you again. I'm sorry to hear about April, but I'm sure things will work out for the best soon. I hope you don't mind, I offered to stand in for her as your witness."

Jade's stomach twisted at the mention of April's name, but she reminded herself that focusing on the ritual was their priority. "Of course, I'd be honored. I didn't know I could invite a guest."

"Oh, yes. Both you and Charlie invite one person to bear witness. We had intended to go over all this with you of course, but circumstances . . . well, the entire coven will be within the inner circle with you, but as your guest I'll be right beside you."

"Are you ready?" Charlie asked. He was dressed in something similar to Jade's outfit, except his neckline was decorated with gold gems and leaves, his own leather tool pouch around his waist.

She removed her cloak and handed it to Willow. Charlie's eyes widened and his mouth hung slightly open as he stared at her. After a moment he mouthed, *Wow.*

Jade couldn't help but smile back. "I'm ready if you are."

His cheeks flushed pink, and he cleared his throat. "Uh, good. Just follow my lead." He held his hand out toward her. She placed her hand in his, and strength flowed from his warm, callused palms. They faced the circle with Mrs. Keepsake by Charlie's side and Ms. Scrivener by Jade's, while Willow stood behind them all.

Willow, Mrs. Keepsake, and Ms. Scrivener spoke at once. "We come to the Sacred Circle to bear witness to the Ascension. In perfect love and perfect trust, we ask for entrance within."

Mrs. Keepsake patted Jade's hand. "I'll see you soon, de—" She disappeared. Jade felt a slight coolness on her hand, like some of the air had been sucked into the void left by her travel.

Charlie spoke in a strong voice. "I come to the Sacred Circle, in perfect love and perfect trust."

He nodded to her and she repeated his words.

Charlie bent down and, using his right index finger, pointed at the lower edge of the circle where it met the ground. He ran his finger up over his head, across to his right, and back down to the ground, essentially cutting a doorway in the barrier. As his fingers traveled, the electric blue shimmer faded behind it. He entered through the clear doorway and she followed, bowing her head humbly. Once inside, Charlie turned and retraced the path with his finger in reverse order, the barrier flowing back into place.

CHAPTER 26

As Jade followed Charlie into the circle, the townsfolk appeared before them. A couple hundred people, they filled the space between the circle and the pony wall surrounding the clearing. They were all smiling at her, and she looked to Charlie, wondering if she was supposed to say something.

"Now we walk the township circle. Think of it like a vote. Each person will either bow their head in acceptance of us or turn their back if they reject us."

She tensed at the thought of her hometown rejecting her. Charlie squeezed her hand gently. "Don't worry. There's always a couple who reject the next coven leader, but most everyone will accept us. This will set our intention to lead and protect the townsfolk with honor."

He began walking and Jade followed behind. He'd been right, and by the time they had returned to where they started, only a few people had turned away.

Willow spoke from behind them, startling Jade. "The township accepts Jade and Charlie as coven leaders. So mote it be."

Charlie said, "Now it's the coven's turn."

She followed him through the opening in the pony wall. Jade looked at her coven members lined up between the inside of the pony wall and the family crypts. They stood tall and still, watching her. They were the leaders of the township and its people. Thirteen Witches chosen by the coven leaders; some were descendants of the founding families, others were chosen for their knowledge or experience or an ability that balanced and empowered the coven.

Charlie told her quietly, "We walk the coven circle to ask their acceptance of us as their High Priestess and High Priest. If only one refuses to let us pass"—he turned to her, his expression unreadable—"then it's over."

She frowned at him and he clarified. "Technically, if any one of the council denies you, then you'd be released from being High Priestess. Of course, that would never happen. It would mean they'd disband. There would be no Sugar Hill coven."

Jade realized even if April was safe, she didn't want to return to Sun City. She no longer felt drawn to it. This was her home, this was her coven, and they needed her as much as she did them.

Charlie went before her, each member quickly bowing their head to him. She set her shoulders and stepped up to the first council member. In a firm voice she said, "I come to you in perfect love and perfect trust to ask you to accept me as High Priestess."

The woman before her was tall and slender, her bright auburn hair curved gently over her shoulders. Her emerald eyes squinted at Jade, and she crossed her arms.

If only one refuses to let us pass . . .

Jade remembered the surge of power that came in the tunnels when she took ownership of her lineage. She raised her head to meet the imposing woman's gaze. "I am Jade Cerridwen, daughter of Rose Cerridwen. I am a Witch of Sugar Hill, like my aunt, mother, and grandmother before me. I am here to take my rightful place as High Priestess and to lead and protect this coven with my life. What say you?"

The woman raised one eyebrow and after a moment uncrossed her arms. With a slightly lilting accent, she said, "I, Selene of the Sugar Hill coven, welcome you with open arms and an open heart, and accept you as my High Priestess." She smiled the kindest smile Jade had seen. Jade smiled back, promising to herself to get to know each and every coven member, starting with her.

She went to each one in turn, clockwise around the circle, and when she arrived back at the beginning, Charlie took her hand again and faced the center. "With perfect love and perfect trust, we enter, gratefully."

Jade and Charlie walked past the eastern crypt and entered the inner area of the clearing. In the center was a raised stone circle with a table, the Ascension altar. Surrounding it were what appeared to be four people in long black hooded cloaks, one standing at each compass point, facing away from the center. Their hoods covered their faces. They were the Elementals, the raw power of the elements, channeled into this plane of existence and given human form for the purpose of ritual.

Charlie whispered to her, "These are Elementals, they guard each . . ."

"I know what they are," Jade said, a little too loudly. "Sorry. Nerves. Question is, what do I do?"

Charlie whispered, "Now that we have the support of the townspeople and the coven, we must walk the Elemental circle to prove our commitment and link to their powers. They will test us each in turn and decide if we may pass. Wait here and listen to what I say. After I've finished my test, I'll move out of your way and you can step forward. Then you say what I did."

Jade grabbed his hand as he pulled it away. "You've been through this before, right?"

"Yes, but now that you're gonna be High Priestess, it's a whole different correlation—"

"No, I get that, I mean." She looked at the figure waiting for them. "They're going to test me how?"

He turned toward her, holding her hand tightly against his chest. "It's different for everyone, so I can't really say, but I'm here with you, Jade. And I've complete faith that you'll come through this just fine. Besides, after what we've been through the last couple of days, this will be easy."

She nodded and he squeezed her hand one more time before letting go. After a deep breath, Charlie took position directly in front of the eastern Elemental. "Element of Air. The inspiration that drives us. The beginning of all things. Intelligence personified. I humbly ask for passage into this Sacred Circle."

Jade watched Charlie intently, waiting for something to happen. He didn't move but his eyes clouded over, becoming solid white. After several seconds Jade was starting to get uncomfortable when suddenly Charlie took a shaky step back, his eyes quickly returning to normal. He took a step to the side, motioning her forward.

She bowed her head and stepped up to face the eastern Elemental. Lifting her head, she gazed under the hood. There was nothing there. It was as she expected. Pure air is invisible, after all. "Element of Air. The inspiration that drives us. The beginning of all things. Intelligence personified. I humbly ask for passage into this Sacred Circle."

She heard the words in her head rather than with her ears: "You already know what you have to do."

Jade waited for something more to happen, but as the seconds ticked by, she got frustrated. "That's all?" She frowned in the face of the most powerful being she'd ever encountered.

Air replied, "You think you know everything; you tell me."

Jade's frown changed from frustration to confusion, then realization struck her. All those years ago she had been so naturally gifted, she only read magic books because she wanted to. Of course, she learned from them but it was effortless. It gave her a sense of knowing it all. Now she realized she really didn't. She had only just started to learn about the mysteries, and now she was so out of practice that she was behind where she needed to be.

She needed to put aside her pride and accept that she had much to learn. "I understand."

Air nodded once and turned away from her, facing the center of the circle.

Jade smiled as she walked to her left, following Charlie along the gentle curve of the Sacred Circle. *If they're all like this, I've been worried for nothing.*

They stopped on the southern edge and faced inward toward the southern Elemental. Charlie took his turn facing the Elemental and recovered much quicker this time. As he stepped aside, Jade lifted her head and gazed into the face of Fire.

It was flame, but not. Human, but not. Her breath came in ragged spurts, her heart pounded in her chest as the heat pressed against her face. She squinted and looked down at her feet, avoiding the blinding light of the flames inches before her. She wanted to run from the sorrow of what her parents had suffered. This image before her, a symbol of their torture. As she cowered before Fire, a small part of her mind scolded her, *This shouldn't upset you. You got through the Fire trial. You faced your parents' deaths. What's wrong with you?*

Fire's voice was ragged. "You will never forget what happened to them. The sadness will never leave you completely. However, you can control it in time, if you are willing to put in the work."

She forced herself to look up at it. "How?"

"Courage is not avoiding pain; it's doing what is right while enduring it."

Enduring pain was not Jade's strong suit, but she focused on the thought of not only April but a whole township needing her. She took a deep breath and pushed forward with her energy. Her voice shook as she said, "Element of Fire. The heat that drives a heart to beat. The cleansing flame leaving only truth behind. Desire, and change. I humbly ask for passage into this Sacred Circle."

Fire lifted its head slightly, and its glowing eyes burned into hers. Its voice seared in her mind, pure thought. "Release the past and step through."

She thought of the night her parents had died. Saw the flames roaring up the sides of the house, bursting from the windowpanes. It still hurt to watch, but not as bad as she thought it should. She thought she should collapse as she had that day, crumpled into the ground, powerless. But she remained standing, watching it all burn, feeling the heat.

This time the rain didn't come. This time she let go and allowed it to happen. Letting herself feel it, she reminded herself, *It's in the past. I can't change it now.*

The flames continued growing higher and hotter. Then they shrank, lowering in intensity and slowly going out like the gas on a stove. The house was still burned, but it stood as tall as ever, roofline intact. It only looked blackened, as if the fire had only touched the outer edge of the wood.

The vision disappeared and she was once again looking into the face of Fire. It turned around and faced the center of the circle.

Jade followed Charlie to the left and stopped before the western Elemental. After Charlie's turn, she stepped forward. "Element of Water. Blood that flows in our veins, emotions that guide our decisions. Water of life. I humbly ask for passage into this Sacred Circle." Jade waited anxiously for what would be asked of her.

Water lifted its head, and Jade looked into eyes made of the ocean itself. "Accept what's right in front of you."

Jade fell forward into that blue and was drowning. She struggled to swim to the surface, but she didn't know which way was up. Suddenly all directions seemed right. In a panic she could only think of one thing, Charlie. The thought of him calmed her immediately. She stopped struggling and held still. She saw him smiling at her, and it warmed her soul. Reaching out to him, she found herself standing before Water once again. It turned around and faced the center of the circle.

They walked left once more and stopped before the northern Elemental. "Element of Earth. Grounding, stability. Mother Gaia from whom we come and to whom we will return. I humbly ask for passage into this circle." Jade was calm now. Each vision she endured was purging something from her that no morning jog or relaxing bath could.

Earth lifted its head. Jade saw two black caves. She accepted it and allowed the now familiar pull to take her where it would.

Opening her eyes, she saw nothing. If she hadn't told her eyelids to open, she would still think them closed. She forced herself to remain calm and waited patiently for some light to appear. Her nose itched. She went to scratch it, but her arm wouldn't move. Nothing could. She struggled at first, fear rising in her chest. Then a thought occurred. Surrounded by Earth, the Earth, she was literally in The Great Mother's arms. It was the safest place anyone could be. She let this idea sink into her fear and disburse it.

As she calmed, she felt herself released. She was standing in front of the Earth Elemental, looking into her eyes, now emerald green. "Well done," Jade heard in her mind. The lady before her was different from the other Elementals. For one thing this was definitely female. With the others Jade couldn't tell. Earth winked at her. "When you get out of your own way, you can accomplish miracles." The voice was unlike any she had heard. It was undoubtedly feminine yet had a strength that was equally undeniable. Earth turned to face the center as the other Elementals had done, and Jade heard in her mind words that wrapped around her like a mother's embrace: "Welcome home." Jade stepped past Earth.

Charlie held his hand out to her, and she took it gently. "This is it. It's all about us now." He led her to the center of the clearing, where Mrs. Keepsake and Ms. Scrivener stood waiting beside the altar. The Book of Shadows was lying open in the center, turned to the Ascension ritual. They stepped up onto the disk, and Charlie stood opposite Jade, facing her across the table. Looking into his eyes, she felt grounded.

Charlie pulled the wand from his pouch and placed it along the eastern edge of the table. He held his hands open over the wand and nodded to Jade. She placed her hands next to Charlie's and glanced down. The words on the page were glowing. Charlie began reciting the words and Jade joined in.

"Wand, element of Air. Directing power, guiding intent, serve us this night in our rites."

He pulled the small knife from his pouch and laid it along the southern edge. "Athame, element of Fire. The heartbeat that drives us, serve us this night in our rites."

Jade pulled the chalice from her pouch and placed it on the western edge. "Chalice, element of Water. Life and change, serve us this night in our rites."

She lifted the disk from her pouch and placed it on the northern edge. "Pentacle, element of Earth. Stability and strength, serve us this night in our rites."

They slowly raised their hands, palms facing each other. As they spoke, Jade's palms began to grow warm. "Air, Fire, Water, Earth, we thank you for your gifts on this night."

Jade felt something shift within her. It was like she could truly feel magic again. There were hundreds of energies bombarding her all at once. Some had a warmth or coolness about them, some energies she could feel tingling in her palms or forehead. There were even new tastes and smells. She started to feel overwhelmed, like someone who had been kept in a soundproof dark room, suddenly thrown into a crowd on a sunny day.

Charlie closed his eyes and she followed suit. She focused on the energy around them. The Earth beneath their feet, the four guardians, the coven members, everything was sending energy toward them. She focused that energy in her heart, preparing to send it to the Keys on the altar to seal and empower them for future spells.

She opened her eyes as the power built to its crest. Just as their hands were about to touch, a spark shocked them. This time she saw it. Blue electricity like the waves that rolled off a Tesla coil. It started at their palms and slowly traveled up to the tips of their ring fingers, evaporating into the air. The blue light left heat in its wake, and Jade looked to Charlie, their eyes meeting with an electricity of their own.

They each took a step back, and the electricity intensified. It shot back and forth between them but didn't hurt. It took the form of a sphere, floating between them at chest level. Jade felt the power rising within her. It swirled round her chest, then down her arms and out of her palms, causing them to tingle. She focused on the energy, sending it out to the sphere. It met the energy coming from Charlie and combined in the sphere with her own. Her energy was cool, like a mountain stream. His was warm, like the sun's rays. She used her mind to gently nudge the energy ball larger and larger until it encompassed both her and Charlie. Their combined power merged.

One by one, each coven member began to chant, "As above, so below." As they did, they raised their hands toward the sky, then after a moment, they threw their hands toward Charlie and Jade. White light shot out and joined with the bluish-white sphere around them. The blue and white swirled around like a glowing soap bubble, the view outside the sphere fading in and out as the glowing lines whirled around.

Jade felt tingling throughout her whole body, like every molecule was ignited with power. She stared at Charlie, eyes wide, breathing heavy, trying to control the energy running through her. The tingling became sharper, then it began to hurt. She focused on containing the energy, but the harder she gripped it, the more it hurt. "Charlie?"

"Don't try to direct it, let it flow."

Jade tried to relax, tried to let the energy travel where it wanted, but it stung her skin, like the static shock when you touch something after scuffing your feet on carpet. The shocks were growing in number, covering more of her body. She tensed, looking down at her palms. Fear rose within her, closing her throat. On the verge of panic, she looked up at Charlie.

He stepped to her, grabbing her hands. "You're okay, Jade. It's just the coven's energy combining with ours. I'm right here with you. We're in this together."

His voice was deep, slow, calming. The prickling on her skin continued, but it didn't hurt anymore. Her focus was on him now. The whole world faded away, and it was just the two of them. She was drawn to him, a magnetic pull, a need. She understood now why many coven leaders were married. It felt like she imagined a marriage should. This man, her partner. The one person who would always be connected to her, in a way no one else would. He was so close to her now, their clasped hands the only thing between them.

His eyes flick downward toward her lips. "Jade . . ."

"Yes?"

"I really want to kiss you right now." He smiled his lopsided grin, but he didn't move closer.

Jade's heart pounded as the seconds ticked by. She lifted on her toes and pressed her lips to his. She was about to stop, but he let go of her hands and wrapped his arms around her. She draped her arms around his neck and leaned into him. He was warm and strong, and she felt at home. When he finally pulled away and she lowered down to her feet, she found she couldn't stop looking at him.

He smirked at her. "While I'd love to stay like this forever, we have a ritual to finish."

"We're not done yet?" she quipped.

"Nope. Whole bunch of people waiting for us to finish."

"Oh. Okay." She pulled away and reluctantly let go of his hands.

Charlie stepped back and began waving his hands in a large figure eight, directing the energy from the sphere through Jade, into the Keys, then through himself and back to the sphere. It was a continuing infinity loop, and Jade became hypnotized watching him. He was strength, power, and beauty, wrapped up in one fluid motion. Jade relaxed and let the energy go, moving her arms as he did, joining him in the flowing dance, moving the energy through them both.

The Keys began to glow and levitate, becoming brighter with each pass of the energy. She looked around the ring of coven members, Willow standing behind Charlie, someone in the distance, Belle to the left . . .

She looked back and into the eyes of Andrew. He was outside the circle, but she could see him clearly. He was saying something and smiling proudly at her.

"No." Jade raised her arms, grabbing hold of the energy and wrenching it away from Charlie's grasp.

"What are you doing?" Charlie yelled.

Jade's anger and hatred flared up within her, merging with the energy in her grasp. She wasn't thinking, she just wanted to stop Andrew. She sent the energy flying toward him. There was a blur in her line of sight. She blinked and saw Andrew's face. He was in shock. Staring at something inside the circle.

How is he not dead? Even being out of practice, I should have at least wounded him.

She could still feel the power surrounding them. She reached out to send another blast his way, but there was a shout, a scream, and the voices of many people in confusion. Charlie quickly ground the energy remaining in the sphere, sending it out of her easy reach. He turned and ran to Madame Belle, who was crouched down, blocking her view of someone lying on the ground.

Jade covered her mouth with both hands. "No," she whispered. All the energy she'd intended for Andrew had gone to someone else. Someone who had sacrificed themselves to protect him. She stumbled forward and pushed Charlie out of the way.

"NO!"

Willow's eyes were closed. Her face contorted in pain. Her hands were clenched to her chest. The last glowing remnants of Jade's magic faded, revealing burn marks and blood seeping from under her fingers.

Jade dropped to the ground. "Goddess! What have I done? Willow, I'm so sorry." Her voice grew instantly hoarse as her throat closed around the words. Tears streamed down her face. Mrs. Keepsake and Charlie were blurry figures on the other side of her, chanting a healing spell, their glowing hands waving over Willow's body.

Jade looked up to where Andrew had stood but he was gone, replaced by the townsfolk, stretching to see what was happening from beyond the iron fence.

Moments dragged by into what felt like hours. Finally, Willow opened her eyes, but her pupils were white with electric blue veins stabbing through the whites of her eyes. In a low voice she exhaled one word, "Jade."

CHAPTER 27

Jade slammed the door to her room open, rattling the bookcase. She grabbed her suitcase out of the closet and threw it on her bed. As she hurled each piece of clothing at the suitcase, she choked back tears. She had left the circle, running through the woods, fleeing the cemetery where Willow's body lay bloodied and broken. As she ran, she had heard Charlie calling out for her to stop, but she couldn't. She'd run all the way, farther than she ever had before, her sorrow and rage driving her on.

She threw her shoes at the case, then her scarf, then she took off her cloak. She would leave it behind along with everything magical. This time she would leave for good, for everyone's good. Losing her parents hadn't been her fault. Losing Willow . . .

She threw her cloak on the bed, and the pendant Willow had given her slipped out of the pocket and landed on the floor. She looked down at it. Things didn't just slip out of Witch's cloak pockets. She collapsed to the floor and clutched the pendant to her. Her tears burned. Her breath came in ragged gasps. *Why? Why did she do that?* She couldn't wrap her head around why she would have protected him. *After everything, why him?*

Sobs wracked her body again as another wave of grief hit her. *It doesn't matter why. It's all my fault. I killed her.*

She pulled herself up with shaking hands and placed the pendant gently on the foot of the bed. It was over. She'd come back and done her duty, she'd tried to use magic, and it had only gotten someone else killed. She shoved the lid of her suitcase shut and fastened the latches. *I'm done.*

As she dragged the suitcase off the bed, movement caught her eye. An envelope landed on the floor. She picked it up and stared at it. The tightness in her throat, the twisting of her stomach, she wanted to run, but instead she plopped her suitcase back down and sat on the bed next to it.

She stared at the envelope for a few moments, her name printed in block letters. Turning it over, she found it wasn't sealed, the flap was simply tucked under the open edge. She opened it and pulled out the single sheet of paper.

Dear Jade,

Something's happening today. Something big. I'm not gonna tell you what, just in case this letter manages to find you, and just in case you decide to care. I don't want you suddenly uprooting your whole life for little ole me. Let's just say it's important to me. Life and death kind of stuff, and I'm scared.

I have to do something that I've never done before, and I'm probably gonna fail. Okay, I'm most definitely gonna fail, but if there's one thing I've learned from you, it's losing doesn't matter. You always try like you know you're gonna win. So, I'm gonna try.

I just wanted you to know that, win or lose, I have no regrets. I'm following your example, and that makes me proud, no matter the outcome. I don't think I ever told you this when we were kids. I mean, why would I? We were kids. I didn't know how to put something like this into words back then. But here it is: I'm proud of you. I was then and I am now.

Sure, things are different now. You're hiding away in your walled-off city. You've turned your back on magic and everything you were raised to believe in, and you've ignored every letter I've sent. Probably will ignore this one too. But you know what? Who cares? You'll always be my friend, and nothing you ever do or say will change that. Because you're awesome.

Yup, I said it. You are awesome. Go ahead, you can gloat.

Thanks again for teaching me how to try.

Love,

Charlie

Jade put it back in the envelope. *Always try. What good is trying if it just gets people killed?* She looked over at her red cloak crumpled on the bed. She rose and picked it up. Her aunt and mom had worn this, her grandmother too probably, though she'd died before Jade was born. A long line of powerful Witches, each taking their turn as High Priestess. And now it came down to her. She stared at the pin while tears flowed readily, creating a pattern of dots on the red fabric as they fell.

While she never cried in Sun City, she also had never been through so much as in the last week. But there was still unfinished business to take care of. Willow's being gone didn't change that. April was her best friend, Charlie was her partner, and for better or worse, Andrew was her uncle. As her aunt had once told her, Witches take care of their own. Each of them was Jade's in a way, and each of them needed her. Though the odds were against her, she would do as Charlie said. She would try.

She wiped her eyes and wrapped the cloak around her shoulders, then returned the pendant to her pocket. She headed downstairs, leaving her suitcase where it sat, and ran all the way back to the cemetery.

***

Jade arrived at the cemetery to find only two parked cars. Charlie and Mrs. Keepsake were walking out and met her at the entrance.

"Where is everyone?" she panted as she placed her hands on top of her head, trying to slow her breathing.

"What do you care?" Charlie walked past her and straight to his car.

Mrs. Keepsake gave Jade a sympathetic look and placed one hand on her shoulder gently. "This has been a tough day for all of us, dear. The coven is . . . well, let's just say they're not very pleased the Ascension wasn't completed. Charlie talked to them, smoothed their ruffled feathers, so to speak." She glanced at Charlie opening the truck of his car. "You two need each other. Still much to do, yes?" She headed for her own car.

Jade approached Charlie, where he was placing some ritual items carefully into a wooden box in his trunk. "I'm sorry."

He threw the bundle of incense he was holding into the box, sending leaves scattering, and slammed the trunk shut. "OH! You're sorry? Well, that just makes everything better doesn't it?"

He walked around to the driver's seat and got in. "I'll be sure to tell Willow you're sorry." He glared at her as he started the engine, then peeled out, sending a cloud of rocks and dirt billowing up like a smoke screen.

Jade turned away, trying to avoid inhaling the dust. She heard the car screech to a halt. He stopped a short distance away. After a moment he backed up slowly and stopped where she stood. He got out of the car and stood glaring at her with tear-filled eyes. Jade's heart broke at the sight.

"I'm sorry," he nearly whispered.

"That's okay. I kind of deserved it."

"Yeah, you did. But that's not why I'm sorry. I'm sorry I drove away. That's something you would do, run from your problems. That's not who I am. I face them, no matter how much it hurts or how uncomfortable it makes me."

He sighed and placed his hands on his hips. "When you first got in town, I didn't think you'd last the day. When you ran from Joy's Crossing Over ceremony, I figured you were done for sure, but I found you at the lake and decided to give you the benefit of the doubt. Through each trial, I kept expecting you to quit, but you didn't. I thought you'd changed. But today I needed you—the whole coven needed you—and you just took off."

"I'm sorry." Before Charlie could respond she said, "I know, it doesn't fix anything, and I have a lot to make up for. But it's a start, and hopefully, given enough time, I will be able to fix it."

"I don't need you to fix anything, Jade. I need you to show me that you're someone I can count on, that this town can count on. Andrew has not only April but the Book of Shadows too. Don't you realize what that means? That book is full of generations of coven leaders' knowledge. In the wrong hands it's a very dangerous thing, and anytime now

Andrew's gonna use it to bring someone back from the dead. I can't stop him alone. I need to know if you're really with me."

"He has the Book of Shadows? You're sure?"

"Pretty sure. We looked for it after you left, but I think with all the commotion he could have easily grabbed it. He's the only one who had any reason to take it."

Commotion. That's not the word I would use. She reminded herself that Charlie didn't do anything wrong. She was the one who had hurt him when they were kids by running away, and she had done it again. She had to prove to him that was the last time. "Well, if we're going to stop him, I guess we first have to find him. And for that we probably need some help. Where is everyone?"

"Mrs. Keepsake and Madame Belle took Willow to the chapel. Everyone else went home. I told them to raise their protection spells. I don't want anyone else hurt."

"Good idea. If Willow was here, we could ask her for help, but I guess I ruined that too." Her heart twisted as she remembered what Willow looked like the last time she'd seen her.

Charlie frowned. "Why don't we ask her?"

Jade stared at him. "I can't tell if you're messing with me or what."

"Messing with you? What are you talking about?"

"Unless you're suggesting we hold another séance." Her voice wavered on the last word.

"Why—?" His eyes widened. "You think . . . oh, Jade." He placed his hands on her shoulders. "Willow is still alive."

Jade's pulse quickened. "She . . . what? How?"

Charlie smirked. "You really think you're more powerful than our oldest crone?"

"No, but I was channeling divine magic."

His grin faded. "She is hurt pretty bad. She may still die, but for now she's stable. She's in the chapel because it's a powerful center of magic. They're using it to try to heal her."

Relief flooded through her. "I need to see her. Now." She ran to the other side of the car and got in.

***

They rushed into the chapel, pulling up short when they saw Willow lying on a bed of flowers in front of the altar. A platform of roots had grown up out of the ground to support her body at waist height. She was in a flowing white dress, simple in design, but beautiful.

Jade's heart was in her throat. *We're too late.* She grabbed Charlie's arm. "Is she—?"

"I don't know." They rushed up to Mrs. Keepsake, who was standing nearby. "What's going on? I thought you said she was stable."

Mrs. Keepsake spoke in a near whisper. "We thought she was. She seems to be coming in and out of it. As if she's trying to decide if she wants to go."

Madame Belle was walking around Willow, placing small herbs and flowers along the edges of her dress. Charlie and Mrs. Keepsake continued talking low as Jade approached Willow.

"Grandma Willow?" she whispered. Her eyes were closed, tiny blue veins radiating from her darkened eyelids. "Please. I . . . I'm so sorry." She swallowed hard.

Willow's eyes opened. A bluish white, they stared blindly at Jade. She lifted one hand slowly, and Jade took it gently in hers.

"It's me. Jade. Do you remember what happened to you? At the Ascension?"

Willow nodded slowly.

She wanted to ask why she did it. Why she sacrificed herself to protect him. But she couldn't bring herself to. *It's all my fault.*

Willow's voice was rough, barely above a whisper. "Blame is a worthless thing, Jade. Focus on what you can change. Andrew must be stopped, but not by killing."

That was a big ask. Jade felt she could probably strangle him with her bare hands right now. "We don't even know where he is."

"You have been gifted everything you need." Her eyes fluttered shut, and her hand relaxed in Jade's.

Jade's heart dropped, until she noticed Willow's chest slowly rising and falling in a steady rhythm. *Thank the Goddess, she's still alive.*

She laid Willow's hand gently on her stomach, then turned and walked over to Charlie and Mrs. Keepsake. "She's so weak." She swallowed against the lump in her throat. She wanted to cry, but she couldn't, not now. "We need to finish the Ascension ritual. Andrew will not get away with this." Forcing Jade through the trials, kidnapping April—he was a threat that needed to be dealt with.

Mrs. Keepsake said, "I'm afraid you can't do that without the Book of Shadows, dear."

Charlie said, "I guess we need to find Andrew first, then. Did Willow say anything about where he might be?"

"Only that I've been gifted what I need."

He raised an eyebrow. "Gifted? Could she be talking about the pendulum she gifted you right before we started the trials?"

"Maybe." She pulled it from her cloak pocket. "You think she meant we should do a locator spell?"

He shrugged. "Worth a try. But maybe try it on April. Remember Willow tried to find Andrew before and it didn't work. He's probably still cloaked."

Mrs. Keepsake said, "Since you've no idea where to start looking, you should probably use a map. Its' a lot faster to pinpoint location that way."

Charlie said, "We should go to my house. I've got an old map of town there, and it's a lot closer than your home."

Jade looked back at Willow. She seemed so small, so fragile. It was too unlike her normal stature. "Sure. I can't help here."

***

They drove down the dirt road and onto the pavement. When Charlie turned into the drive for the mayor's house, Jade said, "You're kidding. You're the mayor?"

"Yeah, your aunt was interim mayor for a while, but a couple of years ago she started saying it was time for someone new. The townsfolk voted and I took over officially."

A couple of years ago? Is that why he wrote the letter? Jade wondered

The driveway turned a large circle in front of the house. It wasn't exactly a mansion, but it was huge and had a spectacular view. The street off the driveway went at a steep slope for a couple of blocks before intersecting Main Street. No houses were built on the hillside, but a few benches dotted the grass. Jade remembered it as a gathering place in the summer for picnics and watching the sunset.

Charlie stopped in front of the front door. Two narrow white pillars held up a small awning, and a spiral topiary framed the entrance. The house was big enough to host a large party, but not too big to get lost in.

Charlie placed his hand on the center of the door. Lowering his head, he whispered, "Reserare" *Unlock.* The door swung open and Jade followed him in.

They walked through the marble and mahogany entrance, down a long hall with crystal sconces, and out of the back of the house. They crossed a flagstone patio surrounded by a low wall, then continued across the large expanse of lawn. She noticed a small shack on the other side tucked into the tree line. "Where are we going?"

"The Accords won't let us keep magical items in the mayor's residence, so we use this." He waved toward the shack as they neared it. The wood was so old and crooked that it looked like the whole thing was about to fall. Charlie walked up to the shack and waved his hands over the rusted padlock. They waited in silence, but nothing happened. He tried it again. Still nothing.

"Well that's not good." Charlie raised his hand. The lock squeaked and shuttered, then popped open with a groan. He glanced at Jade. "We need to finish that Ascension." He opened the door and stepped into the dark doorway, dropping out of sight.

Jade blinked, wondering if it was another portal. She stepped forward and peeked into the darkness. There was a steep set of stairs leading down, and Charlie stood at the bottom, holding a lantern.

"Come on down, but watch your step. It's even steeper than it looks."

She followed his advice and managed to arrive safely on the dirt floor. Looking around, she realized they were in a root cellar. The walls, ceiling, and floor were all dirt. Shelves lined the walls, and there was a waist-high bench in the center of the small room. The legs were thick wooden spindles, but the top was some kind of hard black material, like the kind used in a chemistry lab at school.

Charlie put the lantern down on the table and started searching the shelves. There were jars and boxes in one section, books in another. Jade felt drawn to one corner of the room where no shelving was. It was especially dark here, as if a shadow was covering the space, though nothing was between the lantern and it.

Jade walked over and inspected the wall. It was the same type of compacted earth as the rest. She was just starting to reach out her hand when Charlie startled her.

"Okay, we're ready. I think." He turned toward her. "You ready?"

Jade stepped up to the table and saw a large parchment filled with a rough sketch of Sugar Hill. It was held down at the corners by four bowls. Their contents seemed to be moving. She looked closer and realized each contained one of the four elements swirling around the bottom of the bowl: soil, smoke, flame, and water.

Charlie pointed at the map. "Time for the pendant."

She stepped up to the table and took the pendant out of her pocket, reminding herself that she'd already worked with magical energy a few times successfully. *It's a simple locator spell. Nothing dangerous.* She held it to her closely, and closing her eyes, she sent her nervous energy out through the ground and pulled in the positive energy she felt from Charlie.

Opening her eyes, she held out the pendant straight in front of her, letting it dangle. As she spoke, she dipped it into each of the bowls. "Power of Earth, power of Water, power of Fire, power of Air. I, Jade Cerridwen, seek out April Goodrich. By the power of self, by the power of family, by the power of the elements, I command you, show yourself to me."

She waited but the pendulum simply swung side to side, giving an answer of *Nope*.

"Great, now what?" Jade frowned down at the parchment. She turned to Charlie, extending her hand with the pendant. "Here. You're more connected to magic than I am now. You should do it."

"But I don't have the connection to her like you do. Maybe you should try your bracelet. The one April gave you?" He pointed to the string of small seashells that looped around her left wrist.

"How did you know about that?"

"When you were going through the Earth trial, April and I had some time to chat. She told me about how you each made one and exchanged them. It's how we found you."

Jade took the bracelet off and looked at it. If he'd been able to find her with the bracelet she'd given April, maybe she could do the same for her.

She held the bracelet in her hand with the ball of the pendulum and let the cone hang down. Repeating the steps of dipping into each bowl, she said, "Power of Earth, power of Water, power of Fire, power of Air. I, Jade Cerridwen, seek out April Goodrich. By the power of self, by the power of family, by the power of the elements, I command you, show yourself to me."

The pendant began swinging in an ever-increasing circle, then the circle began to shrink. Finally, as if pulled by a magnet, it settled over a spot right of center. The parchment began to darken at the spot, as if ink were being spilled. The darkness spread out in lines, and soon Sugar Hill was covered with a spiderweb of thin lines. The spot that had formed first turned red as blood.

CHAPTER 28

Jade leaned in close and recognized where the red mark was. "Isn't that Mary's Tavern?"

Charlie nodded as realization spread across his face. "It makes sense actually."

"What?" Jade asked sarcastically. "Andrew's out partying to celebrate his win?"

Charlie smirked. "I doubt it. What makes sense is that he's gone to one of the town's major ley line markers."

Jade tilted her head. "I feel like I've heard that word before."

"Ley lines are the Earth's natural lines of power. Like veins, they crisscross all over the world." He waved his hand over the map, and the thin bloodred lines glowed, emphasizing their connection at several points. "As you can see, there's quite a few running through Sugar Hill. When these lines cross, the power running through them is concentrated, and these points are called markers. The chapel is a natural one, and the cemetery was built on one."

"And Mary's Tavern is one too?" Jade almost laughed.

"No, but the well behind it is. Water is one of the most powerful markers. The well is even older than the town. It was built back when this was just a trading post.

"Since Andrew took the Book of Shadows, he has the correct spell, but he needs more than that to bring his daughter back from the dead without a coven leader's help. A ley line marker will channel a ton of elemental energy." He paused, frowning at Jade. "Which will help, but it still might not be enough power."

"This is a dark magic spell, right? Bringing someone back from the dead?" Charlie nodded, and Jade saw it again, the darkness that passed over his face, like the ghost of a shadow. It happened every time dark magic was mentioned. "And you know a lot about dark magic, don't you?"

Charlie met her gaze. "What makes you say that?"

Jade tilted her head. "You really want to play that game with me, or do you just want to tell me what you've been trying to hide?"

Charlie shook his head. "I'll tell you all about it when this is over. Right now we don't have time."

"Fine. Then tell me what's needed for a dark magic resurrection spell. Everything that's needed."

"There's two ways to do this spell. The first is by using divine magic. But that's something only accessible to a coven leader."

"Which is why he wants me to help."

"I think so. He probably thinks your relationship will make you want to help him."

"Well he messed that up when he let me find out he killed my parents. What's the other way?"

"The other way, the way I think he's been planning for, is to sacrifice an innocent. Particularly someone who's not a Witch."

Jade realized who he was suggesting. She whispered, "April."

Charlie nodded. "I think that's what he meant when he called her 'insurance.' He's still hoping you'll change your mind and help him do that ritual, but if you refuse—"

"Then he'll sacrifice April? But Willow spelled her. How could he get past that?"

He frowned at the table for a moment, then realization spread across his face. "With Willow being so injured, her power's weakened and so are her spells. It wouldn't be immediate, but he'd probably be able to break through, eventually."

A shiver ran through her. She wasn't cold or even afraid. It was the same way she felt whenever she was faced with something unbearable. She wanted to run, but running wouldn't save April. "No. Not this time," she muttered.

"What?" Charlie asked.

"Never mind. So how would this resurrection spell work? I assume you've read it?"

He nodded. "First, he needs a place that is sacred and clean."

"By 'clean' you don't mean freshly mopped, I assume." She smirked.

"Exactly. It means not having blood spilled. Not used for dark purposes. Kind of like an innocent space." He pointed to the well. "The most likely spot is here, since water is a cleansing element. He'd place an item from the deceased in the focal point of power, in this case the well, then he'd speak the right words, which are in the Book of Shadows. The next part depends on whether he gets you to help him or not."

"Definitely not."

"Right, but he doesn't know that. He's probably setting up for that possibility but positioning April in case you refuse." He thought for a moment, looking at the map. "If you helped him, there isn't much else to do. You just step up to the well and place your hands over it, channeling the divine while he speaks the words.

"Without your help he'll need to sacrifice April. He'll have her standing right next to the well, probably tied to one of the posts that support the bucket. He'll need to sacrifice his own blood first. A lot of it. Doing that would leave him a bit disoriented. But once enough of his blood is spilled, he'll kill April with the same knife. Then he'll toss the blade into the well, along with both their blood. Once that's done, the deceased, his daughter, would return."

Her stomach turned at the thought of April being dead. "All you need is a few moments to cast a binding spell, right? So, I tell him I thought it over and want to help. While he's focusing on me, you bind him. Easy peasy."

Charlie looked doubtful. "Not that easy. Certain times of day are more conducive to high-powered spells like this. He'll need to wait until the moment the sun hits the horizon. That's when he'll stab April. Doesn't give us much time, and I'll need time to get set up properly. There are short-cast binding spells, but to make sure it's strong enough to hold him, I'll want to use one that is a longer cast. Also, he's had plenty of time to plan this and get the area set up. What if he suddenly decides to go ahead without you?"

"He won't. I may have been wrong about who he is, but I know who he's been the last twenty years. He gets what he wants, and he wants me on his side."

Charlie didn't look convinced.

Jade put her hand on his shoulder reassuringly. "Hey, we can do this." She looked into his eyes. "Remember all those spells you helped me with when we were kids? You didn't think half of them would work, but they turned out all right. Not to mention all the trials we just went through. I wouldn't have been able to make it through them without you. Together, we can do this."

Charlie nodded and gave a small smile. "Okay. Let's get going."

Jade was so grateful he was there. Blood magic was something she'd never been comfortable with. Not because blood grossed her out at all, but because it usually tapped into energies that were dangerously close to dark magic. Now they were going to be there for a full-on dark magic spell. She had no idea what to expect from that kind of energy or how it would affect her.

As they walked to the car, Jade watched Charlie. They had been inseparable as kids. After all the years apart, it had taken some time to become close again, but they were slowly getting there. He'd been indispensable during the trials and seemed genuinely upset at April's kidnapping. And then there was the Ascension. When their magic had combined, she'd never felt so close to someone. When he'd kissed her, she'd never wanted him to stop.

***

When they arrived at the tavern, Jade could feel the energy rising, charging the air like static. Charlie parked in front of Mary's Tavern and jumped out of the car. He stepped onto the curb, looking around. "You feel that? I think he's already started."

Jade frowned at the alleyway leading to the back of the tavern. "Great. Let me go first. I'll tell him I've changed my mind and . . . I don't know, distract him. You stay out of sight as long as you can."

"Sounds like a plan, but I'll go around the other side and approach from the opposite direction." He pointed to the other side of the tavern. "Less chance he sees me that way. Just keep him talking. The spell I'm going to cast takes time."

She nodded once and started toward the alley. Charlie grabbed her hand.

"Hey." He looked into her eyes for a moment, then over her whole face, like he was trying to memorize her. He reached out and tucked one of her curls behind her ear. "Be careful. I don't want to lead this coven without you."

She smiled back. "Out of time, remember."

He cleared his throat. "Right. Sorry. See you." He ran off one way and Jade went the other.

When she arrived at the back, she peeked around the corner of the building. April was tied to the well as Charlie had thought, but she looked unharmed as she struggled against her restraints. Andrew was pacing back and forth on the patio, all its tables and chairs in a pile on the other side as if a storm had blown them over. He was muttering to himself and gesturing animatedly with an athame in one hand, as if arguing with someone.

Jade slowly stepped out from the building. Andrew hadn't seen her yet. If she could just get to April.

"You're here! I knew you'd come." Andrew was approaching her, arms outstretched as if to hug her, a joyful smile on his face.

She put up her hand. "No!" Her hand tingled, her magic begging to come out. *Patience,* she reminded herself. *Need to give Charlie time to get into place.* Andrew was standing still, waiting. "We . . . need to talk first."

He eyed her suspiciously. "About what?"

She continued quickly before he could measure the truth in her words. "I've been thinking over what you said. It wasn't fair that Abigail was taken from you, especially so young. In fact, the only thing worse than a child losing her parents would be a parent losing their child."

He grinned. "See, you get it." He turned back to the space next to him. "I told you."

"I want to help you," Jade continued, "but I . . . need some assurances first." She glanced at April. She'd stopped struggling and was standing tall, calmly, as if nothing were wrong.

Andrew glanced at the horizon. "Whatever you want, it's yours." He yelled to the side, pointing his knife at a spot in the air. "No! I said I'll handle it, so let me handle it, you bitch!" He looked back at Jade. "I'm sorry." He pressed his hands down to either side and looked back and forth. "I'm sorry, look. Heh. It will all be okay. I promised . . . I promised I would do this—fix this. Just, Jade, honey, what do you want?"

Jade was frozen for a moment. His outburst was so irregular, talking to the air. She felt the same cold energy she had at the séance woosh past her. *Great, it's her.*

She focused on Andrew and saw movement behind him. *Hurry up, Charlie.* She gave her best smile. "I just want to know that . . . well, I'm not sure if you can—"

"Just tell me!" His face was twisted in rage. He seemed to struggle to calm himself and in a lower voice said, "Please, tell me what you want."

"April . . . can you promise she'll be unhurt?" She had nearly reached April's side by this point.

Andrew looked to April, then squinted at Jade. Tilting his head, he said, "I already told you she'll be fine, if you help me."

As Andrew approached her, Charlie stepped out from the shadows. The glowing orb in his hand pulsed with a strange combination of swirling light and darkness. He threw it at Andrew's back.

A gust of wind blew past Jade. In its wake she felt the dark energy again. It flew toward Andrew. He turned and blocked the orb at the last minute. It rebounded straight back toward Charlie on the patio, enveloping him, surrounding him in the swirling shapes, blocking him from view.

Andrew turned slowly toward Jade. "You really shouldn't have done that."

Jade scrambled for a way to placate him. She couldn't face him alone. She wasn't strong enough. "No. Wait! I—he did that on his own." Andrew glared at her, but he wasn't attacking. "Yeah, I told him, I told him we were wrong. I said we—"

Andrew flicked the point of his knife blade downward. Jade crumpled to the ground. Everything was so heavy, as if she weighed hundreds of pounds. She was slouched over, unable to lift her head, she could only stare at the ground while Andrew talked.

"I thought you understood. I thought . . ."

Jade's ears strained to hear anything other than the wind and thunder.

Boots walking on stone, just to her right. *That must be Andrew going to the well . . . or—*

April said. "Jade, don—" Her voice was cut off, as if something was placed over her mouth.

Jade's heart beat heavy in her chest. She tried to pull the energy to her palms. Nothing. All those times the tingling of energy had come unbidden, now it refused her call.

Andrew's voice, more distant: "I'm sorry to do it this way, but I'm out of time. You have no idea what you're capable of, Jade. When this is over you must find your destiny."

Andrew's quick intake of breath, hissing through his teeth.

Water drops, echoing.

Jade struggled to sit upright. She had to. She had to see what was happening. She remembered when Charlie had lifted her at the cliff. She didn't have a feather as a trinket, but she remembered the sensation, lightness, airy.

The space between Charlie's ears.

The quip came unbidden to her memory, but it worked; she felt lighter. She raised her head, and as her body slowly followed it, she began lifting up.

The first thing she saw was Charlie. He was still in the orb, but it was beginning to degrade, slowly becoming clear.

She turned toward the well and saw Andrew standing behind April. There was nothing covering her mouth, but her lips were pressed tightly together. Her hair whipped around her face as her wide eyes pleaded at Jade, overflowing with tears.

Andrew's hand rested gently on her head. "You were like a daughter to me. No . . . wasn't my daughter . . . She was a good girl . . . . did everything I asked." He looked up at Jade. "Why didn't you help me when I asked?" He was crying now. "No one would have had to die."

He said, "If I can bring her back, I can bring everyone back." Andrew raised his hand holding the knife. Both it and his hand were smeared with blood. It dripped down from his wrists toward his elbows. Jade tried to run toward them, but she was so slow, the effects of Andrew's spell not quite gone. He shoved the knife into April's back.

Everything stopped. For a moment Jade and April were locked in each other's gazes.

The wind died. The lights went out. The constant background hum of life was silenced. It was like the moment before a storm hits. Only the world wasn't holding its breath. It had inhaled as much as it could and was about to scream.

April's eyes went wide, mouth slightly open like a freeze frame. For another moment nothing moved. In a strange kind of slow motion, Andrew released April and she slowly fell to the side. Jade rounded the well and managed to catch her as she collapsed into her arms.

The screaming began.

The wind hit her like a slap to the face. The darkness smothering the area was punctuated by random flashes of light. Andrew and Charlie both started chanting their own spells, their voices booming loudly in Jade's ears, competing with the pounding of her pulse.

Blood poured from April's back, and Jade desperately tried to push it back in. Put it back where it belonged. But it was too late. They were too late. And Jade had been wrong. Wrong about Andrew, wrong about saving April, wrong about everything.

Jade cradled April to her, rocking her while she looked around frantically for help. *Willow will fix it.*

Willow's dead. No, ill. Her mind struggled against itself to find reality. *She's not coming to help.*

Charlie, he's High Priest. She looked over to where he was battling with Andrew.

It wasn't much of a battle, more like a tussle. Charlie had Andrew pinned to the ground. Andrew was laughing and pushing against Charlie to let him up. "I did it! You'll see, it'll work. Let me go."

Jade looked down at April, her eyes staring blankly at nothing. Her head lolled back, her limp body held up only by Jade's embrace.

Jade was breaking into a million pieces. She could feel it. Everything hurt. Her sorrow was wrenched through her throat. "No. April, no. Please, don't go. I'm so sorry. I can't—"

Andrew did this. The thought twisted the pain in her heart to anger. The heat flowed outward until her whole body burned with hatred.

She slowly lowered April down to rest. She straightened her hair, the blood from her hands staining it red. "I'm sorry," she whispered. Kissing her forehead gently she choked out, "I'm so sorry."

She pulled herself to her feet and turned toward Andrew. He was still on the ground, and Charlie was standing over him, hands outstretched. A softly glowing light flowed down toward him as Charlie intoned a healing spell. Andrew was muttering to himself, barely audible.

Jade stormed toward them, her eyes pinning Andrew. "You piece of—"

"Jade, no." Charlie stepped between them.

She stopped in her tracks and focused on him. "Get out of my way."

"I know how you feel, but he needs to be brought to justice."

"Oh, I'll give him justice all right. Just step aside and let me."

"Jade, we don't execute people without a trial, and he's lost too much blood to have one right now." He looked over her shoulder. "April?"

Hot tears stung her eyes. "We need to make him pay for this."

A voice behind Jade asked, "Pay for what?"

CHAPTER 29

Jade whipped around. April was standing there, looking down at her dress. She lifted her head and smiled at Jade, that familiar sweet smile.

Jade ran to her and threw her arms around her. "April! Thank the Goddess." She pulled her close, eyes squeezed shut, ignoring the questions that threatened to ruin this moment. Her friend was alive, and she didn't care about anything else.

April hugged her back, resting her chin on Jade's shoulder. "Of course I'm okay. I always will be." She gripped Jade's head and whispered in her ear, "*My little lamb.*"

Jade struggled to pull away, but April's grip was too tight.

She whispered again, "Now, the lessons begin." She released her hold, and Jade stumbled back into Charlie.

What was once April stood there, looking herself over. She looked up, her smile too smug, too condescending as she looked down at them, head held high. The pale blue of her eyes was being enveloped by black masses, spreading out slowly from her pupils.

Charlie glared at her. "You're not April. Who are you?"

"Look who's a smart puppy." She reached out her hand to Charlie. "We haven't met yet, have we? I'm Raven." Every time she spoke, her voice sounded different. Emotions moved across her face like leaves on a windy day. She was a mess, but there was power. Jade could feel it flowing off her in waves.

Charlie looked at her outstretched hand and back to her face. "Like you said, smart puppy." He gave her a smile that nearly matched her darkness.

Raven withdrew her hand and turned away, flourishing her hand as if dismissing their presence. "No matter." She looked down her arms as if they were new. She rubbed her hands the length of her torso from her hips, over her abdomen, and cupped her breasts. She shrugged. "It'll do, I suppose. Though I was kind of hoping to get yours." She pointed at Jade.

Jade looked into the black eyes of her best friend. She hadn't thought there could be anything worse than April dying. She'd been wrong.

Raven stepped to the well and leaned back against it, tilting her head down, resting her fingertips to her forehead.

Charlie took this opportunity to try casting a spell at her, thinking she was distracted. Raven didn't move but to raise one finger of her free hand. "Stay."

Charlie froze in place, like a statue. Only his eyes moved, changing to a look of fright and confusion.

Jade said, "What did you do to him?"

Raven raised her head, gently wiping her blood-stained blonde hair off her face. She looked at him and pointed. "Who? Him?" she said innocently. "Nothing permanent I assure you. I just won't abide interruptions during my monologue. Now hush or I'll do the same to you."

She looked over her fingertips. "First thing I'm going to do is change this polish. It's just too pink. Don't ya think?" She smiled at Jade. At her angry expression, she asked, "Too soon?"

Jade tried to take a step toward her, but her feet were stuck in place. She gritted her teeth. "When I get my hands on you—"

"Aw, poor Jade, her best friend was killed and now she's mad at the world. Actually, a lot of people you love have died, haven't they? I'd almost say it's a health risk just knowing you. I've been watching you for a long time, and you're right about one thing, you have been lied to. But not by who you think. See the real story goes like this. Once upon a time there was a very bad man named—"

"I don't care!" Jade was pulling the Earth's energy, using the fact that her feet were grounded but it was a heavy energy, and she needed more time. "All I care about is getting my friend back."

"Aw, my little lamb, you're going to be very disappointed." She stretched her neck to one side, then lowered her gaze at Jade. The black had completely enveloped her eyes. "April is gone. You were too late." She pouted and batted her eyes at Jade. "Boo hoo."

Jade clenched her fists, focusing the energy her flare of anger raised. She flung it toward Raven. As soon as it left her hands, she regretted it. The black cleared from her eyes, and Jade looked into the terrified blue eyes of her best friend. All Jade could think was, *I just killed my best friend.* She frantically reached out, trying to grab the energy and pull it back, but it was too strong, and she couldn't even get a grip on it.

It was slow moving, though, and Raven had plenty of time to block it. Jade watched as the black flowed into her eyes again and the energy bounced off her palms into the ground.

Raven laughed. "Oh Jade. If you could have seen your face! You were all like *No! Wait, I take it back.*" She laughed a moment more, then her face dropped into serious thought. "Your cast wasn't bad though. Not very good either. Try this." With lightning speed Raven threw her hand as if to slap Jade with the back of it.

The power landed so hard Jade was ripped out of the spell holding her down and she spun off her feet. A sickening splat accompanied her landing, facedown in blood. The ground was covered in it. Raven laughed at her. First a snicker, then a giggle. Soon it was an all-out cackle.

Jade slowly got to her feet. "She needs to pick a style," she muttered to herself. Glancing at Charlie, she noticed him wiggling his fingers. Raven's spell was weakening. He only needed time to break free.

Raven's laughter stopped short. "What was that?"

Jade turned toward her, pulling energy from her anger. "Your laughter, it's ridiculous. You giggle, you cackle, I'm surprised you didn't snort. Pick a style." She threw energy bolts at her, as she had at Andrew. More controlled now, they were narrower and brighter. Like lasers, they shot forward and bounced off Raven's hands as they had Andrew's. She had expected they would. All she needed was to keep Raven busy. She stalked away from Charlie, keeping her eyes on Raven.

"You are not in a position to tell me to do anything." Raven made a fist toward Jade, raising her up by her throat.

Jade struggled to breathe. She clawed at the invisible fingers holding her up. Higher and higher she went. Raven examined her as she held her easily ten feet in the air. She squinted at her a moment more, then released her grip. Jade fell several feet, twisting her ankle as she hit the muddy ground and landed on her back. She cried out in pain and grabbed her leg.

Raven chuckled. "Amateur." She turned toward Charlie.

His arm had been moving, but he froze back in place, just before Raven faced him.

Jade yelled, "What? That's all you got?" She struggled to stand on her good leg as Raven turned toward her. "I haven't even gotten warmed up yet."

"Really? All right. Let's see what happens when you get warmed up." Raven pressed her palms together in front of her.

Jade could feel the heat all around her. Like flames from a bonfire, it pressed in on her. She began to sweat. She pulled on her anger, but the pain in her leg and worry for Charlie was dulling it. Trying desperately to think of a way out, she realized, *I need a trinket, or element, or—*

As a sweat bead rolled into her eye, she thought, *Sweat is water.*

"That wasn't very smart." She wiped her face with both hands, held them in a circle above her eyeline, and focused on Raven. Softly chanting, "Aqua." *Water.* The sweat spun off her palms in a circle, growing until the space between them was filled with swirling water. Throwing her hands down toward the Earth, she launched her spell.

Raven raised her brow at Jade. "What was tha—" Gallons of water crashed out of the sky onto her head, nearly knocking her off her feet.

As soon as the water hit, Jade was rushing to Charlie's side, hoping to break him free with a spell. He was already moving and Jade could feel the air around them cooling. She looked back at Raven.

She was wringing out the front of her shirt. "Nice one. Used that on your parents' house, if I remember correctly." She looked up at them. Her eyes widening when she saw Charlie. "That won't do." She raised a hand toward them, palm up, and blew across its surface.

Jade took a breath, and another, but no air filled her lungs. It was like all the oxygen had been taken out of the air. Or maybe she no longer had lungs. Charlie seemed the same, his mouth open wide, gasping for air that wasn't there. They collapsed to their knees.

Raven focused on Jade. "I really don't have anything against you. In time, you could be fairly powerful. But you were a means to an end, and right now? It's the end." She turned to Charlie. "But, what to do with you?" She raised a fist, and he lifted to eye level. She looked him up and down, and a smile began to spread across her face. As she opened her fist, Charlie dropped to the ground, and he and Jade both gulped in air.

She watched them fall. "Well, I'm bored now, so I guess it's time to go find somewhere more interesting." She walked back to the well and picked up the Book of Shadows. "But know this; if you ever try to get in my way, I won't hesitate to do to you what I did to your parents and your precious aunt."

Jade raised her head slowly to glare at her. "What did you just say?"

Raven feigned surprise. "Oh sweetie, you didn't know? Your parents didn't die in just any old fire, and your aunt didn't have just any old heart attack." She leaned toward her with that sinister smile. "I drained every drop of their power." She straightened again. "Now you know." She turned her back on them and started walking away.

A shiver rocked Jade's body. A Witch's power was connected to their life force. For it to be drained away would cause a very painful death. All three of her family members hadn't just been killed, they'd been tortured by this—"Sadistic. Evil. Bitch!" Jade struggled to her feet, keeping her weight on her good leg. Raven slowly turned toward her. She had her attention, but now what?

"Excuse me?" Raven looked down her nose at Jade. Her grin was so smug, so self-assured.

There was one thing Jade knew would work. One thing she could use that would deal a blow even Raven would be surprised by. And the fuel was all around her. Covering her in fact. She knew it was dangerous. Knew after using this, dark magic was only a step away, but she had no choice.

Raven frowned at Jade like a disappointed teacher. "I said, excuse me."

Jade felt the energy all around her calling out. She reached for it, and its dark silky warmth responded gladly. It was copper, and salt, and life itself. And it was eager to bow to her will. She clenched her fists around the energy, sinking into it. Raising her fists up; the blood on her clothes, on the ground, and in Raven, all connected. It was all April's blood, after all. "Suspendat." *Suspend.*

Raven's eyes grew wide. Her blood was turning, twisting, and rising within her. She lifted her head slowly, struggling against the pressure within her. Arms outstretched at her sides, she dropped the Book of Shadows. Every cell in her body was being squeezed by Jade's will. She managed to whisper, "No."

Jade felt the connection break, but it had taken its toll. Raven slumped from the strain of breaking free. "Looks like that's my cue," she croaked, and turned to run.

Jade fell to her knees. Just like in the fight with Andrew, her energy was drained. Charlie had recovered though and threw energy at Raven. As she stretched out her hand to block it, the nearly invisible shock wave hit, crumpling her hand as if it were made of clay. Raven screamed and pulled her deformed hand to her chest. Charlie was hurling vines up from the ground. She brushed them away with her good hand. They withered and died in midair. But there were too many, and soon they began to take hold.

Jade felt the fiery static collecting in her palms once more. She fanned the flames with her anger, focusing everything into her fists. She put everything she had left into throwing the energy at Raven, focusing it at the center of her face.

This time it connected. Raven's head snapped back. When she righted herself, her expression was of disbelief. Her eyes focused on Jade. "So, little lamb does know how to bite. I may have use for you, after all."

Charlie had built up power in both hands and sent it flying toward Raven in the form of two lightning bolts. They stopped midway between them for a moment, then began creeping forward, as if in slow motion.

Raven frowned at them, beads of sweat dripping down her face. She was pushed backward a half step, the vines keeping her from going further. She looked to Jade. "To be continued." With one last smirk she faded away as if she'd been made of smoke. The energy bolts shot through the space she'd been, caught fire to the vines as they passed through, and landed on a tree behind where she'd stood, turning it to ashes.

CHAPTER 30

"No!" Jade limped to where Raven had vanished, looking around frantically. "Where is she?" She looked behind the well, as if Raven was playing some twisted game of hide-and-seek. "We have to find her!"

Charlie stared at her as if she were a stranger. "You . . . please tell me you didn't use blood magic on Raven."

"Who cares about that? We have to follow her. We have to get April back." She turned toward the well, but Charlie grabbed her arm.

"April? April's gone!"

"No. She's trapped inside." She had seen a possession once and it had stuck with her. "Raven's possessing her, that's all. We can get her back."

"Jade, this isn't a possession! From the moment Andrew stabbed her with his blood on the blade, she stopped being April." He grabbed her shoulders roughly. "You need to get that one thing straight in your head. April is gone."

No, she can't be. Jade stared at the well where April had been minutes before. Tied to it, helpless. She'd looked so scared, her eyes pleading for Jade to save her. She'd failed.

Charlie released her and murmured, "Listen to me. Now is not the time to fall apart. If you want Raven to pay for what she did, then you need to pull yourself together. The coven needs us now. Until we finish the Ascension, magic will continue to fade and we won't have the power to stop her when she returns."

Jade couldn't stop looking at the well. It was as if April stood there still, a ghost.

Charlie's voice sounded far away. "Are you listening to me? Jade!"

She snapped her head to look at him.

"Raven will need time to recover from not only your magic but rising from the dead. It's not something you can just jump up and start running after. We need to use this time to finish the Ascension, repair the coven's magic."

Jade sniffed and took a deep shuddering breath. "She seemed to be able to run just fine."

"No, she didn't. I was watching her closely. The fact that she was able to perform magic at all is only because of how strong her spirit is. But it takes time to adjust to a new body, and she is weakened, at least for now. I'm guessing she'll need at least a few weeks to regain her strength fully."

Jade could see the wheels turning as he walked over to pick up the Book of Shadows. "We have that much time to reconvene the coven and finish the Ascension. Then we work on controlling your powers. When Raven comes back, we'll be ready for her, together."

Jade looked over at Andrew still lying on the ground. She walked over and stood looking down at him. The bleeding had stopped, and his breathing was shallow. *What do we do about you?* She wanted to kill him where he lay. Rip him to pieces and scatter him to the wind. Make him feel the way she did right now. *She didn't deserve what you did to her.* The static was building in her palms and she clenched her fists to contain it. It would be so easy to strike him now.

Charlie took her fist in his hand, gently opening her fingers and entwining them with his. She looked up into his eyes.

"I know." His voice was soft and low, like a gentle hug. "It's hard. But I'm here, Jade. Whatever you need. We'll get through this. Andrew will pay for what he did, after he heals."

She nodded at him. He didn't understand. How could he? He barely knew April. He had no idea what she meant to her. For now, she would let him lead. She would wait until Andrew was healed, and then they would have a little talk about what he'd done and how she could get April back.

***

Jade and Charlie carried Andrew to the car and drove him to Sophia's, the town's main healer. When she opened the door and saw them, her eyes widened for only a moment before she got straight to business. "Where are you hurt?" she asked Jade.

"Nowhere. I'm fine." She felt anything but fine, but other than a little soreness in her ankle, she wasn't injured.

"Good." She looked at Andrew held between them. "Andrew?" Charlie nodded and Sophia said, "Follow me please."

She led them to a back room and held the door open for them. "Put him on the bed there." She went to a cupboard and began removing items, putting them onto a tray. "Now please leave me to do my work."

Jade threw one last glare at Andrew as Charlie closed the door. The moment it shut Jade felt a shift within her. Like the closing door had closed off her heart. All the anger, hatred, pain, and fear of the last few hours dropped away. As they went into the living room, Jade came to the logical conclusion: she felt numb.

Mrs. Keepsake entered the front door, carrying a basket of herbs and several crystals. She took one look at Jade and gasped, "Oh my poor dear!" She plopped the basket down on a chair and ran to her. "Are you all right? What happened?"

She was looking her up and down, and Jade realized she probably looked terrifying. "It's not my blood," she said, surprised at how matter-of-fact she sounded.

Mrs. Keepsake looked at Charlie, then back to Jade. "Oh. Well . . . I think maybe a nice hot shower is in order, then. Yes?" She led Jade to a bathroom as she explained, "Grandma Willow's condition hasn't changed, but she's resting comfortably in the guest bedroom now. The chapel's magic has done all it can for now."

"May I see her?" Jade asked. She frowned down at her red hands. Shouldn't she be crying, screaming, doing anything other than speaking calmly and coherently?

She smiled at Jade. "Of course, dear. But, perhaps, a shower should come first?" She placed a hand ever so gently on her shoulder.

Jade nodded and shuffled into the bathroom. She undressed and stepped into the shower. Turning it on, she stood with the nearly scalding water running over her, the blood that was covering her turning pink as it was diluted by the water and ran down the drain. She couldn't relax completely, but she felt protected here. Like time had stopped, and as long as she stayed in the stream, the world didn't exist. But all too soon the water ran clear, and she knew she'd have to face reality.

It was then that she finally broke down. Her knees buckled under her, all their strength gone. She collapsed to the floor under the barrage of water. Every drop beating on her back was much too hot, but she didn't care. Let it burn her away. It was nothing compared to the pain in her heart. Her tears mixed with the shower water, her sobs echoing in the slate-tiled space.

Eventually, her crying slowed. For a moment it surprised her that she didn't just cry forever after what just happened. But then she realized it wasn't over. Possessed or not, she couldn't just let Raven have April's body. She needed to get her back. Until that happened, she needed to keep going.

Then there was Andrew. All her life she'd looked up to him, admired him. Now she couldn't stand the thought of him getting to exist in a world where April didn't. She needed to make sure he paid for that. She didn't even want to think about Raven yet. Charlie said they had time, and she would use that time to deal with the fallout of everything that had happened. She turned off the water and stepped out to find her clothes cleaned and neatly folded on the sink.

She dressed quickly, and when she entered the living room, Sophia immediately stood and led her to where Willow was. As she opened the door, the smells of rosemary and mint welcomed her, healing herbs often used for pain. The room was softly lit with dozens of white candles. Willow lay on a bed in the center of the room, a circle of twinkling lights like fireflies surrounding her. One of them shot toward Jade. It stopped inches from her face and danced in place for a moment before returning to its place in the circle.

Sophia whispered, "Some of the fairies have returned and are quite determined to help in any way they can, including protecting Willow while she heals. Don't be too long, she needs her rest." She turned and left.

Jade approached Willow's bedside, and the fairy line parted for her, closing again behind her. Grandma Willow had always seemed larger than life to Jade. She carried herself with such power and grace. Now, she looked so small and helpless. As tears threatened to spill for what seemed like the millionth time that day, Jade turned to leave. She couldn't bear the sight of her like this, helpless.

"Going so soon, child?" Willow's voice was stronger than before, though not quite as commanding as it usually was.

"I'm sorry." *For so many things.* "I didn't mean to wake you."

Willow lifted her hand slowly, and Jade took it as gently as she could. "You didn't, I was just . . . resting my eyes." She opened them and Jade was saddened to see her eyes were still white. "It's good to see you."

Jade tried to smile, to be strong for her. She had never seen Willow looking anything but regal. When Jade was little, Willow was the sun and stars to her. She could do no wrong. Why she would sacrifice herself to save someone like Andrew . . . it didn't make sense.

Willow squeezed Jade's hand. "What is it? Ask your question."

"Why did you do it? Why did you save Andrew?" Jade waited, expecting another crazy bombshell, like he was her son or something. For a moment, time seemed to stop.

"My dear Jade, I didn't do it for him. I did it for you. Becoming High Priestess is such a delicate time. I didn't want you to bear the burden of having killed someone for revenge. Killing out of hatred mars the soul. The shadow it places on your heart is tainted. In time it will scar you permanently. Affect your abilities as coven leader. I couldn't let that happen again." She closed her eyes, her breathing heavy. It broke Jade's heart to not only see her this frail but know that she was the cause of it.

"Now you listen here, child." Grandma Willow opened her eyes and looked right at her. "Guilt will do nothing for you. Everything happens for a reason," another labored breath, "including this."

Jade fought back tears, but they escaped, falling on their clasped hands. *No. Not now.* She took a deep breath and cleared the boulder in her throat. "April—" She broke down. Sobs mixed with her words as she poured them out. "Andrew killed April and Raven took her body. She's possessed or something. I held her when she died. There was so much blood, and I didn't know what to do. I tried to stop her, Raven I mean, but she teleported. And Andrew"—her anger flashed white hot—"he caused all this. He . . ." Willow's breathing was so shallow, Jade could hardly see her chest move. Andrew may have started it, but Willow was her fault. "I'm sorry, Willow. I'm so sorry. I just—I don't know what to do."

Willow squeezed her hand slightly. "You become High Priestess. You and Charlie heal the coven's magic. There's nothing more important than that." Her eyes closed and her hand relaxed as she fell asleep.

Jade placed Willow's hand gently down. "I will. I promise." As she headed for the door, she told the fairies, "Thank you for protecting her."

***

Charlie called back the coven, except for Sophia and Mrs. Keepsake, who stayed with Willow. This time, when Charlie and Jade's powers combined, nothing interrupted them. Jade felt the same rising of power as before, but now there was something different about it. It had a flavor, a lightness, like citrus.

This time, while Jade helped Charlie loop the energy through the Keys, she stayed focused, unconcerned with who may be outside their sphere of energy. She felt him looking at her and glanced up at him. He nodded at her and she understood, it was time. In synchronicity they pulled the Keys' elemental energy up and into the sphere.

Four energies now swirled around them: their own, the familial, the coven's, and the Elementals'. All that was left was the divine. Jade looked upward, both excited and nervous for what was to come.

Charlie took her hands, and Jade knew the words they should speak. She didn't know how, but as Charlie began, she knew what would come next.

"By the blood and bone . . ."

"By the pulse and breath . . ."

"We invoke divinity," they said together. "The way is prepared, the vessels are ready. Bless us with your power to defend this coven and its people. So mote it be."

The sphere of light around them grew in intensity until it was too much to bear. Jade closed her eyes, gripping Charlie's hands to keep from falling back. A shock began at her head and traveled down through her whole body like a lightning bolt. She was shaking, in pain, and floating all at once.

Then it was gone. She was standing in front of Charlie next to the altar with the Elementals and coven surrounding them. She blinked and looked around. Everything looked the same, but she felt different somehow. It felt like she'd been hollowed out, and the space within her was filled with air and light.

Charlie was staring at her with a look of amazement, his eyes wide. "Whoa. You feel that?" He looked down at his hands and arms, turning them over.

Jade asked, "Is this different from when you became High Priest with Joy?"

He looked up and smiled at her. "Yeah. I'm not surprised though. We're connected in a different way than Joy and I were. But my body feels . . . clean." He picked her up and spun her as he laughed. "It worked!"

Jade couldn't laugh, too much had happened. He looked so happy though. It was as if a weight had been lifted from his shoulders, the dark shadow that haunted him banished from his face. She smiled back at him, grateful that one of them was able to move on. "What do you mean it worked?"

He was still holding her arms, and as he looked down into her eyes, she could swear she saw tears forming. "What? Nothing. It doesn't matter. None of that matters. All that does is that we're partners. High Priestess and High Priest of Sugar Hill."

Turning, he straightened up and raised his head slightly. "I hereby release the Elementals. Stay if you will, go if you must, the circle is open to you." They each drifted away until only the coven members remained.

Charlie said, "Madame Belle, please release the Sacred Circle."

She nodded once and walked the barrier counterclockwise, its energy flowing into the crystal she was carrying. As the circle dissipated, Jade could feel the energies around her. Before, it had nearly overwhelmed her, but this time she recognized it and took control. She directed each sensation downward into the Earth to be dispelled.

All the plants and trees were greener. There were tiny multicolored flowers scattered in the grass that she hadn't even noticed before. Even the stone of the buildings was a richer gray. She felt she'd been watching a black-and-white TV all her life and suddenly there was color. In the middle of this cemetery, life was thriving all around them. She realized what the final tarot card had been telling her. All the chaos, all the trauma she'd endured, it was all leading to this. A blossoming of her power manifested in the vibrant colors around them. If only it hadn't come at such a high price.

Charlie asked, "Are you all right?"

She wanted to scream at him, *Of course I'm not, what's wrong with you? Aren't you worried about Willow? Don't you care April's dead?* But it wasn't his fault. He barely knew April, and he probably assumed Willow would be fine. Jade nodded, "Just trying to get used to this new feeling."

"You will. It'll fade away in time, but you'll be able to access it when you need it."

He turned to face the gathered coven members and spoke in a commanding voice. "The ritual is complete. Let it be known; the Sugar Hill coven is whole once more. This township and its people are under our protection."

Jade felt the urge to speak, though she had no idea what she'd say. She stepped up next to Charlie and took his hand. Suddenly the words flowed. "Only those with good intent are welcome here. Anyone following the darkness is hereby banished from our borders." A spark passed between their clasped hands, and Jade felt her palm warming. She looked at Charlie as she continued, "So mote it be . . ."

He repeated, "So mote it be . . ."

Together they spoke: "So mote it be!"

Charlie winced and let go of Jade's hand, turning away from her toward the altar.

"What's wrong?" she asked.

"Nothing, we just have a lot to do." He closed the Book of Shadows and began gathering the four Keys.

Madame Belle approached and handed him a small box. Jade recognized it from the chapel. As Charlie placed each Key gently into the black velvet-lined container, Madame Belle told Jade, "Congratulations, ma chere. Oh, I'm so proud of you both."

Charlie said, "Thank you. Would you and the rest of the coven please spread the word to the townsfolk that they can lower their protection spells. The danger is past."

Jade picked up the Books of Shadows. It felt so familiar to her, like it belonged to her, though she'd only held it a handful of times. She asked Charlie, "So what now?"

"Now we attend to coven business." He picked up the box with the Keys and marched toward the car.

Jade walked beside him. His silence was screaming at her. She could almost hear his thoughts, like a word on the tip of her brain. "What are you trying to keep from me?"

"A lot happened while you were gone. I'm fine now." He looked down at his palm. "I should be fine. This really isn't the time to talk about it."

Jade grabbed his arm and he stopped walking. "Charlie. If we're going to be partners, we have to communicate better. Please, just tell me."

"You're right." He started walking again, slower this time. "A few years ago, we were attacked by a dark coven, North Devonshire. It was—" His eyes darkened for a moment. "Our battle magic wasn't as strong as it should have been. We were losing. I resorted to blood magic. It worked, we won. Problem is, killing another Witch, even in self-defense . . . it leaves a mark." He looked down the footpath. The coven members had left, it was just them. "The last few months, I've felt that mark growing, like some kind of dark shadow inside me." He placed his hand to his chest.

Jade remembered what Willow had told her, that in time, the damage would become permanent. "Does Willow know?"

Charlie nodded. "Without my even telling her." They had reached the car, and Charlie opened the trunk for the ritual items. "I wanted to step down as High Priest, but she persuaded me to wait while she did some research. When Joy was killed and you agreed to come back, she said the Ascension ritual should cleanse me. And she was right. I feel so much better now, Jade." His lopsided grin beamed at her. "And with the two of us as coven leaders, we'll be able to heal this coven completely."

They got in his car and Charlie drove through Main Street, headed back toward his house. The town was slowly coming back to life. The lights in Katie's Emporium shone brightly, and carousel music could be heard from inside. Fairies flitted from lamppost to lamppost, lighting them as they went, bathing the street in their soft glow. Everything appeared more alive, the colors more vibrant than seemed natural. This was more like the town she remembered from her childhood.

Suddenly Charlie screeched to a halt. Jade looked up in front of them to find a lion standing in the street. Even with the magic all around them, she blinked, unbelieving. As tall as the car, its breath steamed out of its mouth as it panted at them. Its fur was gray as stone, and the tip of its left ear was missing. She looked in his glowing golden eyes for a moment. He shook his mane and trotted off the side of the road, disappearing behind the firehouse.

"What was that?" Jade asked. "I mean it was a lion but . . . what was that?"

Charlie looked at her. "I'm not sure, but I dare say, Sugar Hill's magic is back." He grinned like a little kid and hit the accelerator.

As he made the turn up Sugar Hill Road, the mayor's house came into view just as the sun was peeking over the horizon. A crowd of people was waiting by the front door.

As Charlie parked on the side of the house, Jade asked, "Any idea what that's about?"

"Being coven leader is about more than just finding lost Keys and battling evil bitches. We have a township to run."

"You mean it's an actual job?" Jade asked sarcastically.

"Yup." They both got out of the car, and Charlie leaned on its roof, looking Jade in the eye. "A lot of these people rely on magic for all kinds of things, and lately that magic's been failing them. While having permanent coven leaders will automatically fix a lot of things, some spells need to be recast. The extra boost of power we have from the Ascension will allow us to cast most spells almost effortlessly, but it'll wear off soon, so this is the best time to do this."

Jade glanced at the group of people waiting for them. She didn't want to deal with people now, but maybe it was for the best. It would help take her mind off everything and give her a chance to practice using the new magic coursing through her. She needed to make sure she was ready when they faced Raven again.

As they walked toward the crowd, Jade felt the same urge to help people as she did in Sun City. But this time she wouldn't have to hide. This time, she would use magic.

EPILOGUE

The great hall had been silent for years, except for the dripping of rainwater through its shattered glass-domed roof and the whistle of wind through its open doorways. Every room in the massive building lay dormant, their floors covered in a thick layer of dirt and dust. No vines had grown here. No rodents nibbled in the walls. There was no life.

If any living soul had been there, they would have heard an eerie sound just then. A hum reverberating throughout the space just before she appeared. The woman collapsed to the floor from thin air. One hand gripped the grime below her, the other was clutched to her chest. She stayed kneeling on the floor for a moment, catching her breath, then slowly raised her head to take in her surroundings. Even in the dark she could see the outlines of broken furniture, the rubble from a partially collapsed wall, a cauldron lying on its side covered in dust. Dust, but no cobwebs. Even spiders dared not come here.

She rose and stood shaking, her breath slowly returning to normal. She could feel the dark energy around her. It was the only thing that inhabited the place. It had been awakened by her arrival and was creeping its way toward her. From the walls and floors it came, slithering down the stairway, coming to embrace her as an old friend. This place had seen violence and death. This place was full of dark magic.

She smiled, looking up to the glass dome several stories above her. It had once been a grand place, but now it was in ruins.

"I think I'm going to like it here." She climbed the winding staircase, which stopped just shy of the dome. The more the darkness filled her, the more she felt her energy return. She held her broken hand out in front of her, examining its misshapen form with an accusing glare. It would take time for her to heal completely, but she was good at waiting.

She reached the top floor and walked over to where the dome became a wall of windows looking out over the countryside. In the distance she could see a slight brightening of the clouds, reflection of the lights of Sugar Hill.

Raven smiled. "Yes, this will do . . . quite nicely."

ACKNOWLEDGMENTS

To YOU. Yes, you, the person reading this book. Without you, this story would be sitting in a notebook somewhere in the bottom of my closet, with all the other stories I wrote for myself. Because of you I spent countless hours writing, researching, and struggling to find just the right words. Because of you I learned about publishing, formatting, and marketing. Because of you, this book exists. Thank you.

To my first beta Emily Hornburg, who help me write before I knew if I wanted to publish or not.

To Jasmine Noble-Shelly, for her inspirational writing and motivational feedback.

To all my CPs and Beta readers, without whom this book would not be worthy of selling. I can't put in words how much I appreciate your time, honesty, and precious feedback. Thank you: Andrea, Brittany, Catherine, Courteney, Danae, Jacqui, Kristy, Lori, Marissa, Melissa, Ross, Sandra, Sathepine, Stephanie, and Tanni. You all have helped me more than you know.

Last, but certainly not least, to my family and friends, who probably never thought I would finish this, but loved me enough to not say that to my face. Thank you for your positivity and support.

About the Author

Michelle Winkler was convinced by her husband to live in the Arizona desert. While skeptical at first, she realized if she could survive hitch-hiking halfway across country at 20 years old, spend eight years in the Navy, and raise two sons, as long as she had air-conditioning, she'd probably be okay.

Since her move she's: started a veggie garden, learned how to shoot a bow, completed three associate degrees, and become a kayak enthusiast. However, she still hates to cook, and will absolutely run screaming from the room at the first sight of a bug. Because bugs are evil.

When writing she's usually supervised by an adorable Brittany (that's a dog breed) named Zen and his mini-me little sister, Pepper.

She's most often found in the digital world on Twitter or Instagram @mwinklerbooks.

Her website, michellewinkler.com has links to all her social media hangouts, info on future projects and more.

CPSIA information can be obtained
at www.ICGtesting.com
Printed in the USA
LVHW041259191020
669155LV00003B/517

9 781734 954326